# THE
# WOOD

# THE WOOD

## CHELSEA BOBULSKI

FEIWEL AND FRIENDS

NEW YORK

⊱───

A FEIWEL AND FRIENDS BOOK
An imprint of Macmillan Publishing Group, LLC
175 Fifth Avenue, New York, NY 10010

Our books may be purchased in bulk for promotional, educational, or business use. Please
contact your local bookseller or the Macmillan Corporate and Premium Sales Department at
(800) 221-7945 ext. 5442 or by e-mail at MacmillanSpecialMarkets@macmillan.com.

Library of Congress Cataloging-in-Publication Data

Names: Bobulski, Chelsea, author.
Title: The wood / Chelsea Bobulski.
Description: First edition. | New York : Feiwel and Friends, 2017. | Summary:
    After her father's disappearance, Winter takes over guardianship of the now-sinister
    magical wood behind her house where time travelers sometimes get lost. |
Identifiers: LCCN 2016039983 (print) | LCCN 2017019408 (ebook) | ISBN
    9781250094278 (Ebook) | ISBN 9781250094261 (hardback)
Subjects: | CYAC: Forests and forestry—Fiction. | Magic—Fiction. | Time
    travel—Fiction. | Missing persons—Fiction. | Family life—Fiction.
Classification: LCC PZ7.1.B64455 (ebook) | LCC PZ7.1.B64455 Woo 2017 (print) |
    DDC [Fic]—dc23
LC record available at https://lccn.loc.gov/2016039983

Book design by Rebecca Syracuse
Feiwel and Friends logo designed by Filomena Tuosto

First edition, 2017
1  3  5  7  9  10  8  6  4  2
fiercereads.com

To Nathan—for your unending
love, support, and faith.

# I

Dad tells me the wood is not a place to play. It is a place for business, and it is more powerful than I could ever imagine.

He tells me I cannot forget the rules of the wood. There are three.

Do not travel from the paths.

Do not linger after dark.

Do not ignore the calling.

These rules are easy to remember. He drills them into my head every day over cereal breakfasts and walks to the bus stop. He meets me after school and reminds me again, but when I ask if I can go into the wood, he says, "Not yet."

I watch them from my bedroom window, the trees that spread out behind our house along the Olentangy River. To everyone else, they are half a mile wide and three miles deep. To us, they're limitless.

I watch the seasons change from that window. Count the

number of leaves that have turned orange and red, purple and gold. I watch them fall from their branches, covering the ground so that the paths are only distinguishable by the weathered logs that outline them.

When the snow comes, the logs are also covered, and I wonder if it makes the rules harder to follow. If it's easier to wander off the paths when they can't be seen. Easier to get trapped in the middle of a limitless space, unable to escape when night comes crawling in. If it's easier to forget things such as duty and honor surrounded by all that white.

Dad tells me it's in his blood. He would know the paths even if he were blind. He feels the night descending like others feel the warmth from a fire or smell rain on the horizon. He never neglects to heed the call.

Even when he wants to.

He tells me it'll be the same for me, when I'm old enough. He tells me it's in my blood, too.

And when he finally begins my lessons in the wood, I know he's right. I feel it, like birdsong. A buzzing melody beneath my skin that keeps me on the paths, guiding me, never letting me go where I shouldn't. I cannot travel from the paths—it is physically impossible. I cannot linger after dark—to do so would be suicide. I cannot ignore the calling—the one time Dad told me to try, the birdsong turned into hornets, boring into muscles and sinew, crippling me with pain and sickness.

It is because of these rules that I don't immediately think anything's wrong when I come down the stairs one morning and Dad's not sitting at the kitchen table. Why I don't understand when I see Mom sobbing into Uncle Joe's shirt. Why a humming clogs my ears as Uncle Joe tells me Dad wandered off the paths. That he got swallowed up by the trees.

That he's gone.

I tell Joe it can't be true. Dad couldn't have walked off the paths—it isn't possible. Joe must have made a mistake. Dad just hasn't come back from his morning patrol yet. That's all.

But I've never seen Uncle Joe look so pale. He murmurs to himself, the same way he does when we play chess and he's thinking of all the possible outcomes. I catch fragments like "must have tripped somehow" and "maybe a fight with a traveler?" and "need to inform the council."

Mom is sitting at the table now, her arms crossing her head like a fort. I lean over her and lay my head on top of hers, even though I can't understand why she's crying. Dad's still out on morning patrol.

He's coming back.

In the weeks that follow, the council's investigation concludes with no evidence of foul play. They determine he simply stumbled off a path. An accident. Nothing anyone could do.

But I know better.

Either he was forced off the path, or he found a way to walk off it voluntarily. If it's the former, if a traveler somehow forced his feet from the path, there's nothing I can do. So I tell myself it's the latter, because if Dad walked off the path, he did so for a reason. If Dad walked off the path, then I should be able to do the same thing. But even as I stand in the wood, surrounded by ice-covered trees that glitter in the sunlight like crystals, throwing bands of rainbows onto the snow around my feet, I can't follow him. My body won't let me.

I ask Uncle Joe what this means.

He says it's in my blood. I can never walk off the paths.

# II

## 20 MONTHS LATER

I have never been so scared, or so curious, as I was the first time I met a traveler. Dad had told me about them, of course, these people who fall through the time-traveling portals—the thresholds, wormholes, whatever you want to call them—that pockmark the wood behind our house. They are the reason for the guardianship. They are the people who need to be protected from the wood, and whom the wood needs to be protected from.

*Our job is to keep them from crossing a threshold into another time,* Dad told me during my first lesson.

*Why?* I asked.

*It's dangerous,* he replied. *For them and for the wood. Travelers are meant to live in their own time periods and no other. To be stuck in an era that is not your own could cause major ramifications.*

*Like what?* I prodded.

*Death,* he answered. *Destruction. Implosion of the space-time continuum and life as we know it.*

I don't think Dad meant to scare me. I think he just wanted me to know, to understand. What we do—what the Parishes have always done—matters. Even in his cynical moments, I don't think Dad ever *truly* believed the work we did was for nothing. But it didn't stop me from seeing an omen of death and destruction the first time I laid eyes on a traveler.

He was tall—double my height—and broad, a mountain of flesh and bone. Dad didn't seem concerned, but I knew if I was out there alone, I wouldn't have been able to handle this traveler the way a guardian needs to. I was too small and he was too big. That's where the fear came in.

But the curiosity was stronger. I had only just begun my lessons in historical fashion—an effective signifier when trying to determine a traveler's origins—but I could at least pinpoint him to seventeenth- or eighteenth-century Europe. I was still trying to master Latin and Greek at the time, so I had no idea what language he spoke, but that didn't matter. Dad knew everything I didn't, and then some. I stuck to Dad like a shadow, watching his body language and facial expressions as he guided the traveler back to the threshold from which he came.

Some things you just can't learn from books.

Now, I stand across from a traveler who couldn't be more different from my first. She is a peasant girl, with a curtain of black hair covering her face and a black, suspicious eye peeking out from beneath the strands. She's shorter than I am, but the dagger in her hand makes her just as dangerous as the man who towered over me all those years ago. Still, I am not afraid.

What a difference six years make.

"Who are you?" she snaps at me in Japanese.

At least, I *think* that's what she says. It's in a more formal style than modern Japanese. Judging by her clothing, I wager a guess at Early Middle Japanese, which is really unfortunate. I'm much more fluent in the modern dialect.

I hold up my hands in front of me to show I'm not a threat. "A friend," I reply. "I want to help you."

At least, I think that's what I said. I mold my face into the same lines of sympathy Dad always used, just in case.

Her gaze narrows. "Where am I? I do not recognize this place."

"A wood," I tell her, "where lost people sometimes find themselves."

I'm not usually so direct with my answers; most travelers jump at the chance for someone to lead them home, even a stranger such as myself, whether their questions are answered or not. But this girl's fear doesn't shut her down; it wakes her up. If I'm going to get her to cooperate, I need to be as forthright as possible.

"Where are you from?" I ask, taking a step closer.

She stiffens. A band of sunlight glints off her blade.

"Please," I say. "I'm just trying to help. Don't—"

But she's already running, barreling toward me like a bull at full charge. I duck at the last second, pivoting myself around her and catching her wrist in my hand. She jerks to a stop. In her split second of shock, I grab her other wrist, pinching her hands behind her back until the dagger loosens from her grip and sticks point-first in the earth.

"I don't want to hurt you. See?" I pick up the knife and throw it into the trees. "I just want to help."

"Why?" she spits.

"Because you're not supposed to be here. Don't you want to go home?"

Her body relaxes slightly at that word. *Home.*

I take a deep breath. "Tell me where you live."

She hesitates, then mutters, "Heian-kyō."

Heian-kyō. The city now known as Kyōto.

"What year?" I ask, but I must not ask it in the right way, because she doesn't seem to understand.

"Who is the emperor?" I try again.

"Takakura."

There is only one Heian-kyō threshold, so I'm not worried about sending her back to the wrong time, but it's important to keep track of the threshold's current timeline for the council's records. I'll have to double-check to be sure, but if I remember my Japanese history correctly, that would put the threshold somewhere near the end of the Heian period.

"I'm going to let go now," I say. "You have two choices here. You can run away and stay lost, or you can follow me and go home. Understand?"

I'm really winging the Japanese now, but she nods anyway. She follows me down the paths without saying a word. A cloud moves over the sun as we walk, and the blood in my veins jerks at the sudden darkness. A primal reaction, but logic quickly takes over, as it always does on cloudy days. The wood doesn't change until night falls, and I know exactly how much time I have left.

Two hours to sundown.

We finally reach her threshold, an empty pocket of space between the trees, only distinguishable by a break in the logs lining the paths and the decrepit shingle hanging above it that bears her city's modern name: *Kyōto, Japan.*

"If you step through the trees here," I say, "you'll find your way home."

"Home?" she repeats.

I nod.

She smiles and carefully takes a step forward, then another, walking underneath the shingle. And then she disappears entirely, as if she were never here to begin with.

This is my favorite time in the wood. The hour just before sunset, when the wind slashes through the green canopy above me, cutting open squares of orange sky like patches in a quilt. Fireflies flit through the trees, little lanterns in the encroaching darkness. I put out my hand and catch one in my palm. Its blue body is different from the fireflies others see outside the wood. Dad told me once that they are an evolved species, that our wood is littered with evolved species the rest of the world will not see for a millennium.

I stroke my finger down its silver-striped back and its wings flutter, revealing the lower half of its body. Pinpricks of light swirl in a clear shell, an entire galaxy of stars and planets and sunshine trapped in its tiny frame.

At least, that's what it's always looked like to me. Dad used to say it reminded him of oil slicks, the way the rainbow would swirl through the black, but he loved working on cars and I love astronomy, so I guess it all depends on what you want to see.

I press my lips against my wrist and blow until the bug flies away. I wish I could stay longer, but the sun is closing in on the horizon, and mist is already starting to unfurl from the trees surrounding me, collecting on the paths like a ghostly blanket. It's as if the mist knows the rules change after dark. As if it would hide the paths and the thresholds from me so I couldn't find my way home.

This is the moment when I wish my feet wouldn't betray me. When I wish I could stay in this exact spot, staring up at the patches in the leafy quilt until they turn velvety black, speckled with stars, and letting the trees take me so I can find him.

But then my feet shuffle toward home. Halfway there, the wood becomes less dense. I see the light from the kitchen through the gaps in the trees, and I remember why I can't disappear.

Mom would be all alone in this world, and she would never forgive me for doing that to her.

I would never forgive myself.

She wants me to stop coming out here. We argue about it sometimes but Mom knows there's no fighting it. The wood calls to me like a siren, tugging an invisible thread that reaches deep into my core, so that I have no choice but to follow. A puppet on a string.

Uncle Joe mediates when he can, but he's not always around.

I know I've stepped over the threshold into the normal wood—the one that everyone else sees when they drive by on 315—when the breath rushes out of my lungs in a single huff and the regular noises of the world, the cars honking and the hum of the streetlights blinking on and the sound of the river, swollen from the previous night's rain and lapping against the edges of our neighbors' yards, slam into my ears.

It's always like this. Heart drumming, lungs burning, as if I've been holding my breath for hours. I feel heavier somehow, rooted to the ground, and yet disconnected from all of it.

I sit down on the giant rock that bears my parents' initials inside a heart and watch the sunset. Mom spots me from the window above the kitchen sink and waves. I try to wave back, but I'm still not completely in control of my body, and my hand doesn't leave my side. I smile at her instead.

Mom shrugs as if to say, *What can you do?* She knows I'm okay. She's seen Dad go through this a million times, what he used to call the decompression stage. The toll the body takes from walking through a world that is not its own is like jet lag times a thousand. She knows in a few minutes I'll be back to normal and I'll walk through the door with full control of my motor skills and ask what's for dinner.

But her shoulders don't relax until I stand and go through the stretching exercises Dad used to make me do to get my blood flowing again. Of course, he used to say chocolate ice cream did the same thing, taking me to Mr. Igloo whenever I skinned my knee or had my blood drawn at the doctor's office. "You eat chocolate ice cream and your red blood cells start to multiply. Poof," he would say, handing me a cone. "Like magic."

Now that I'm older, I know it isn't true, and I'm not certain the stretching does anything, either. Still, it feels good. Lets me forget he's not here next to me, doing the same stretch with his hands on the ground between his feet. For a moment, I can almost hear him breathing, and I think if I peek through the curtain of hair covering my face, I'll see him there in front of me.

But I never allow myself to actually look. It would hurt too much.

I start down the path toward home. Mud squishes up into the treads of my hiking boots. Crickets and cicadas buzz around me, static noise that didn't reach me farther back in the trees.

And then there's something else, a whisper that swims by my ear, soft as the tip of a feather stroking my skin. The breathy sound shifts and stretches itself into too many syllables, but it sounds like it says my name.

*Winter.*

I turn back to the wood, half expecting to see my dad standing there in the same plaid shirt he wore the first time he took me into the wood, when I was ten and he seemed indestructible. A constant in my life that would never change.

But there's nothing. Just a darkness that stretches beyond what most people see.

# III

Uncle Joe sits on the back porch, cloaked in shadows and cigar smoke. I'm fairly certain he wasn't sitting there a moment ago, but that's nothing new. Joe's magic allows him to bend the normal rules of nature and space.

"Any travelers?" he asks, a stream of blue vapor seeping out of his nostrils.

The old porch beams creak under my weight as I sit next to him. "One. A peasant girl from Heian-kyō. She put up a fight, but that was my fault. My Japanese is rusty."

"Course it is," Joe says. "That threshold rarely opens."

I shrug. "I should have been prepared."

Uncle Joe scratches his chin. His black stubble is salted with white, and the silver strands weaving through his hair seem to multiply every time I see him. Joe is forty-three years old, or so he likes to say. Age is kind of relative when you're immortal. He doesn't have a line on his face, and his body is more ripped than our star quarterback. Age has no hold on him anywhere else, which makes me wonder if the white in his hair has anything to do with age at all, or if it came from the wood. If the things he's seen over the last thousand or so years are finally catching up to him, or if his guilt over what happened to Dad is eating him alive, same as it's doing to me.

It's easy for Mom to tell me I shouldn't feel guilty, that there's no way to know if I could have prevented Dad's disappearance by being out there with him that morning, but it doesn't help. All I see when I look in a mirror anymore is my selfishness. I should have gotten up when my alarm clock went off that morning. Should have helped Dad with the morning patrol. But it was a Saturday, and my bed was warmer than the air surrounding it, and I knew Dad wouldn't begrudge my sleeping in.

That's the worst part about it, knowing that Dad wouldn't have even said anything to me for missing it. For not being there. For failing him.

But whatever I'm feeling, I know Joe's guilt must be worse. Joe has worked for the council as the Parish family intermediary for hundreds of years, a sort of liaison between the soldier (me) and the bureaucracy (the council). He checks on me, reports back to them. He's supposed to keep me safe, just like he was supposed to keep Dad safe.

I don't know if the other guardians are as close to their intermediaries as Dad was to Joe, but even if they hadn't been like brothers, Joe would have still felt responsible for what happened to Dad.

I think that's why Joe doesn't come around the house much anymore. He can't stand looking into my mother's pale, lifeless eyes, not when it was his failure that stole the light from them.

Joe takes one last puff of his cigar, then makes a flicking motion with his wrist. The cigar disappears. Like magic.

"Council meeting tomorrow afternoon." He stands. "I'll find you when it's time."

He starts down the porch steps.

"Hey, Uncle Joe?"

He turns.

"Do you want to come in for dinner?" I ask, even though I already know the answer.

His gaze flicks to the back windows, through which we can see Mom bustling around the kitchen, carrying plates to the dining room table. He watches her a moment longer, an unreadable expression hardening his face, then shakes his head.

"Maybe next time," he says, his body already dissolving and scattering like a million grains of sand in the wind. I suppose doing something as normal as walking or driving is too passé for someone who can teleport.

"Yeah," I reply, even though he's already gone. "Maybe."

⟿⟾

A platter of roast chicken sits on the dining room table surrounded by bowls of mashed potatoes, sautéed green beans, and a leafy salad tossed with tomatoes and cucumbers. Mom and I both eat like birds. The leftovers will feed us for days, but she refuses to cut recipes.

She also refuses to move Dad's clothes out of the closet even though it's been almost two years. Uncle Joe says she's not grieving properly. He says I need to talk to her, but I don't see what good that would do. I'm holding on to Dad as tightly as she is.

Mom stands behind her usual chair. "Dinner's ready."

I kick off my mud-splattered boots, eyeing the third empty plate she always sets in front of Dad's chair, and make my way into the kitchen to wash off the dirt in the cracks of my palms. "Thanks."

Not many would expect my mom to be a great cook, considering that most mothers who spend ten hours a day at work would rather order takeout when they get home, but cooking's always been a stress reliever for her. As soon as she gets home, she changes out of her professor uniform of tweed slacks and a white blouse into her sweats and trusty apron. She digs through the fridge, opens her cookbook, and doesn't say a word until the meat's roasting or stewing or frying and the whole house smells like fresh herbs and melted butter.

One time I joked that this was her own form of decompression, her way of becoming human again after a long day in another world wearing a hat that wasn't labeled MOTHER or WIFE. She smiled at me and said, "Yeah. I suppose you're right." And then I sat down on the stool on the other side of the kitchen island and she asked me what I learned in school that day. Before Dad disappeared, it was our usual routine—me sitting at the kitchen island while Mom cooked, both of us waiting for Dad to return from his evening patrol. Both of us anxious for him to get home before the sun went down, although we hid it well behind small talk and smiles that never quite reached our eyes.

Now, I'm the one who patrols the wood every evening, and Mom waits for me in the kitchen by herself, with no small talk to keep the anxiety at bay.

Water sluices over my hands. I pump a dollop of soap into my palm and scrub out the creases with my fingers. The polished obsidian coin hanging from the leather straps around my wrist clinks against the sink. I turn my hands over and notice a splotch of dried blood on my forearm. Peasant girl must have nicked me when she charged. I wash it off quickly before Mom notices and walk over to the table.

"Looks delicious."

"I hope it tastes as good as it looks," Mom replies, pulling back her chair. She always says this, even after cooking one of her tried-and-true recipes. She's always been so humble that she's never known how to take a compliment. It was one of the reasons Dad said he fell in love with her.

I tell her about my history paper, due at the end of the week, and the A that I got on my English test. It's been three weeks since I had to skip a class to take care of a "disturbance" in the wood, so Mom doesn't feel the need to remind me homeschooling is an option as she's done on other nights. Instead, she tells me about her students and some archaeological dig in Turkey she's thinking about joining next spring.

We both know she won't. I can't leave the wood, and she can't leave me, even though I'd be fine on my own. Even though Uncle Joe would check up on me.

But neither of us says this.

Only ten minutes into the meal and there's nothing else to talk about. Silence fills the room like water in a bowl, pulling us under into our own thoughts and fears and white noise.

# IV

Dad sits me down in the study on the morning of my tenth birthday. It's February, and nearly a foot of snow glitters outside the frosted window. He's made me my favorite drink, a mug of cranberry cider warmed over the stove with cinnamon sticks and a dash of orange juice. Flames crackle in the fireplace, consuming bits of old newspaper with the freshly cut wood. A bowl of scented pinecones sits in the middle of the coffee table, where it has sat since Christmas. The pinecones have lost most of their scent, but Mom sees no reason to throw anything away that still serves a purpose, even if that purpose is purely decorative.

Dad folds himself into his favorite reading chair, ice-covered branches fracturing the window at his back, as I curl my legs up underneath me on the couch. There are presents on the dining room table and sticky buns baking in the oven, but he tells me they can wait. It is a hard thing to hear at ten years old, especially when one of the presents is shaped like the Barbie dream car I've wanted for months, but I scrunch my eyes down into my "serious" face anyway and set the mug on the coffee table.

"You're old enough now," he begins, "to know about the wood."

I no longer have to try to forget my presents. They have left my mind completely.

He launches into a story that begins here, in this old country house made of strong timber and river stone, in the year it was built, 1794, though the Parishes had been protecting the thresholds for nearly eight hundred years before that. One of our ancestors journeyed to America when he heard of a particular patch of trees in the Northwest Territory, a piece of land the Native Americans called sacred and the settlers called cursed, where people went in and never came back out. Not a totally uncommon occurrence back then, of course, but the fact that the trees in question were located next to a river made our ancestor wonder if it was connected to the wood between worlds he was sworn to protect.

"You see, rivers are the power sources that connect the wood to our world," Dad explains, but he must see something in my face that says I don't understand, because he adds, "The wood is like a carousel, a spinning wheel that has no real beginning or end, just the platform where the conductor controls its power. Without power, the carousel does not turn."

I frown at the carpet. "But with a carousel, there's more than one way to get in and out, right?"

He smiles. "There are many points of entry, yes, just as there are many points of entry into the wood, but there are only a few power sources which keep the wood grounded in the space between worlds. Unlike other thresholds that open and close throughout time, the threshold behind our house and the thresholds located next to rivers around the world that act as these power sources are always open. This is why the guardians live next to these thresholds, so they can have constant access to the wood."

"There's more than one guardian?"

"Oh yes," Dad says. "Ten families in all."

He explains a lot to me that morning, things I don't fully understand until he begins my proper lessons, with old journals and guided walks through the wood. He explains how the thresholds work and talks about ley lines, points of power that intersect, and the way the never-ending flow of the river gives the wood a unique source of power. He says worlds were never meant to be crossed, and it is our job to protect the wood from travelers, and to see those travelers home safely.

I learn that the thresholds always open at the same locations—in an alley in Los Angeles that used to be a grazing meadow, or in a market in Shanghai, or in some tiny corner of a place no one would even think to look at twice—little rips in the fabric of time. Some open for fifteen seconds, others for fifteen minutes. The longest open threshold on record was an hour, back when my dad was still in diapers. Grandpa sent a group of seventeen travelers back through the same threshold in one afternoon, herding them like cattle.

And then the thresholds close, like scabs over a cut. Days, weeks, even years in the human realm can pass before the scab is picked and the timeline rips open once more, bleeding travelers into the wood until it scabs over again. This continues until the threshold closes for good, the cut finally healing into a scar, although this doesn't happen as often as Dad would like.

He grabs a book from the shelf and hands it to me. It's an old book bound in leather with the title and author's name etched in green. The copyright reads 1936. It is a collection of stories, paranormal events that have taken place around the world that have never been fully explained. He tells me to turn to chapter twenty-three, titled "Time Travel." In it, there are a dozen stories of people disappearing from their time period only to wind up in another. One story in particular catches my eye, about a traveler wearing medieval clothing, who, according to onlookers, appeared out of nowhere in the middle of a street in downtown Chicago. One witness told police that the man shouted at passersby in Shakespearean English and stared at the buildings surrounding him as if he'd never seen anything like them. In his confusion, the man was run over by an Oldsmobile and died instantly. Some thought he had possibly escaped from an asylum, while others thought he was an actor who'd had too much to drink. Whatever the case, his identity was never discovered, leading some to believe he may not have been from their time at all.

"These people pass through the thresholds unknowingly and end up in our wood," he explains. "They become disoriented, and it is our job to take them back to their own time, but a few of them have slipped through the cracks in the past thousand years, since the guardians were called. These travelers journeyed through a threshold that was not their own and ended up in another time. This is dangerous for many reasons but, most important, it upsets the natural order of things. We are all supposed to exist only in our own timelines. To be dropped into another could rip apart the very fabric of our world."

I flip the page. There is a copy of the newspaper article detailing the accident, along with a sienna photograph of the body splayed underneath the car.

"I want you to read that book before we begin your lessons," he says just as the oven timer dings. He ruffles my hair. "Enough talk for one morning. I believe you have presents to open."

But I am not as excited about the Barbie dream car or the sticky buns. I hug the book to my chest and keep it on me at all times over the next week, reading whenever the opportunity strikes, making notes in the margins in purple ink under the notes made by my dad and my grandpa and someone else before them.

# V

Trevor watches me in fifth-period chemistry from the other side of the room. Meredith notices and nudges me with her elbow. A drop of distilled water sloshes out of the beaker.

I sigh. "You're lucky that wasn't hydrochloric acid."

"You should go out with him," she says, doodling fat hearts onto her lab packet. "He's clearly into you."

"I did go out with him." For one week in sixth grade. It was enough.

Mr. Craft walks by and Meredith fiddles with the Bunsen burner until he moves on to the next worktable. "But he's *mature* now. And he's a quarterback."

"Second-string," I mumble as I watch the solution and jot down my observations.

"Yeah, but those abs ain't second-string."

I roll my eyes.

Meredith became boy crazy right around the time Dad started teaching me about the wood. She'd talk to me about her latest crush and I'd nod as if I were listening, when really all I thought about was my next lesson. And then she would notice I wasn't listening, and I'd spend the next hour apologizing. We had our biggest fight in eighth grade. Meredith called me a freak and I called her immature. We weren't friends for a week.

It was the longest week of my life. And even though she still calls me a freak sometimes for making it to junior year without having one steady boyfriend and I call her immature for caring more about gossip and boys than our upcoming ACTs, I don't know what I'd do without her.

She reminds me that there's a normal life outside the wood. Reminds me that there's something to protect that goes beyond me and my family, even if it's something that I'll never fully be able to enjoy. Meredith hits it on the head every time without meaning to.

I am a freak.

"Yeah, well, I have it on good authority that Trevor's hoping he'll see you at the game Friday night." She bounces in her seat as she says this, the fluorescent lighting making her perfectly straight teeth look even whiter than usual.

"Did he say that?"

"No, Tommy D. did. I think he wants to ask you to homecoming."

"Tommy?"

She rolls her eyes. "*Trevor.* Honestly, Win, I don't know how you function sometimes."

I don't know, either. It's not like I don't notice boys at all. Not like I don't wish I could be more like Meredith and actually have time on my hands to go to football games and parties and homecoming dances. But even if I did have the time, there wouldn't be any point in it. I don't care how mature he is for his age; I doubt there's a single high school boy in the country who would believe me when I'd inevitably have to cancel a date to send a time traveler home where he or she belongs.

Frustrated, I huff out a breath. "Well, then why doesn't he just ask me? Why does he have to get Tommy D'Angelo to tell you to tell me to go to the football game so he can ask me out to a dance that's still two weeks away?"

"Okay, look. No offense or anything, but . . . you're kind of scary, Win."

I cut my eyes to her. "What's that supposed to mean?"

"Okay, maybe *scary*'s not the right word. You're . . . intimidating. You never talk to anyone besides me. You're totally unapproachable."

My brow furrows. "I talk to people."

"Teachers don't count."

"There's this girl in my English class who's always asking for pens. Anna something."

"Arianna Andrews, and she doesn't count, either."

"I talk to people," I say again, but the bell rings and Mr. Craft is clapping his hands and telling us to turn in our packets, and I don't think she hears me.

It's a lie anyway. When it comes to any semblance of a social life, I am as tiny and insignificant as the fly currently slamming its body against the window behind Mr. Craft's desk. That's the way it has to be. If I get too involved, make too much noise, people will notice me as more than just the brainy girl who skips class a lot and, apparently, scares people. And since being noticed can only lead to questions I can't answer, I think I'll stay in my silent, scary corner, thank you very much.

Meredith takes our packets up while I clean our work area. She isn't the greatest lab partner. She always skips steps in the instructions and never helps me clean up, but I prefer to do things on my own anyway.

*There's no one you can count on out there to save you,* Dad used to say. *When the guardianship passes, you're on your own.*

Meredith returns and shuffles her books into the crook of her arm. "You coming over this afternoon?"

"Crap, I forgot. I'm—"

"Busy." Meredith sighs. "The ACTs are in three weeks. I need you, Win. I got a nineteen on my last practice test."

"I can't tonight, but we'll study all through lunch tomorrow and I promise I'm all yours this weekend."

She stares at the tessellated floor, brown and pitted from past chemical spills. "My parents'll kill me if I have to go to community college."

I swing my backpack over my shoulder and put my arm around her as we head toward the door. "You're not going to community college. Your GPA's not bad, and you're on student council. You'll be fine if we can just nudge your score up a few points."

"Easy for you to say. What'd you get on your last practice test? A thirty?"

Thirty-two, actually, but I don't say this. It's not like it matters anyway. I can't go to college. I already know what I'm going to do for the rest of my life, and it doesn't require a four-year degree. The only reason I'm even taking the test is to make Mom feel better, to make it seem like I have options when I really don't.

We push our way through the congested hall. A couple of guys throw a football back and forth over our heads, holding up the stampede and nearly braining every single person between them. Meredith shouts at them to knock it off, but in a teasing, flirty voice that gets her nowhere.

"Make us," one of the guys says, tossing the ball back to his buddy.

The next time it zooms over our heads, I catch it one-handed.

Both guys stare at me, dumbfounded.

"Mine," I growl, tucking the football underneath my arm.

"See?" Mer says as the guys skulk away, darting pissed-off looks in my direction. "Scary."

I roll my eyes. "So you *wanted* to get smacked in the face with a football?"

"No, but that isn't the point." She pauses at the door to my French class, sighing like she can't believe a person could actually be this clueless. "You sure you can't come over? Mom's ordering Chinese."

I wish I could, but it's dangerous enough to take the afternoon off from the wood on a regular day, let alone on a day that falls between the autumnal equinox and the winter solstice, when the veil thins and the roads between worlds are easier to travel.

I shake my head. "Sorry."

She stares at me, her mouth hanging open slightly. She wants to ask me something, but she stops herself. It's not the first time the question has hovered in the air between us, an unspoken conversation that's practically written in our eyes.

*Why do you keep secrets from me?* she seems to say.

I have to.

*Does it have to do with your dad?*

Yes.

*I could help.*

You'd get hurt.

*I don't understand.*

You're not supposed to.

It's a gap in our friendship that's been widening lately, but we never actually talk about it. It's made even worse by the fact that I can't even tell her what really happened to Dad. As far as Mer and every other outsider know, he walked out on us. It's the worst sort of lie, because no matter how bad things got for him, Dad would never voluntarily leave us. But Mom didn't want people thinking he died, just in case. If he does come back someday—hope swells in my heart just thinking about it, but hope is dangerous, and I crush it the moment it tries to poison me—it'll be a lot easier to tell people he and Mom are working on their marriage than to convince everyone he's back from the dead.

Mer watches me a moment longer, debating something, then says, "Okay. I'll save you a fortune cookie."

"Thanks."

She walks across the hall and ducks into her classroom just as the bell rings.

I take a seat in the back and nibble on a protein bar when the teacher isn't looking.

# VI

It doesn't happen until I've been in the wood for an hour, walking the paths that never end, flicking Dad's Swiss Army knife open and closed.

But it's inevitable. A traveler always comes.

The sound of footsteps behind me starts as a whisper, a shuffling. A sound that could be explained away as something normal if I were still in my world—a squirrel skittering across a path, leaves rustling overhead. But this sound is neither of those things. I stop, my body rigid, as it draws closer.

*Thud-thud-thud.* Boots pounding against packed earth.

This traveler is running, which makes him unusual. Most stumble their way onto the paths without meaning to. They walk in circles, their breathing labored as they try not to panic. I've found some cradled in the fetal position on the ground, crying to go home. I've found others trying so hard to keep it together that they refuse to look at me. They think I'm a figment of their imagination. They don't know I'm more real than they are.

Running is rare. Running implies fear. Implies purpose. This one is either desperate to be found, or desperate to escape. Either way, desperation makes for a dangerous traveler. Speed and a poor sense of direction can lead to a traveler falling through one of the many thresholds that hide between the trees, and then they'll be lost. In another time, another place. Somewhere I can't follow. I have to stop him now, before it's too late.

I wait until I hear rushed breathing over the footsteps, the faint rustling of leaves as arms swing past overgrowth, and then I turn and run toward the intersection behind me.

He comes out of nowhere, but so do I. He doesn't even notice me until my arms are already wrapped around his body. He hits the ground hard. I scramble on top of him, my knees pinning his arms at his sides. He struggles against me. He's strong, and he's got at least forty pounds on me, judging by the solid wall of corded muscles trying to throw me off. Swearing, I pull my knife out of my back pocket and press the blade against his throat.

Two scuffles in less than twenty-four hours. Either these travelers are getting feistier, or I'm becoming crotchety in my old age.

"From whence do you come?" I ask him. Blue veins swell against the paper-white skin of his neck as he bucks against me. I dig the knife in deeper in case he gets any ideas, just enough to dent his flesh. He won't be able to move now without seriously injuring himself. I ask the question again, this time in Latin.

"Off with you, woman," he spits. English, then.

"Not until you answer the question."

I usually try to have more tact than this. The last thing I want to do is frighten someone who's already losing his mind, but he's not afraid, at least not of the wood. I've seen what it looks like to be afraid of this place, in the faces of travelers who have begun to give up hope, and in my dad's face toward the end, when he had finally given up hope, as well.

This guy *wants* to be here. He stares up at me. He's young— seventeen, maybe eighteen. His dark blond hair hangs low in his eyes, which are the same color as the shaded grass surrounding him. "I will not return."

"I'm afraid you don't have a choice." I decide to take a different route. "What year is it?"

He laughs, a mocking sound that rumbles through my chest. "You cannot fool me with that, Madam. Time is of little consequence here."

My brow arches. "So you know about the wood, then?"

"I told you, I will not return," he says, his voice tight as he strains against me. "Not until I have done what I must."

"Unfortunately for you, I can't just let you waltz right out of here. It goes against my job description."

His face screws up like he's trying to make sense of what I just said. He knocks his head back against the ground and sighs. "You cannot make me go anywhere."

"Oh, I beg to differ."

I need to get him out of here, and this back-and-forth stuff isn't working for me. It may be a slow afternoon so far, but that doesn't mean anything, and I don't want to be distracted by another traveler and accidentally let one—or both—slip through the cracks.

I press the knife harder into his throat. "I'm guessing by your accent and your clothes that you're British, from the eighteenth or early nineteenth century. Close enough?"

His chest rises and falls as he tries to catch his breath. "You cannot send me back if I do not say. Travelers must be returned to their own time and place and no other."

My eyes widen. "How do you know that?"

"I would rather not say."

There was a time, or so I've been told, when the wood's secrets were common knowledge in our world, before they passed into the realm of fairy tales. So I guess it's not that surprising that I would eventually come across a traveler who knows what this wood is, what it does. But that knowledge doesn't give him the right to cross into my time—which seems to be where he was headed, judging by his trajectory—or any other, for that matter.

"You're right, I do have to send you back to your own time and place." I shrug. "Give or take fifty years."

"You lie," he says, but there's the tiniest spark of doubt—or maybe fear—in his eyes, and it's all I need.

"It isn't an exact science, you know. So you have a choice. I can send you back through the right threshold, or I can guess and send you back anyway. I may be right; I may be wrong. It won't matter much to me either way. But if I am wrong, you'll live without your family, without your property, and without everything else you've built for yourself for the rest of your life. Which will it be?"

He moves fast, pulling an arm out from underneath my grasp and laying his hand over mine, pushing the blade away from his neck. The knife nicks him in the process, and a drop of blood beads on his skin, lazily dripping down his collarbone. He lifts his head and stares into my eyes.

"Even were that true, which I know very well it is not, I have lost everything already." His voice cracks, and the brittle sound pierces my heart. "That is why I am here. Please. Let me pass."

"I can't." I say it with conviction, with all the authority my position bestows upon me, but I can't quite meet his pained gaze. He lets out a frustrated breath. I decide to try one more time. "From whence—"

"Brightonshire. The third of June in the year of our Lord, 1783."

I exhale but don't move. "Now the question is, are we going to do this the easy way, or the hard way?"

"I will not give you any trouble."

I don't believe him, so when I push away from him and stand, I grip the coin dangling from my makeshift bracelet and rub my thumb over the ancient glyphs carved into its face. The glyphs light up, pure white on black obsidian.

He stands slowly, wipes the dirt from his breeches. The silk stockings beneath his knees are torn, his leather shoes flecked with mud. The white linen shirt he wears beneath his open coat is damp and clings to his chest. Muscles that would put Trevor's to shame stick to the fabric, looking sharp enough to cut diamonds.

My stomach flutters, and I silently curse my hormones. Even if it weren't highly unprofessional, this is no boy to be checking out.

In my time, he's long past dead.

I tuck the knife into my back pocket and gesture toward the path behind him, where sunlight filters through the canopy in lemon-yellow strips. "After you."

He straightens, tugging on the hem of his coat. "I apologize, Madam, for I have no intention of returning. Please move aside. I would rather not harm you."

I smile, and it catches him off guard. "The hard way works, too."

He hesitates, just a moment, but it's enough. By the time he's started running toward me, I've already opened my mouth.

"*Sahabri'el*." The word rushes past my lips in a voice that is not entirely my own. This voice trills its *r*'s and practically chokes on its *h*'s. It is a dead language that has not been heard outside the wood for thousands of years, and it stops him cold.

The coin pulses against my wrist as the word travels through the trees. It all seems slower to me—the sound of the voice drifting on the air, growing louder as it moves farther away; the widening of the boy's eyes and the falter in his steps as the odd language tickles his ears—but I know, for him, it takes less than a second, and then he is surrounded by a net of blue fireflies.

My last resort.

He lifts his hand toward them, their light shining against his palm.

I shake my head. "I wouldn't do that—"

There's a zap, and the smell of burnt knuckle hair singes my nostrils. The boy pulls his hand back and cradles it against his chest. Small, red burns dot the tips of his fingers. He grits his teeth hard and starts to barrel forward.

"Stop!" I yell.

He does, eyeing me with distrust.

"You can try to move through them faster or harder or whatever it is you think you need to do," I say, "but the burns will only get worse. Now"—I cross my arms over my chest—"are you ready to follow me like a good little boy?"

The emotion flickers through his eyes so quickly I almost miss it.

Defeat.

But it isn't what I expected. It's deep and filled with a pain so intense, I've only ever seen it once before, in my mother's eyes. On the day our world shattered. And I can't help but wonder, *What the hell happened to him to leave him looking so utterly devastated?*

No. I can't read too much into his life. Can't let myself become curious. Everyone feels pain at some point or another. It doesn't give him the right to cross time and muck everything up.

He follows me down the path without saying a word. The fireflies buzz like static around him as we twist and turn through the trees. Ten minutes pass. Twenty. I can feel his eyes on me, but I don't look back.

Even though I want to.

We finally reach his threshold, the words *Brightonshire, England* carved into the shingle hanging above it. The fireflies unfold from their net, allowing him to move forward, through his threshold, while creating a wall behind him, blocking his escape.

He gives me a sidelong look. "I will return, and I will find a way around you."

I shake my head. "I don't think so, Jack."

"That is not my name."

"It's an expression."

"It is an odd one." He studies me. "You are not what I expected."

"What's that supposed to mean?"

But he doesn't answer me. He takes a step forward, through the threshold, and disappears. Back to Brightonshire, in the year of our Lord, 1783.

I glance down at my hand. There's a scrape on my wrist from my less-than-graceful tackle. I'll have to hide it from Mom. It's hard enough for her to accept what I do without seeing evidence of the occasional scuffle. I rub my thumb over the coin and leave a message for Uncle Joe. *Trouble at the Brightonshire threshold. Sent home a traveler who seems desperate to come back. It'll need to be watched until we can find a more permanent solution.*

I don't have to actually say the words—the coin records my thoughts. It's a safety precaution, so that guardians can communicate with members of the council without giving away their position to any unsuspecting travelers who might hear their voice and run. I get its importance, I do, but sometimes I wonder if that's all the coin is—a magical walkie-talkie with another couple of neat tricks attached. Or if it's more than that. If someone could use it to read the thoughts I don't want them to read.

I swear, the more time I spend in here, the more I start to sound as paranoid as Dad.

An hour later, I've returned two more travelers to their homes—one in Los Angeles, 1986, another in Shanghai, 1450—and Uncle Joe has replied to my message.

*You* are *the permanent solution*, his voice echoes in my head.

I was afraid of that.

# VII

For my second lesson, me, Dad, and Uncle Joe sit down at the kitchen table, and they tell me about the Old Ones, the Compact, and who Uncle Joe really is.

Dad starts by reassuring me, telling me this is a lot for a ten-year-old to take in, and if they go too fast, if I need to ask questions or need more time to wrap my head around all of this, I just need to say the word. And maybe he's right. Maybe this is a lot for a ten-year-old to take in, but I'm not a normal kid. I've lived my entire life next to a wood full of magic and mystery, and I am so ready to learn its secrets that I'm certain if I have to wait a second longer, my insides will burst out of my skin.

Mom sets two cups of coffee in front of Dad and Uncle Joe and a mug of hot chocolate in front of me. I pretend mine's coffee, too, to feel more grown-up. Mom kisses Dad's cheek, then returns to the sink, where she scrubs dirty pots and pans to the melody of her favorite oldies radio station emitting from the little red box on the windowsill.

I know she doesn't like me learning about the wood. I heard

her talking to Dad one night from the top of the staircase when they thought I'd gone to bed. She wishes she could protect me from it, like it's something bad, but I don't see how it could be. Dad said she knew what she was getting into when she married him, which made her exhale a long, deep sigh.

"I know," she replied. "I just didn't expect it to come this soon. She's still so young."

"I'll protect her," Dad promised. "I won't let anything happen to our baby girl."

*Yeah*, I wanted to say. *Dad will protect me*. I didn't know what from, but his words must have made Mom feel better, because now she seems totally fine with Dad and Uncle Joe giving me my second lesson.

Although, she is scrubbing that pan a little hard.

I stare at Dad, expecting him to speak, but Uncle Joe is the one who clears his throat.

"You know I am not a normal uncle, right?"

I nod.

Mom turns the volume up on the radio.

"Your father and I are not brothers by blood, but sometimes family is more than blood. Neither am I a normal human. In fact, I'm not really human at all. My people are called many things by many people—Immortals, Tuatha Dé Danann, Fae—but the guardians have always called us the Old Ones."

I screw up my face. Joe doesn't look that old to me. He must read my mind, because Joe laughs and says, "It's part of the magic, Winnie girl. We age far more slowly than our human counterparts."

Uncle Joe, whose Old One name, I learn, is Josiah, tells me between sips of coffee about how his people have lived in the wood for thousands of years. How they used to stay clear of the time-traveling thresholds so as not to invite trouble into their world.

"But the thing with doors is," Uncle Joe says, "they open both ways."

Although humans were frightened of the wood at first, and the way its magic disoriented them to the point of madness, some started to see it as a valuable resource.

"These portals were a precious tool in a time when land was king and power was measured by how many people a person had killed or enslaved," Joe says. "How much easier would it be if one could gain land by changing a few things in the past? By stopping an enemy force from invading, or by learning from a past mistake? Perhaps a battle that occurred in an open field, resulting in failure and countless deaths, could be moved to a narrow passage, somewhere the enemy would never expect you to strike. You see how appealing such possibilities could become? To never have to settle for what is, when you can always go back in time and change it into what you want it to be?"

Joe pauses. He has a faraway look in his eyes, like he's remembering all of this, and then I realize he probably is. He would have been there, being immortal and all. *How awesome is that?*

Dad gives him a funny look. Uncle Joe shakes his head, and they share the same kind of silent conversation between them that Mer and I always have. I know better than to ask what it's about, though, so I just sit back and wait for one of them to speak.

Finally, Joe clears his throat and continues. "This is when the council was formed and the human guardians were created. We chose people pure of heart, people who could be trusted. Their lineage would mark the passage of time inside the wood in a way our people, being immortal, never could, and through the powers we had given them, they could protect the wood from being used for nefarious purposes."

Ten humans signed the Compact, binding their bloodlines to the wood. Each guardian became responsible for a different section of the wood, sections that the descendants of those guardians still patrol today. There is no intermingling of the guardians outside of the council meetings, at least not in the wood. We keep to our own territories.

"It does not happen often," Joe says, "but you must understand that it is possible you will one day come across a traveler who knows more about the wood than he should, who may even try to cross into another time on purpose. These types of travelers are more dangerous than the others, because they want what you're protecting, and they won't let you stand in their way. This is why your father and I will teach you how to fight."

I know I need to sound and act just as serious as Dad and Uncle Joe, but I can't stop the grin from splitting my face. "Cool!"

Uncle Joe chuckles.

"Winter," Dad warns.

I glance down at the table. "I mean, I understand."

The first strains of "The Way You Look Tonight" trickle out of the radio. Joe smiles to himself, then pushes his chair back, wooden legs squeaking across the floor as he stands and crosses the room. He taps Mom on the shoulder.

"May I have this dance?" he asks.

Mom is elbow deep in soapy water, but she arches a brow and nods. She towels herself off, then slips her hand into Uncle Joe's. They smile as they dance back and forth across the kitchen. They don't gaze into each other's eyes like Mom and Dad do, all lovey-dovey-like, but they stare at each other knowingly, like old friends reliving a lifetime of memories.

Dad watches them, looking happier than I've seen him look in weeks. It is only then that I realize the lines around his eyes are a little deeper, and his shoulders slump down a little more than before.

Something's different with Dad. I don't know what, and I don't know why.

Maybe if I did, I would've seen the changes coming—the nights he spent holed up in his study and the constant smell of alcohol on his breath—but right now, in this moment, I am too wrapped up in the wood to think about it for long. And when Dad scoots back his chair and cuts in, taking Mom in his arms and pressing his forehead against hers, I forget about it completely.

# VIII

Ninety minutes to sundown, Uncle Joe finds me at a fork in the road, where twelve paths cross and unfurl like a starburst, winding through a particularly dense cluster of trees. A drop of sweat rolls from my hairline down my temple as I stare at my feet, willing them to move just six inches to the left and off the path. My shins burn, and my fingernails mark my palms with thin red crescents, but nothing moves below my ankles. Not even a twitch.

"Winter?"

Uncle Joe's voice is deep and loud, like thunder rolling across my thoughts. The toe of his leather boot stops next to my heel, and I can see the shoulder of his black suit out of the corner of my eye, but I don't look at him. I just keep staring at my shoes, waiting for something to happen.

After a beat of measured silence, I ask him, "How did he do it?"

Uncle Joe gives me the same answer he always does. "I don't know."

I let out a breath and look up. There's a sharp throbbing behind my eye, like someone's trying to drive a pickax through my cornea, and my pulse is a drum in my ears, racing toward something it can't find. My gaze stops on a low branch in front of me, where the top of a leaf is turning yellow. The color globs down the leaf like paint and rolls over the pointed edge.

*Drip. Drip. Drip.*

I look for the puddle of yellow paint that logic tells me should be at the base of the tree, but there's nothing. The color evaporates midair.

When I was younger and first witnessed the wood's transformation from summer to fall, I told Dad it was beautiful.

He said it wasn't beautiful. It was sarcastic. It was mocking our world, taking the things we knew to be true—leaves changing in the autumn, dying on the branches, only to be reborn in the spring—and turning them on their heads.

It was the first time Dad ever referred to the wood as having a conscience, as being a living, breathing spirit that could make decisions and change fates and stop time.

"Things will get harder now," Uncle Joe says.

"They always do this time of year."

Unlike the thresholds the guardians use to enter the wood (the thresholds tied to power sources), the thresholds travelers fall through are typically open for only seconds or a few minutes at a time, so not many travelers have the serendipity to walk through them at that precise moment and fall into my wood. But there's something about the time between the autumnal equinox and the winter solstice. The wood becomes restless as everything surrounding it moves closer to death.

Uncle Joe's theory is that this transition causes the veils

between worlds to weaken, opening thresholds for longer periods of time. Some of the thresholds even become more apparent, taking on the shape of actual doors travelers can see. One such door led to the creation of Stonehenge, a monument to outline the portal between worlds. Luckily, the Stonehenge threshold closed for good a couple hundred years ago. I don't even want to think about how many tourists would wind up in the wood if it still had the ability to open.

Needless to say, if I don't stay on top of things this time of year, a deluge of travelers could flood the pathways, making it easier for one to slip by me while I'm dealing with another. This is also the time of year I skip the most classes.

Dad didn't believe Joe's theory about thinning veils, however. He thought the trees were just hungrier for fresh meat this time of year. Stockpiling for the long, dead winter.

Uncle Joe sighs. "You need to stop doing this."

"Doing what?"

"Trying to follow your father. It's a very selfish thing to do."

I know it is, but I can't stop trying. Not if there's a chance he's still out there. Not if there's a chance he needs me. But Mom needs me, too, and therein lies my dilemma. My split loyalties cleave my heart in two. What would I do if one of these times it actually worked? If I found my feet veering off the paths? Would I follow Dad, or stay for Mom?

I clear my throat. "Got anything on Brightonshire?"

Uncle Joe exhales. "Nothing. First-time offender. You could bring it up to the council if you like, but they'll need evidence he's actually trying to cross over, and even then there isn't much they can do."

"He wasn't just some guy who walked into the wrong

airspace and ended up here. He wanted to be here. He said he'd be back."

"Yes, but can you prove it?"

I sputter. "I don't have to *prove* it, Uncle Joe. He said those words. To my face."

He sighs and takes a seat on the wrought-iron bench behind him. There's an old-fashioned streetlamp next to him with a silver spiderweb hanging like a tiny hammock underneath the lantern casing. None of these was there seconds before.

"Unfortunately, you do. The council laws permit us to interfere with a traveler in rare cases, but only if they are certain the traveler poses a threat to the wood."

"What sort of interference?"

He pats the seat next to him. "Sit."

I slowly lower myself onto the bench and wait for it to dissolve under me. For Uncle Joe to disappear and for me to find myself alone in this wood, going crazy from the constant twists and turns.

But the bench is solid. Loops of cold iron dig into my back.

"It is possible for the council to force a threshold closed, but it requires strong, ancient magic. Dangerous magic. You know that saying, whenever a door closes, God opens a window? It's like that, only the outcome could be worse than a window opening. It could be a Grand Canyon. So, the council has to be certain closing the Brightonshire threshold is the right thing to do."

"Do I have any other options?" A Grand Canyon–sized hole that potentially hundreds of travelers could fall through doesn't sound too appealing.

"Stop him."

"Excuse me?"

"Every time he comes through. Stop him." He says this easily, like I have no life outside the wood.

"First of all," I say, "that sounds exhausting. Second of all, I have this little thing called school."

"You could always do as your mother suggests and enroll in a homeschooling program."

"No, thank you." I'm enough of a freak as it is. Besides, I know what my life's going to look like when I graduate: all guardian duties, all the time. These last two years of high school are the last two years of my entire life in which I can pretend to be somewhat normal. Two years to experience a life that isn't completely consumed by destiny and duty and wishing to be someone else, *anyone* else, even if just for a day. And I won't give that up just because some traveler feels like playing red rover with my threshold.

Dad wanted me to have a normal life for as long as possible, and that's what I'm going to do.

"It won't be forever," Joe says. "The boy will tire of it eventually."

I don't think so. I don't know what Brightonshire wants, but I think he's just going to get more determined, and I think he's going to keep coming until he finds a chink in my armor.

I cross my arms over my chest. Sweat rolls down the back of my neck. Even with the sun setting in front of me, showering the trees with strips of orange light, the temperature hovers in the space between uncomfortable and suffocating. Strange for mid-October, and highly inconvenient. All my back-to-school clothes are long-sleeved shirts, jeans, boots. Cover-ups and layers. August-hot autumn days like this one mean digging through the back of my closet for the few pieces of summer clothing I haven't boxed away.

"This is your job, Winter," he says, quietly. "It must be your first priority. This is not the first time someone has discovered the wood and purposely tried to use it to cross over, and all the guardians before you did exactly as I said. They waited for those travelers, they found them, and they stopped them. Every time. It may be exhausting, but it's the only way."

I wipe my sleeve across my damp brow. "I don't know how many more classes I can skip before I get suspended."

Uncle Joe stands and buttons his suit jacket. He doesn't even look mildly uncomfortable in this heat. "Your duty is more important than perfect attendance," he says. "Besides, you could get straight As in your sleep."

I wish. There'd be a lot fewer late nights catching up on homework. "It's not about that—"

"Then what is it about?"

But he wouldn't understand. Somehow, I don't think Uncle Joe's ever wanted to be a normal sixteen-year-old girl.

"Nothing." I push off the bench and it disintegrates into thin wisps of gray smoke. "I'll figure it out."

"Good girl." He clears his throat. "Now, then. We should be on our way. Don't want to keep the council waiting."

I place my hands in his. My stomach plummets to my toes, the same feeling I get after a roller coaster crests its first hill. The world shifts sideways and there's a pressure in my ears, like someone's trying to squeeze toothpaste out of my head.

And then we're gone.

A split second later, we're standing in front of a stone arch-way on the outskirts of my patrol area. Every guardian zone has one, an ancient monolith of a doorway inscribed with the runic language of the Old Ones. A silvery, transparent mist flows inside the archway. Looking through it is like peering through a rain-soaked windshield, making the trees beyond it look blurry and distorted.

Before Dad disappeared, I had been through this archway only once, when he took me to the council for approval to begin my guardian training. Since Dad disappeared, I have gone through it once a week.

For the first ten weeks or so, I always looked to Uncle Joe first, uncertain if I should cross without permission. Now, I take my hands from his, ball them at my sides, and barrel through the archway without a second glance.

In the space between one step and the next, there is an absence of sound—an odd sensation, considering even in the quietest moments of life, there is a sound track. The hum of electricity through the walls. The hush of the wind rustling the leaves, or causing the old beams in our house to groan. Even the sound of my breath entering and leaving my body, or the sound of my stomach growling, or my bones cracking, or my footsteps smacking the ground. But the complete and total vacuity of sound is a feeling I haven't grown accustomed to, although I guess that shouldn't surprise me. Dad told me he'd never gotten used to it, either, and he'd been traveling through the portal on a weekly basis for over twenty years of his life.

I come out the other side in a stone antechamber lit by torch-light. Sound rushes in as if someone has just flipped the switch in my brain that turns my ears back on. The torches crackle on either side of me, while a vein of water trickles down the wall to my right.

"This place is located beneath a lake," Dad explained the first time we came here. "That's where the water comes from."

"What lake?" I asked.

He just shook his head. "You wouldn't know it," he said. "It's not of our world."

Uncle Joe steps through the portal and we walk side by side down the hall, our boots slapping the wet stone floor. The hall opens into a large room with a vaulted ceiling and three rows of wooden benches curving in a horseshoe shape around the dais against the far wall. Antique broadswords, daggers, and cross-bows line the walls. Very medieval chic. The other guardians are already here, along with the intermediaries who watch over them as Uncle Joe watches over me.

The other guardians are all in the same age range as my dad was—forty or older—except for Anaya, a twenty-two-year-old girl from India who always makes it a point to smile at me. There's also a guardian-in-training, a boy from Romania named Valentin who, along with his mother, looks like the descendant of Van Helsing in his leather jacket and perma-scowl. He tried to talk to me about American movies once, something about John Hughes and the Brat Pack movies being his "favorite of all time," but his mother hissed at him to act professional, and he fell silent. I haven't really gotten to know anyone, at least not well enough to move beyond the awkward realm of acquaintance. It isn't like we all stand around the watercooler after these meetings are over. Still, they nod at me in greeting as I take a seat in the back with Uncle Joe.

Even now, nearly two years later, there is still pity in their eyes when they look at me. At first, it was nice, to know that my dad was being missed, that others understood on some small level what I was going through. But now, it just reminds me all over again what I've lost, and I want to scream at them that their sympathy isn't helping. How can I expect to even start the process of moving on if all they ever see when they look at me is the girl who lost her father, forcing her to become the youngest guardian in over a hundred years? When they look at me like that, I just want to crawl under my bed and pretend the world doesn't exist.

The council members enter last, taking their seats on the dais behind a long stone table. I don't know how old they are, but unlike Uncle Joe, their hair is all white, and their skin is thinner than parchment, making it appear blue or purple or green depending on the color of their veins.

I glance at the empty space to my left on the bench, and I can almost see Dad sitting there, looking like he did the first time he brought me here, shortly after my tenth birthday. "They looked that old the first time your grandfather brought me here, too," he whispered, making me giggle. "I was surprised clouds of dust didn't spew out of their mouths when they spoke."

At that time, he'd already explained the basics to me of who these people were, of who Uncle Joe really was, but I was still fascinated to be in a room filled with an immortal race of people who weren't *really* human. At least not if your definition of human was someone born in our world.

Now, one of the council members, a man with a long hooked nose named Alban, taps the gavel against the table, officially calling the meeting to order. He waits for the hushed conversations around the room to die down.

"We have some troubling news to bring forth today," he says. "Two of our council members, Augustus and Celia, of House Tara'né, have gone missing. They were last seen at our previous meeting." He raises his voice to be heard over the sudden whispers. "We have no leads as to their whereabouts at this time, but we are investigating the matter. Anyone who has any information of their whereabouts or who would like to help in the search, please see us after this meeting is concluded. Now then, Guardian Ballinger, please stand and give us your report."

Tom Ballinger, a guardian from Cornwall, stands and recites the number of travelers he sent home in the past week from his patrol sector. Seral, the council member on the far left-hand side of the dais, records his words in her ledger in shimmering gold ink. When he is finished, Guardian Kamali Okorie, from Nigeria, stands and does the same.

I glance at Uncle Joe. "Has this ever happened before?"

"What do you mean?" he murmurs.

"Two council members disappearing like that?"

He nods. "Sometimes we can lose track of time, forget where we're supposed to be. It's an easy thing to do when you've lived as long as we have. It's too early to worry. I'm sure they'll turn up somewhere." But the skin between his eyebrows pinches and he speaks a little faster than normal, and I know he's worried anyway.

"So . . . you don't think this has something to do with . . ." The words claw into my throat. I can't force them out, but I don't have to. Uncle Joe can read my mind like a scrying mirror.

"Your father?" I nod. He's just like Dad in that way, always knowing what I'm thinking, feeling. I guess you can't bottle-feed or potty-train a person without becoming weirdly attuned to them.

"No," he says. "I don't. I'm sorry."

"It's all right." It was silly of me to hope anyway. To think that maybe if they found Augustus and Celia, they'd find my dad, too. It doesn't make sense—I know that—but if I've learned anything these past twenty months, it is that grief and logic don't usually go hand in hand.

When it's my turn to stand, I'm horrified to find my voice is thick and scratchy, and that my eyes are burning. My thoughts went to that place again, where all I can think about is how unfair it is, the fact that I could go to sleep one night with a father and wake up the next morning without one. It's a dark, dangerous hole of a place, easy to stumble into but difficult to crawl out of.

I take a deep breath, force the pain and anger away behind a thick cinder-block wall of denial. "I sent home ten travelers this week." I list all the places and times they were from—San Francisco, 1923; Heian-kyō, late 1100s; Thebes, 2300 BC—

finishing with the boy from Brightonshire, England, this afternoon. The scratch of Seral's quill underlines my words.

Alban nods and waves, permitting me to sit back down and allowing the next guardian to speak, but I remain standing.

"Was there more, Guardian Parish?" he asks, his old voice gritty like wet sand.

"There was a problem with one of the travelers," I say. "I'm not sure how, but he seemed to know things about the wood that no traveler I have ever encountered before has known."

"Such as?"

"How the portals work, what my job as a guardian entails, that sort of thing."

Alban tilts his head, thinking. "That is not so unusual. There are many families who still pass down tales of the wood in the oral traditions, even to this day. Most assume they are fables, works of fiction, but sometimes a child will look deeper into the stories and search out the thresholds for themselves."

"Yes, but he wasn't just in the wood to check out the scenery," I say. "He wanted to use the thresholds to cross over into another time."

One of Alban's white, fuzzy eyebrows curves like a caterpillar. "Do you know where it was he wished to go?"

"No, but I think he's going to try again."

The other council members sit up a little straighter.

Alban narrows his eyes. "Do you have reason to think this boy is a threat to the wood's survival?"

I think about what Uncle Joe said, how dangerous it can be for the council to forcibly close a threshold. How it could open up a giant hole through which hundreds of travelers could appear. And then I think about the boy—Brightonshire. The paleness of his skin and the dark circles beneath his eyes. He looked like he hadn't slept in days.

*I have lost everything already.*

"Guardian Parish?" Alban asks.

"I'm not sure."

He sighs. "Let me ask you this instead: Do you think you can handle this boy on your own, or do you need the council to look into other means of controlling the situation?"

My nails bite into my palms. I wish I could say it was out of some extreme confidence in my abilities that I respond with, "No, that won't be necessary. I can handle it," but it's the image of those green eyes boring into mine with the same hopelessness I see every time I look into the mirror that makes me say it. I'm not sure what the other means of control would be, if they would go straight to closing the threshold, or if they would do something to Brightonshire. If they would find some way to make him—I don't know—disappear, or mess with his memories. And even though I have no reason to care what happens to him, a boy who lived hundreds of years before I was born, I do.

Alban nods. "Very well. I expect another full report on the situation next week."

"Yes, sir," I say, sitting back down.

Two more guardians give their reports, and then Alban closes the meeting by striking the gavel a second time.

Uncle Joe walks with me in silence back through the portal and into my section of the wood. The sun is even lower on the horizon now, a ball of orange flame vertically sliced by tree trunks, as if one of us—the sun or me, I'm not sure which—is trapped in a cage.

"Let me know if that boy gives you any more trouble," Joe says.

"I will."

There's a sudden twinge in my stomach and my head whips to the path on my right, where instinct tells me another traveler will be waiting to go home, and my instinct is never wrong. It's just another bonus to being a guardian. Instinct is a primal urge evolution never bred out of us.

Uncle Joe follows my gaze as he starts to disappear, just as the bench and streetlamp he conjured disappeared earlier. "Better get on with it," he says as the side of his face scatters on the wind. "Twenty minutes to sundown."

⊱⊰

It doesn't take long to find the traveler. The man standing in front of me is middle-aged, with thick blond hair swept off his face and a suit that is simple and clean, double-breasted with wide lapels. Early 1990s, most likely, although it's always harder to tell with suits. They haven't changed all that much in the last fifty years.

He's breathing heavily. He rubs the palms of his hands against his eyes, whispering in French, "*Ce n'est pas le cas, ce n'est pas le cas . . .*" *This isn't happening, this isn't happening . . .*

"*Pardon, monsieur,*" I say gently, my brow crumpling with practiced worry.

He drops his hands, meeting my gaze.

"*Êtes-vous perdu?*" *Are you lost?*

"*Oui,*" he replies, but when I move toward him, he backs away. "Stay right there!" he shouts in hurried French. "Don't move."

"I'm here to help."

He folds in on himself, gripping his knees. For a moment, I think he's going to throw up. Instead, he sobs. "It was dark, so dark . . ."

I frown. The sun is setting, but its light still shines through the trees, painting the path gold and brown. There is shade here, but it isn't dark, and there is no way this man has been in the wood overnight. I feel the travelers as soon as they breach the thresholds. My body hums and my legs carry me to them.

"What's it like?" I asked Dad once. We sat on an overturned log, munching on the trail mix and apple slices Mom had packed for us. "For the travelers?"

"Disorienting," he said. "A maze of vertical bars and a never-ending green ceiling. Every turn looks the same. Every path contains their footprints, even when they're certain they've never walked that path before. The more time they spend in here, the more they lose themselves."

I nodded as if I understood, but the truth was, I had never felt disoriented in the wood. I always knew where I was going, where I had been. I knew the paths as if they were etched into my brain. I still do, even when they change, even when an old threshold closes for good and a new one pops up in its place. I have never lost myself here.

I keep Dad's explanation in mind, trying to empathize with what the French man is going through, hoping that empathy will show in my face and in my posture as I approach him. But he eyes me like he's in a bad dream, and I'm the monster stalking him.

"Monsieur," I start again, "from whence do you come?"

"I was walking back to the office from lunch," he mutters,

more to himself than to me. "I was in the middle of the city. How did I end up here?" He slaps his palm against his brow. "*How did I end up here?*"

"Please, sir, I need you to stay calm. I'll help you find your way back—"

I reach for him, but he slaps my hand away. "*Non!*" he shouts. "Where am I?"

"Tell me where you came from," I say, "and I'll tell you where you are."

He scoffs at my questioning. A strong wind rustles the leaves overhead, dousing us with sunlight. A moment later the wind dies down. The leaves settle, shrouding the man in a dense patch of shade. His eyes widen as he takes in the trees surrounding him. "*Non, non, non, non—*"

He scrambles out of the shade.

"Monsieur," I say very slowly, very calmly. "Tell me where you came from and this will all be over."

"How do I know I can trust you?"

"Don't I look trustworthy?"

He squeezes his eyes shut.

"Please," I say. "All you have to do is trust me, and you'll go home. I swear it."

He stops breathing, and for a moment I worry he's going to pass out. Then one eye opens, followed by the other. "Paris."

"What street?" There are three active thresholds in Paris, thresholds being much more common in older cities.

"Rue Mazarine," he says. "That's where I live. But I was walking down Rue Princesse when I somehow ended up in this godforsaken place."

"Good. What year?"

He narrows his eyes. "That's an odd question."

"Humor me."

"1993."

I smile to myself for guessing right. "Come on. I'll take you home."

The walk isn't far, which only cements the fact that he couldn't have been wandering in the wood long enough to become quite so paranoid. Then again, maybe I'm overthinking it. Maybe he's just paranoid by nature. If I were a regular person, with no knowledge of the wood, and I was walking down a street in Paris and suddenly walked onto a path in the middle of an enchanted forest, wouldn't I be a little less than trusting of the random girl who showed up asking me where I was from?

"If you walk through the gap between those two trees, you'll find yourself back on Rue Princesse," I tell him, stopping at his threshold.

He gives me a quizzical look. "Thank you, Mademoiselle . . . ?"

"Winter," I say.

"Winter," he repeats, nodding and starting forward—

"Wait."

He looks back at me.

"Why were you saying it was dark?"

"*Pardon?*"

"When I found you," I say. "You said, 'It was dark, so dark.' But the sun's still up, and I know you weren't here overnight."

He shakes his head. "It only lasted a few seconds, but the sun—it was like it had been blotted out of the sky. I couldn't see anything." He laughs a little and scratches the back of his neck. "Perhaps I had a panic attack."

"Do you get those often?"

"Only once before."

"Did you black out then, too?"

"*Non*," he admits, "but this is a most unusual circumstance."

"Of course." I gesture toward the threshold. "Go on, before someone worries about you."

He swallows, his Adam's apple bobbing in his throat. "*Merci*." His voice echoes through the trees even after he's disappeared.

I'm less than a quarter mile from my threshold—the kitchen lights wink at me through the trees, blotches of yellow that dapple and move across the bark—when I hear the footsteps. They're too quiet this time, like someone's trying to sneak through my wood, and I know there's only one person it can be.

I take a deep breath. There is almost no light left in the wood. The sun is just the edge of a fingernail on the horizon, where a splotch of Easter-egg pink sky fades into dark purple clouds. The path slithers under my feet, flecks of dirt skating forward like miniature tumbleweeds. The wind has returned, howling through the spaces in the trees, blowing thin wisps of curling mist onto the path.

I don't have time for this.

The footsteps are closer, coming up the path to my right. I edge forward on my toes, careful not to make any noise. The wind flows in and out like the tide, and I can hear Brightonshire breathing through the quiet pauses.

Dad would tell me to leave him. If he's stupid enough to travel the wood at night, he isn't worth saving.

I would say that's cruel. We don't get to play God here.

Dad would say we have no idea what goes on in the wood after dark. We don't know if the thresholds close or stay open. How many people stumble their way past the thresholds, only to never make it back out—a steady stream of travelers feeding the monster the wood becomes at night. That doesn't mean we stay and become the next course on the menu.

That was why, in his darkest moments, Dad didn't think our job actually meant anything. Why he thought we were just wasting time, protecting something that can protect itself.

But I have to believe what we do has a purpose, and I have to believe that everyone in this wood is worth saving because if I don't, if I let myself think the way Dad used to, then his sudden disappearance from our lives would have been for nothing.

And I couldn't handle that.

The boy rounds the bend, and again I grab him before his eyes even register I'm there. I hook my arm around his neck and drop him to the ground. All around us, the wood creaks and groans. Darkness seeps in like spilled ink across paper.

"We have to go," I say, dispensing with the formalities. I grab his arm and wrench him up.

"I will not leave." He tries to twist out of my grip, but fear has made me stronger than he is.

I fist my hands in his shirt and tug him forward, so he can see the whites of my eyes. "If you don't come with me now, we're both dead."

"Then let me pass so that I might find shelter."

There's a crack next to us, like lightning. The trees are morphing in the darkness, branches reaching out with knobby fingers.

"Not happening, Brightonshire." I have to yell to be heard over the wind. "Way I see it, you have two options. You do what I say or I leave you here to die. Which is it?"

His hand locks around my wrist. "If what you say is true, we do not have time to return to my threshold. We must go through yours."

"Nice try, but I have one thing you don't."

"And what, pray tell, is that?"

"Friends." I push off him, grab the coin, and signal the fireflies. They surround him as he gets to his feet, a buzzing fire-blue mob. "Take him to the Brightonshire threshold, quickly."

They push him forward, singeing his clothes, his hair, until he finally gets the message and jogs down the path toward his threshold.

"And don't come back at night," I yell after him, when really I should have yelled, *Don't come back at all.*

Thirty seconds to sundown.

I sprint for my threshold. I don't know if the fireflies will still be on my side come full night. They could just as easily turn on him, burn him to nothing, but he's no longer my concern. I did everything I could with the time he gave me. If he survives it, maybe he'll be more cooperative next time.

Because I know, if he survives, there will be a next time. There's something he wants desperately, and desperate people do crazy things. I've come across my fair share of them in my time here, but none of them, not one, have been desperate to pass through the wood into another time. They've all just wanted to go home.

So what's Brightonshire's endgame?

My feet stick to the path as I draw closer to my threshold, like running through tar. A figure moves across our back-porch light, and then Mom is standing there, her hands wrapped around the porch railing as she stares into the wood, bouncing back and forth on the balls of her feet. I try to call out to her, to let her know I'm here, I'm coming, but she can't hear me. She only hears and sees what anyone else who isn't a direct guardian descendant would: a thick patch of trees that has yet to be torn down by a developer or some millionaire looking to build another mansion along the Olentangy.

I pump my legs harder, until my feet are barely touching the ground. The path morphs into quicksand, sucking me down with every step. Unnatural shadows swim past me on either side. A vine lashes out from the darkness, curling around my calf and pulling me to the ground. I grab the knife from my back pocket, flick it open, and cut the vine. It slithers back into the trees.

I push myself out of the muck and crawl forward. Ten feet away, five. The path pulls my ankles under, followed by my shins, my knees. I'm half swimming, half dragging my body to the break in the trees.

This is it. Full night.

I'm not going to make it.

Mom senses it, too, even though she can't see me. She runs for the entrance to the wood, her hair swinging behind her.

The quicksand pulls me under with incredible ease, folding around my body, enveloping me in its womb. My knees are gone, my thighs. I dig my fingernails into the silt, stretching for the solid land that is just inches from my reach. The path bubbles over my hips, my back, rushing up my shoulder blades.

Mom stares at me from the edge of the threshold, her daughter dying right in front of her, but all she sees is the path, looking as solid as it always has.

My heart squeezes. I can't leave her all alone in this world. She won't survive it.

I kick my legs out behind me and *reachreachreach* for the threshold, my fingertips inching just outside the tree line as a wave of silt crashes over my head, pulling me under.

*Winter*, a voice whispers in my ear. *I've missed you.*

*Dad?*

Something closes over my outstretched fingers and pulls. My arm releases from the muck, followed by my head. I take a deep breath as black silt drips from my hair. My forearm crosses the threshold and the silt disappears, no trace of it on my skin or the sleeve of my white tee. My head breaches the threshold next, and the muck that had clung to my eyelashes and gotten crammed up my nose is gone as well.

Mom pulls the rest of my body out of the wood. She scoops me up into her shaking arms. Her voice chips on her sobs. "I was so scared. I was so scared—"

I wrap my arms around her. "It's okay," I say. "I'm okay."

She shakes her head, her fear turning to anger. "Where were you? Why didn't you come home?"

"I'm sorry, Mom. I—"

"You are never going back in there again."

I don't say anything. We both know she doesn't have any control over that. It's bigger than she is. Bigger than I am. But it makes her feel better to say it, even if only for that brief second.

I think she wishes she could have said it to Dad. Like she

believes if she'd been more vocal about her concerns, he might not have walked off the path.

Mom wipes her hands under her eyes. "Come on," she says. "Dinner's ready."

I follow her into the house. My legs tremble beneath me and my upper body is numb, but I won't do my stretches here, so close to the wood. Not when it feels like something is still in there, waiting for me to come back.

"Why can't I go in the wood at night?" I ask Dad as we practice my first foreign language—Latin—at the dining room table.

"Your conjugation is terrible," Dad replies, looking over my shoulder at my worksheet.

I cover the paper with my scrawny arms. "Why can't I?"

He sighs. "It's dangerous."

I roll my eyes. "But *why* is it dangerous?"

"It's dangerous," he says, "because the wood changes at night. It takes on an entirely different personality."

I arch my brow, and he laughs.

"That isn't enough of an explanation for you?"

I shake my head.

"Well, I was saving this lecture for a different time, but I suppose it doesn't hurt to give you a sneak peek now." He scoots his chair closer, takes the pencil from my hand, and pulls my workbook out from under my arms. He sketches something in the corner as he speaks. "Just as there are nocturnal creatures in our world, there are creatures in the wood who come out only when night falls. These are dangerous creatures, and the little we know about them comes from what the Old Ones were willing to tell us, and what some past guardians who stayed a little too long in the wood after sunset were able to see before just barely making it out alive. Of course, there were guardians who did the same thing who didn't make it out alive, but we can hardly get any information from them."

He smiles, but when he catches my eye, the smile disappears and he clears his throat. "I don't tell you this to scare you, Winnie girl. These creatures can't enter our world, so you have nothing to fear from them here, and it will be a long time before you'll have to enter the wood without me by your side. Even then, so long as you leave the wood before the sun sets, you'll be safe. Understand?"

I nod, my fingernails digging into the edge of my seat.

He stops sketching and passes the workbook back to me. The empty space running along the top of the page is now filled with monsters. Big, fat ones with skin that looks like tree bark; tall, skinny ones that look like humans if humans could be pulled out like taffy and given an extra row of teeth; long ones that slither on the ground like snakes; and stocky ones with leathery wings that look like a cross between a bat and a bald eagle.

I point to the dark blob shape in the corner. "What's this one?"

"A shadow creature," he says. "The Old Ones call them Sentinels. They're flesh-eaters, travel in packs. They freeze their victims, keeping the meat fresh so they can take their time skinning them alive."

My eyes widen.

Dad ruffles my hair. "I told you not to worry about them, didn't I? The chances that you'll ever run into one are slim, especially if you keep your wits about you. That's why these lessons are important, so you'll be prepared for any and all situations, including avoiding danger whenever possible. Take me, for example. I've been doing this for over thirty years, ever since I was your age, and I have yet to leave the wood after sundown. I only know what these creatures look like from my own studies, not because I've seen them for myself. There, you feel better now, don't you?"

I nod, even though it's a complete and total lie.

"And then," he says, "as if these things weren't enough, the wood itself changes at night. It will turn on you. If you're lucky, it will kill you before any of the monsters find you. But if you're smart, you'll never be in that position to begin with, so you won't have to worry about it. Got it?"

"Yes, sir."

"Good. Now that we've got that settled, let's run through your conjugations again."

I roll my eyes. "Daaad. Do we *have* to?"

He taps his finger against the monster sketches.

"Oh," I say. "Right."

I pick up Latin pretty quickly after that. It helps that I can't sleep for a week after Dad's lecture. I lie in bed for hours every night, counting conjugations instead of sheep.

⟶⟫⟩⟨⟸

Mom tries to call Uncle Joe after a silent dinner, in which the silverware screeching across our plates was the only sound, but he doesn't answer. I sit in the living room, curled up on Dad's favorite leather recliner, his bookcase full of first-edition Yeats and Emerson and Fitzgerald behind me. The leather still smells a little like black coffee and sandalwood cologne. I wrap his favorite blanket around me and stare at the wood through the back window.

It has never looked as terrifying as it does tonight.

My thoughts drift to Brightonshire, whether he made it out or not. I hope he did. No one deserves that kind of death. But why was he in the wood at night in the first place? If he knew the wood as he said he did, why risk it? What is he trying to find? My mind turns it over as condensation gathers on the windowpane.

The phone rings and Mom shuffles into the kitchen in her pajamas. She frowns at me. "What are you still doing up?"

I glance at the clock on the mantel. Ten thirty.

I must have fallen asleep.

Mom answers the phone and, after a few seconds, says, "She's not going back in there, Joe. Find someone else."

She crosses her arm under her chest, and I don't have to hear Uncle Joe to know what he's saying. *There is no one else, Grace. You knew that when you married Jack. This is the way it has to be.*

She listens to him, tears swimming in her eyes, then looks at me. "He wants to talk to you."

It takes me a second to register the phone being held out to me, and another second for my body to actually move. My sock feet pad across the carpet of the living room and onto the linoleum. I take the phone from Mom's hand and wrap the cord around my finger.

"Hello?"

Mom slips out of the kitchen and up the stairs, the old floorboards creaking beneath her.

"You okay?"

He sounds tired. The bone-deep kind that only starts to show on the surface after it's already rotted away the core.

"Not really."

"What happened?"

"Brightonshire," I say. "He came back at sundown."

Joe pauses. A teakettle whines on the other end of the line. I imagine him walking through his studio apartment overlooking the river, passing the artifacts he's collected over the years: a funerary-instructions tablet from ancient Egypt, a vase from Babylon, a Renaissance tapestry from Venice. I guess those are the perks of being immortal. Dad used to say there were downsides, too, darker parts of Joe that he never showed anyone except Dad.

"Your mom said she had to pull you out," he says, and now I imagine him sitting at his claw-foot Victorian dining table with a mug of tea. "That all she could see were your fingers and that something had ahold of the rest of you."

I nod.

"Win? You there?"

"Yeah," I say, leaning against the counter. "The path. It . . . it turned on me."

"You're lucky you made it out."

"I know."

"Don't let it happen again."

It's his good-bye voice. I learned to recognize it when I was young. He has a habit of hanging up the phone before I'm ready.

"Uncle Joe—" My breath hitches in my throat.

"Yeah?"

"I heard his voice again."

Joe sighs. "He's not in there, Win. He's gone."

He says more, but I don't listen. It's nothing I haven't heard already. I just stare at the moon breaking over the trees, striping the darkness with silver, like Uncle Joe's hair, until he hangs up.

I place the phone back in its cradle on the wall.

I don't know why I'm so shaken up. My dad, Uncle Joe— they both warned me what would happen if I stayed in the wood after dark. Still, it feels like my family dog contracted rabies, and now it's sitting in there, hiding in the trees. Waiting for me.

I dread going back in tomorrow.

# XII

I sleep in.

I don't know if Mom turned off my alarm or if I forgot to set it, but it's the first time in years I've missed my morning patrol. Not a big deal when I wasn't the sole guardian of my territory, but Dad isn't here to pick up the slack anymore.

I throw on a tee and a pair of jeans, not even bothering with brushing my hair or my teeth. There's no time. Mom has a mug of coffee and a bran muffin waiting for me on the counter, along with a note. *Working late. Leftovers tonight?*

I look at the oven clock. Ten minutes until I'm supposed to pick up Mer. Twenty-five minutes until we're officially late for first period. I pour the coffee into a travel mug, wrap the muffin in a napkin, and head out onto the back porch.

I check my watch—nine minutes—set my backpack and thermos on the porch steps, then head into the wood with my knife out and ready.

It looks like my wood again. No tar-like quicksand on the paths. No tree limbs reaching for me like witches' hands. The sun is a finger's width high in the sky to my left. I can almost believe last night was a dream if I try hard enough.

That's the thing about the wood. It blurs the line between what's real and what isn't. Makes you think you're crazy for seeing things no one else sees, like dead people walking and uncles who fade in sifts of sand. If I ever told Mer what goes on in here, she'd send me to an institution.

It feels like my wood again, too. No cold blasts of phantom air, no shadows shifting between the trees. Everything looks as it should. The trees sigh like they're happy to see me. The paths stretch out in front of me in dizzying swirls and tangled knots, paint dripping off the leaves, slowly changing the wood from summer green to autumn fire.

I don't have time to do a full sweep—though *full* is a relative term in a never-ending forest—so I stick to the paths closest to my threshold, listening for any sign of disturbance, but I don't feel another presence, and I'm confident no travelers have slipped through this morning. At one point, I think I hear a child crying, but it's only a robin warbling in the tree to my right, just outside the wood.

I check my watch as soon as I cross my threshold. Great, I have exactly two minutes to make an eight-minute drive. I tuck my knife into my backpack, swing the backpack onto my shoulder, and grab my thermos. Then I jump into Dad's car, throw my backpack on the backseat, and peel out of the driveway.

Meredith's sitting on her porch when I pull up. Her brow furrows as she slides into the passenger seat.

"Well, don't you look radiant this Thursday morning," she says as I pull back onto 315. "You sick or something?"

"Overslept."

"Well, we can't let Trevor see you looking like this." She takes out her makeup bag and almost shoves a mascara wand up my nose.

"Must you?" I ask, groaning as the light in front of me turns red. It'll be a miracle if we make it on time.

"Oh, I'm afraid I must."

"At least save the mascara for when I'm not driving."

She hands me a hair tie as we sit there, and I let her dab some concealer under my eyes as I pull my hair into a ponytail. I learned long ago that there's no point in fighting Meredith when she's made up her mind about something. At least not about something as unimportant in the grand scheme of things as makeup.

We pull into the parking lot with three minutes to spare, and I skid into first period just as the bell stops ringing.

I try to concentrate in my classes, but I'm tense and my mind keeps drifting back to the wood, my body waiting for the inevitable tug I'll feel when Brightonshire decides to make his next move. I test out various explanations to give my teachers if I need to leave. With Mr. Harris, my precalc teacher, it's a known fact that all I have to do is go up to his desk and whisper "female problems" and he'll hand over a hall pass, no questions asked, even to a no-good truant like me. Madame Bent, my French teacher—French, of course, being the one class I don't have to try in *at all*—will give one away if you say you need a mental break, but only on the days she isn't properly caffeinated.

When I make it to seventh period without feeling even a twinge that something might be wrong, the anxiety swirling through my stomach starts to subside. Maybe I won't need an excuse after all.

Too bad my life just isn't that simple.

With ten minutes left in class, I feel it, like a dodgeball in the gut. My breath huffs out of my lungs and my skin prickles, hair rising on my forearms and neck. My legs cramp from the urge to move, to run, to get into my wood and not stop until I've done my job. My neighbor side-eyes me as I squeeze my hands into fists. I bite my tongue to keep from whimpering.

I stand abruptly, cutting off Mr. Abbott's lecture about the symbolism of the moors in *Wuthering Heights*. "I need to go to the nurse's office."

He blinks at me. "Can it wait for the bell?"

This seems like a reasonable request. Even my classmates are staring at me like I'm crazy. There's no point in leaving school now, with only one class period left after this one. But sixty minutes is worth several lifetimes in the wood. I can't risk it.

"No, it can't." I cough into my hand, but it doesn't sound very convincing.

Mr. Abbott studies me, no doubt weighing the number of times I've already skipped his class this year against the fact that I still have the highest grade in the class and participate more than anyone else when I am here. Staying on top of my schoolwork is my way of making up for my absences to my teachers. It also helps me talk the principal down from a suspension to a detention when I'm in serious trouble. Or at least it did, before I discovered Principal Edwards has a Lake Erie–size crush on my mom. I even overheard him call her a "babe" once to the guidance counselor, a fact I've used to my advantage on more than one occasion.

My calves cramp again and I double over, slapping my hand on my desk to steady myself.

Mr. Abbott's eyes widen. He hands me the hall pass. "Feel better."

I thank him, scoop my books into my arms, and head out into the hall. I already feel better now that I'm *doing* something, but the buzz beneath my skin won't subside until I've emptied the wood of travelers. I make a quick stop at my locker and throw everything in my backpack. There's no time to weed out what I need from what I don't.

I text Mer once I get to my car, telling her something came up and asking if she'll need a ride after school.

She replies: *Nope, dance troupe until four thirty. Someone else can take me home. Have fun skipping class, loser ;)*

I don't know what Mer thinks it is that I do when I skip school. If she thinks I'm a stoner or meeting up with a boy or what. It started right after Dad disappeared, and I think she assumes it's my way of coping with my loss. Either way, she gives me my space and pretty much leaves me alone like everyone else. Sometimes I get the sense that she's a little jealous, though, that I manage to skip school and still get good grades. She wouldn't be so jealous if she knew *why* I skipped, or that I have to study into all hours of the night just to keep up.

I speed down 315, going forty-five on the curves and punching it to just under sixty on the straight stretches. I know I should slow down, but I can't. Every fiber of my being is telling me to *move, move, move. Faster, faster, faster.*

A mile from my house, I have to drop down to forty as I pull up behind a garbage truck. Good thing, too. I pass a speed trap around the next bend. The cop doesn't even look at me as I pass, just keeps his radar gun pointed at the curve. I let out a sigh. It's killing me to go this slow, but it'd be even worse if I had to actually stop and waste time getting a ticket.

*Finally*, I swing into my driveway, pull the keys out of the ignition, and head into the wood.

I know where Brightonshire is as soon as I step over the threshold, a predator sniffing its prey. He decided to circle around this time, like that would make him harder to find. I veer to the right, not even bothering to hide my footsteps. It's not like he isn't expecting me. My knife flashes under the afternoon sun.

I find him less than a mile in, standing in front of the Amsterdam threshold, staring at the glyphs carved into the branch that hangs over the invisible doorway between the trees. His head tilts and his hand cups his chin. His eyes move right to left as if he can actually read them.

But that's impossible—it's a dead language. Only an Old One or a direct guardian descendant can read the glyphs.

I stop five feet behind him, watch the dancing strips of sunlight filtering through the trees turn his hair from dark blond to caramel to gold and back again. The wind is light, a toddler blowing out its birthday candles after an extra-special wish, but it still manages to rustle the thin cotton of his shirt.

He doesn't look away from the carving as he asks, "Must we go through the same charade every time?"

"What charade?"

"'From whence do you come,' 'return to your threshold,' 'don't come back.' It is getting rather tiring."

"No," I say to his spine. "I need some information from you first."

He turns away from the threshold, and that's when I notice the leaf turning black at the edges. The black is running down the green in thick globules, like blood instead of paint. It covers the leaf and drips to the ground, but the color doesn't disappear. It sizzles into the earth, smoldering in the grass, creating a pool of black glass.

My eyes widen as I step forward. "What is that?"

I glance around at the other trees, at the leaves on the lower branches that have already been painted the colors of orange flame and yellow sunbursts and red candy apples. There are a few dark purple leaves that flip up to show pink undersides as the breeze kicks by, but nothing that could be called a true, endless-abyss black.

"I'm not certain," he says. "There's naught like it in the journals."

My brow furrows as I look at him, *really* look at him. I take in the small scar on his chin, like an off-kilter dimple, the slash of his eyebrows hanging low over his eyes. "Who are you?"

"I will not give you my name," he scoffs. "Not until you have earned it."

"Is that some kind of eighteenth-century rule they don't teach in our history classes?"

"Names have power," he says, watching our reflections in the black puddle. "You can control those of us who do not belong here more easily if you know them." His eyes flick to mine. "I am surprised your father did not teach you that."

"How do you know my father?"

"I do not know him personally," he says, "but I know of him."

"I don't believe you."

He shrugs. "Believe what you like. That is all the answer I am prepared to give."

"Fine." I cross my arms over my chest. "If you won't tell me who you are, then at least tell me what you're doing here, and how you know so much about the wood."

"Only if you promise not to send me back."

"Nope, sorry," I say, grabbing his arm and turning him back toward his threshold. "Not that interested."

He wrenches his arm from my grasp.

I sigh. "Don't tell me I'm going to have to send my friends after you again. They're not very pleasant."

He takes a step toward me, shadows clouding his eyes. "Something's happening here." His breath whispers across my lips. It tastes of black tea and cinnamon, mixed with the campfire smell that clings to his shirt. "The wood is changing. You must feel it. The darkness that creeps in during the day. The eyes watching when no one is there."

His physical presence is so big, so strong, it makes me want to step back. But that's not how I roll. Not here. Not in my wood. I lean my head forward instead, so that our brows are almost touching. "I don't feel anything."

"Liar."

The wind kicks up harder and the smell of the wood—bark and raw earth and autumn leaves—slinks up my nostrils.

I exhale. "Okay, maybe there's something . . . off," I say, thinking of the French traveler—*it was dark, so dark*—and Dad's voice, welcoming me home as the path pulled me under. I point at the leaf turning black. "And that's not exactly normal."

"It's worsening," he says, "whatever it is."

"How do you know so much about this place?"

"My family is connected to it, like yours."

"You mean . . . you're a guardian?" It makes sense—I don't know why I didn't think of it before. But why would a past guardian be using the wood for his own personal use? It goes against everything we are, our entire purpose for being.

"I wish," he says, blowing my theory to hell. "My parents are cartographers, record keepers, members of—"

"The council?"

"Precisely."

This makes even less sense than the guardian theory. I've never met an Old One who looked so . . . young. "So"—a million questions swirl through my mind; I grab one at random—"that means you can walk through the wood without getting lost?"

"Unfortunately, I cannot. My parents adopted me when I was very young. I do not share their gifts."

"You're human?"

He nods.

"Then how—?"

He holds up his arms. His sleeves fall to his elbows, revealing dark maps inked on his skin. If it weren't for the smudging near the wrists, I would swear they were tattoos, they look so perfect. Pathways shoot out from his threshold, marking other portals along the way and alternate routes to take to reach my own.

"I copied these from their library," he says.

I nod at the sign he was reading. "And the glyphs?"

"My parents taught me how to read them."

"Well. Isn't that convenient." I shake my head. "Look, I can't help you if you don't tell me why you're here."

He studies me a moment, his gaze drifting down my face. He lingers on the mole on my collarbone before returning to my eyes. He takes a step back, and though the tips of our shoes are still nearly touching, it feels like an ocean of space opens up between us and I can breathe again.

"My parents are Augustus and Celia," he says, watching me carefully.

"The council members who disappeared?"

He swallows. "Yes."

"Oh. I'm . . . I'm sorry."

He doesn't say anything for a moment, and neither do I. My voice is quiet when I speak again. "The other council members seem to think they'll turn up soon. That they just lost track of time or something."

He stares at the ground. "I do not think so."

"Not to be insensitive, but I still don't see what that has to do with you running around this wood like you're Lara Croft."

His forehead scrunches up. "Pardon me?"

"Never mind," I say, waving off his confusion. "I need you to tell me *exactly* why you're here."

He catches his bottom lip between his teeth. "I've already taken a great risk by telling you as much as I have."

I cross my arms over my chest.

He sighs and glances at the wood around us. We're the only ones here, but he lowers his voice. "I think their disappearance has something to do with what's happening in the wood now, in your time, and I cannot just sit at home and act as though everything is all right. Yet, I . . ."

"You what?"

He stands rigidly straight, his hands behind his back. "I do not think I can do it without your help."

I frown. "What exactly are you asking me?"

"I need you to let me through," he says. "Into *your* time."

# XIII

Brightonshire watches me, hope and uncertainty rolling across his face in equal measure.

"You're asking me to break the most important rule of the wood," I say. "The rule that isn't even spoken because it should be known, without question. The rule that encapsulates my entire purpose as a guardian." No traveler can ever pass through a threshold into a time that is not their own.

"Yes, I am asking that of you, but I am also telling you, if you do not let me through into your time and work with me to discover the truth of what is happening here, there may no longer be a wood for you to protect." His Adam's apple rolls down his throat. "There may no longer be a *world* for you to protect."

I rub my palms into my eyes, where a dull ache has sprouted behind my corneas. "This is insane. If what you're saying is true, why didn't you tell me this from the beginning? Why run?"

"I had not planned on involving anyone." He glances at the trees, his voice dropping lower as he says, "I don't—" He takes a deep breath. "I'm not sure who can be trusted."

"But you trust me? That's funny—you didn't seem to trust me yesterday. What's changed?"

"You have not given me much choice in the matter." He runs his hand through his hair. "And I believe the disappearance of my parents may have something to do with the disappearance of your father. I believe you are the only one who can help me."

Whatever I was expecting him to say, it wasn't this. "What?"

"I will say no more of it here. It isn't safe. I can explain properly in a more private setting."

"Yeah, well, that isn't going to happen. If you have something to say, say it now."

"Please," he whispers. "I cannot risk someone overhearing."

"There *is* no one else," I say. "Just you and me."

He shakes his head.

"What are you afraid of?"

"I'd rather not say. Not here."

"You're not giving me a lot to go on, Brightonshire." I roll my eyes. I can't believe I'm even humoring this lunatic. "Why should I trust you?"

His hand reaches tentatively toward me, his fingers stretching until they lace through mine. Heat sparks along my knuckles, up my arm, and down my spine. My stomach tugs as I stare at his hand. A hand that, for all intents and purposes, was laid in a coffin with the rest of his body over two hundred years ago and should not be here, intersected with mine.

He holds my gaze. "Trust is not simple. It is not something that can be bought or earned within moments of meeting each other. But I promise you, if you let me through to your time, I will do everything you ask of me. I will follow your orders and be where you want me to be and say what you want me to say.

If I ever once step out of line or give you any reason to doubt my intentions, you need simply order me back into the wood, and I will go."

"Just like that?"

He nods.

My lips tug into a half smile. "That's kind of hard to believe, given your record."

He doesn't smile back. "I swear on the lives of my parents, I will not let you down." His hand tightens around mine. "I need to know what has happened to them. I need to . . ." He swallows. "I need to know if they can be saved."

And with that one statement, he unlocks the deepest secret of my heart. The belief that I can still save my dad, despite everyone telling me it's impossible. I see the same desire in his eyes. Wonder if others have told him it's useless, too.

"I can't believe I'm doing this," I say after a moment's pause, in which I think about the reasons why I shouldn't do this and shove them aside, all because one thought keeps rising above them: *If there's a chance Dad's connected to this, if I can finally find out what happened to him, don't I owe it to myself and my mom to try?*

I huff out a breath. "You have to do everything I say, no questions asked. Starting with my afternoon patrol. You need to stay by my side and not make any trouble, understand? Then I'll sneak you into my house and you will tell me *everything*. If I don't believe you or don't like something you say, I'm bringing you right back here and you will never come barging through my wood again. You okay with that?"

Confusion scrunches his face. "Okay?"

"It means, 'Do we have a deal?'"

"Yes," he says, holding out his hand. "We have a deal."

My brow arches. "Try to keep up."

We start down the path, cutting deeper into the wood.

After several minutes of tense silence, in which I am distract-ingly aware of his footsteps next to mine, I ask him, "You know this is dangerous, what we're doing? If the council finds out, we're dead. As in coffins six feet under and worms wiggling between our decaying toes."

"I fear it will take quite some time to become accustomed to your unusual vernacular."

I glare at him.

"Yes, I know," he says, quietly. "And yet it is worth it."

I think of Dad, waiting for me to rescue him. I think of Mom, waiting for me to come home for dinner, wishing she could set a third plate at the table. I think of me, of all the times I've wished Dad were still here to finish my lessons. To give me some sort of validation and make me feel like I might actually know what I'm doing. To just . . . be a dad.

"Yeah," I say. "It is."

⊱───❧

The little girl is curled up on the path. Her peach-colored dress is smudged with dirt and her hair has fallen out of pearl-encrusted combs. There's blood on her arms, thin scratch marks trailing from her shoulders to her wrists. At first I think she must have wandered into a patch of brambles, but then her hands move up her arms. Blood coats the crescents of her fingernails. She digs them into her flesh and pulls down as she stares at trees she can no longer see.

Brightonshire pulls up short. All the blood seems to drain from his face at once. "What's the matter with her?"

My throat constricts as I stare down at her. "The wood's the matter with her. It makes people delirious." I glance back at him, my eyes narrowed. "That's why I'm still not certain I can trust you. With all the time you've spent in here, you should be just as crazy as she is." Well, maybe not *just* as crazy, since I've never seen anyone lose it this quickly before, but at least a little perturbed. "Why aren't you?"

"I took precautions."

"What sort of precautions?"

He doesn't answer.

"You said you'll say anything I want you to say, and if you don't I can send you right back to your time. So? What's it going to be?"

He hesitates, then pulls his topcoat away from his body, revealing a silver flask at his waist. He lowers his voice and leans into my ear, his breath tickling my neck. "It is an elixir my parents were perfecting to help mortals keep a clear head in the wood. It is forbidden by the council, so I would appreciate it if you did not mention it to anyone." His gaze flicks back to the girl. "Can we help her?"

"She'll be back to normal once she goes home. We just have to get her there."

What I don't tell him is this: I have only seen three travelers look this lost in my time in the wood, back when I was first starting to get a feel for the paths without my father's presence by my side. They had all spent hours wandering through trees that never changed, and their last shreds of hope had seeped out of them along with their sanity.

I didn't trust my instincts then. Didn't know the tingling in my spine and the tightening in my calves was alerting me to another's presence in the wood. Didn't understand it was guiding me to the travelers. I'd never really had to trust my instincts before, with Dad. I just followed his.

But this girl couldn't have been in here more than half an hour—enough to frighten her, certainly, but not enough to break her. I'd have felt her presence as soon as I entered the wood, just like I felt Brightonshire's.

It doesn't make sense.

I crouch down next to her, laying my hand gently on her shoulder. "From whence do you come?"

Her skin grates into her nails, a soft sound that reminds me of the river. She doesn't speak.

"What is your name?" I try, remembering what Brightonshire said about names. Maybe if I know hers, she'll be more willing to follow me.

Her fingers catch on her wrists, and she reaches up to her shoulders once more.

I grab her bloodied hands. Fingernail shards stick out of the gashes on her arms. My stomach pitches, and I grit my teeth to stop myself from vomiting. "You don't need to hurt yourself anymore," I say. "We're here to help."

Something flickers in her eyes, a spark of recognition. "The shadows said no one could help me," she whispers. "They said I was going to die in here, like the others."

I don't know what she means by *others*. I've watched people go insane, but there have been no deaths that I know of since I began my lessons, not during the day at least. (I can't account for what happens in the wood after dark.) And I don't know what she means by *shadows*, but the fact that she's hearing voices concerns me. I need to get her out of here before this place permanently damages her.

"They shouldn't have told you that," I say. "It's not true."

"They said they'd come back for me, at night. They said they wouldn't let me get out alive."

Brightonshire drops down next to me, pushing the girl's hair out of her eyes. "We will not let any harm come to you, little one."

"Can you tell me your name?" I ask her.

She swallows. "Sophie."

"Where do you come from, Sophie?"

She frowns and turns her head once more to the trees. The light begins to fade from her eyes.

"Don't look there, Sophie," I tell her, placing my finger under her chin and forcing her eyes back to mine. "Look at me. What year is it?"

She laughs. The sound is thin and too high-pitched. "That's a silly question."

"I know, but please answer it anyway."

"1914."

Brightonshire shakes his head. "Remarkable. Over a hundred years separate us, and yet here I am, speaking with her."

I narrow my eyes at him. "*Shh*, you'll scare her."

He squeezes her hand. "I apologize, Sophie. Can you tell us where you live?"

"Boston," she says. "I'm supposed to be getting ready for my sister's engagement ball."

"Don't worry," I tell her. "We'll get you there. Just follow us, okay?"

She hesitates. "The shadows told me not to move. They said they'd come back for me."

"They can't hurt you, Sophie. Not if you come with us."

But I've already lost her. She stares through me, her eyes fuzzy.

I open my mouth, but before I can say anything, Brightonshire scoots in front of Sophie, forcing her to look at him. "Have you ever played hide-and-seek?"

Her lips pull at the corners. "It's my favorite game."

"Marvelous!" He claps his hands together. "My friend and I play it all the time in this wood. Your home is hiding between the trees, you see, and we must seek it out. The first person to find it wins the game."

She tilts her head. "Really?"

He arches a brow. "Do I look like I would lie to you?"

Her cheeks turn pink as she shakes her head.

Brightonshire takes her hand. "Come. Let us go find your home."

She smiles up at him, unconcerned with the thin trails of blood running down her arms. "All right."

They start down the path. I let Brightonshire lead the way, tapping him on the right or left shoulder depending on where we need to turn. I know the Boston threshold well. It's situated in a park, and it opens frequently. I tend to get at least two children or nannies from there a month. I even got a rider on a horse once who didn't even realize he was no longer in the park. I told him he'd just wandered off the main path and if he went back the way he came, he'd find himself in familiar territory. It didn't hit me until after he'd returned home how true a statement it was.

When we get to her threshold, I pull back on Brightonshire's shoulder, making him stop.

"Ah, here we are," he says.

Sophie frowns. "I don't see my house."

He puts his hands on his knees, dropping down to her level. "It's right through the trees there. You only need take a step forward and you'll see it."

She takes a small step, then stops. "I only see more trees."

"One more step should do it."

She sighs and walks forward, disappearing through the threshold.

He straightens and looks back at me. "I hope she will be all right."

"She's home now," I say. "She'll have some explaining to do, but her parents will just be happy to have her back."

He nods. "Where to now?"

"This way."

Our footsteps are muffled by the wind shaking the leaves overhead. They're almost all painted now. Sunlight glitters across them like Dorothy's ruby slippers, if she also had purple and orange and yellow slippers. Dad laughed the first time I said that, but he wouldn't be laughing now. Not with the black leaves speckled in between, spreading like disease.

I clear my throat. "Thanks for helping me with her," I say. "You're really good with children."

He shrugs. "I only wanted to see her home safely. She looked so broken."

"The wood will do that to you." Even without some unknown power turning the leaves black.

"It is odd."

"What's that?"

"The shadows Sophie described. Have you ever encountered aught like them before?"

"No," I say, though that's not entirely true. But last night, when shadows that shouldn't have been there without light to cast them darted through the trees, it was after the sun had already set. Not in the middle of the afternoon. "There are stories about the shadow monsters who live in the wood after dark, but there's no way Sophie was in the wood that long before we found her."

"How do you know?"

"I would have felt her presence earlier," I explain.

"Can you feel everyone's presence in the wood?"

"Yes," I say, ignoring the doubt tugging at my heart.

"Do you think these shadows have something to do with what's happening here?"

"I don't know."

We walk on, down the twisting, curving pathways. I watch Brightonshire, his steady footing, the crystal-clear focus in his eyes, all from an elixir that defies the very reason the guardians were selected in the first place: to protect the wood from the travelers who would use it for their own personal gains. Augustus and Celia must have known how dangerous this elixir would be if it fell into the wrong hands. Were they really willing to take such a risk simply so their adopted son could . . . what? Partake in their legacy? Or was there a different motive behind the elixir? Maybe they didn't disappear because something bad happened to them, but because *they* were doing something bad.

*And if that's the case, can Brightonshire even be trusted?*

# XIV

Twenty minutes to sundown. I hold up my hand, and Brightonshire comes to a stop next to my threshold. "Wait here."

My first steps out of the wood are wobbly, and my head feels like it weighs a thousand pounds, but I can't do my decompression exercises, not until I know the coast is clear. Taking deep, steadying breaths, I cross the backyard and check the driveway. No car, no Mom.

I grab my backpack from the car, then stick my head through the threshold and say, "All right. Follow me."

He steps through the threshold and immediately lists to the side. I grab him and stand him upright.

"What's wrong with me?" he asks, his face turning a sickly shade of green.

The fabric of his shirt is soft and delicate in my palms. Homespun. Nothing at all like the clothes we wear today. I clear my throat and let go of him. "It's just an aftereffect of the wood. Sit down for a second."

We sit next to the rock. I check my watch. I don't know how long I have until Mom gets here. For a moment, I think maybe I shouldn't hide him. Maybe I should tell her I'm bringing a two-hundred-fifty-year-old boy home from the wood, not because I think he's cute or anything, but because he's going through the same thing we are, and maybe we can help one another. Maybe if we find out what happened to his parents, we'll find out what happened to Dad, too. But we need to keep it a secret, because if the council finds out I've broken the most sacred rule of the wood, I don't know what they'll do.

Yeah . . . I don't see that going over so well. Besides, I don't plan on keeping him here long. I'm just going to hear him out, then send him right back where he belongs. He'll be here one night, tops.

I show him how to stretch and touch his toes, and then how to circle his head to loosen the knots in his neck. "Better?"

He nods.

He stays close as we head for the back porch, his eyes catching on the road, the telephone lines, the satellite dish sticking out of old Mr. Whitman's roof across the street. He sucks in a breath, his steps faltering as a man on a Schwinn speeds down the road. "What in God's name was that beast?"

"That was a bicycle," I say. "Don't worry, it won't hurt you."

"I find that highly unlikely."

I take my key out of my back pocket and twist it in the lock.

"Does everyone dress in such a fashion in your time?"

I glance over my shoulder at him. "What do you mean?"

"Do women wear pantaloons often? Or shirts that expose their arms so?"

I turn the knob and open the door. "Believe me, buddy. You

look just as weird to me as I do to you. Boots off," I tell him, chucking mine off by the heels. "I don't want to explain a mud trail to Mom if she gets home before I can clean it."

Brightonshire takes off his boots and holds one in each hand. "You do not wish to announce my presence?"

I snort. "God, no. My mom doesn't do so well with anything related to my job, and she definitely doesn't do so well with random boys in the house." Not that I've ever tested the theory, but I can guess what her reaction would be, and it would involve her favorite meat cleaver.

"So I am to remain hidden for the duration of my stay?"

"Hidden and silent." My keys clatter on the kitchen countertop as we cross to the back staircase off the pantry. "Think you can manage that?"

"I am not an imbecile," he grumbles.

I lead him upstairs to my room, through the first door on the right. I swing my backpack into the far corner, next to my desk, and spin around. Brightonshire stands in the doorway, staring at the ceiling fan. His hand reaches out, fingers curling in on themselves before getting too close to the lightbulb.

"What sort of candle is this, that it may burn so brightly without flame?"

"Um, it's called electricity," I say, even though I know I shouldn't tell him anything. Unspoken rule number two: If a traveler somehow makes it through a threshold into the future or, God forbid, is *invited* through one, he should not be informed about anything that may alter the course of history. This includes, but is not limited to, advances in technology and medicine, information on current world politics, or historical events that have occurred after the traveler's time.

He reaches for it again. "Amazing."

I move forward and snatch his hand in mine. There's a jolt, an awareness that shoots up my veins and makes my stomach churn as my skin touches his. Static—from my socks sliding across the rug next to my bed. That's all it is.

I clear my throat and let go of his hand. "That's not important right now. You need to tell me everything you know about what happened to your parents, and why exactly you need to be here, in my time, to save them."

"It is a long story," he says. "I am not certain of where I should begin."

"I have time."

He crosses his arms over his chest. "How much do you know about the council?"

I sit in my desk chair, fold my knees into my chest, and start counting off everything my dad ever told me on my fingers. "I know it was created a thousand years ago to protect the wood from humans who wanted to use its power to conquer lands and vanquish their enemies and all that villainous, medieval he-man stuff. I know the council members are immortal, and that they chose ten mortals they could trust to physically guard the wood from outside threats. One of those mortals happened to be my ancestor, and the guardianship has passed down through our bloodline ever since. Which is why I'm a little confused that your parents would make an elixir that would give travelers such an advantage in the wood."

"The elixir was never meant to be used by anyone else. It was only for me."

"Still, they must have realized it could fall into the wrong hands."

Brightonshire's eyes narrow. "Why so interested in the elixir?"

I give him the same look. "Why so *dodgy* about the elixir? How do you know it isn't related to what happened to your parents? I mean, they did go behind the council's back to make it. Maybe they've been doing other secret things, too."

"That's absurd," Brightonshire says through clenched teeth.

"Why?"

"My parents didn't disappear because they were doing something wrong," he says. "They disappeared because they knew too much."

My brow furrows. "What do you mean?"

He takes a deep breath. "What would you say if I told you my parents had reason to believe there was a conspiracy within the council?"

"What sort of conspiracy?"

"It all started with your father's disappearance. Naught like it had ever happened to a guardian before, not in broad daylight. My parents were far from pleased with the scope of the council investigation that followed. They spoke at the dinner table every night about how nothing was being done—"

"Wait, back up. What year did you say you're from?"

He blinks. "The year of our Lord, 1783."

"So how does someone who lives in the year 1783 even know what happened to my dad in the twenty-first century?"

"Forgive me," he says, his tone taking on a professorial quality. If he wore glasses, he would be cleaning them or pushing them up his nose right about now. "I did not realize you were unaware. Members of the council are permitted to live in whichever time period they prefer. This, of course, does not apply to the intermediaries who watch over the guardian families, as their duty requires them to remain within the current guardian's own time period, but immortals can choose which time period they will live in because, for them, time is circular. The only element that counts the true, linear passage of time in the wood is the life and death of each guardian, and so, as long as they do nothing to affect the course of history, the council members may live wherever and whenever they wish, and still possess the ability to participate in what is happening in the wood's present timeline."

This is starting to make my head spin. "So, wait. If you live in the year 1783, but your parents just disappeared a week ago, how do you even know about it? I mean . . . wouldn't they still be around in your time?"

"My parents choose to live in the year 1783 just as your mother chooses to live in your house. When my parents attend the council meetings in your present timeline, it is no different than when your mother leaves your house. You expect her to come home when her day is done. My parents disappeared in your timeline, and so they never came home in mine."

"Okay," I say, only somewhat understanding. "Continue."

He frowns. "With which part?"

"The part about my dad," I say, my mouth suddenly dry. "Uncle Joe—our family intermediary—he told us there was an investigation, and that the council decided Dad somehow found a way to walk off a path."

He leans forward, his fingers creating a pyramid in front of him. "My parents did not believe the investigation was conducted properly," he explains. "No guardian has ever been able to walk off the paths before, so why would such an anomaly occur now? My parents decided to perform their own investigation, and what they found—"

"Winter?" Mom's voice floats through the house.

Crap. The front door shuts, followed by the sound of Mom's keys clattering onto the countertop next to mine. "Are you home?" Her voice has that tinge of worry in it, the one she gets when the sun's about to go down and she has no idea where I am.

I hold up my hand. "Hold that thought." I walk out into the hallway. "Be right there!"

The fridge opens and closes, followed by the static buzzing of the microwave. "Hurry up," she calls back. "I'm starving. You'll never believe the day I had."

"Tell me about it," I murmur as I glance back into my room, where a boy from the eighteenth century stands, touching the lightbulb in my fan before pulling his hand away. I take a deep breath and tiptoe back in, quietly closing the door behind me. "Look," I whisper, "I need to get down there before she suspects anything. What did they find?"

He glances at the door. "Should you not venture downstairs before your mother comes searching for you?"

I wave his comment away. "Tell me quick."

He sighs. "They overheard a conversation they were not meant to hear. They couldn't be certain exactly who was speaking as they could not see their faces, but it became clear a plot to overthrow the council was brewing."

I frown. "Overthrow them? What do you mean, 'overthrow them'?" The council has always been and always will be. Who would want to overthrow it, and why? For what purpose?

"I do not know the specifics—my parents were very careful to keep this from me. I only found out about it by eavesdropping on them when they were discussing the matter in the library."

"Okay, but what does this have to do with my dad?"

He lowers his voice, so that I have to lean closer to hear him. "After my parents disappeared, I found a name on the desk in their study. One name. One clue as to what could have possibly happened to them." He pauses. "Jack Parish."

My heart squeezes painfully. All this time, I've hoped for this—a reason to think Dad didn't just walk off the paths, that there was something else going on, something *more*. I still don't know if I can trust Brightonshire, but if there's even a chance Dad's connected to all this, then there's only one question that matters.

"What do you need me to do?"

He scratches the back of his neck. "I'm not exactly sure where to begin, but I believe the Parish journals are a good place to start," he says. "Your grandfather's and your—"

The microwave beeps in the kitchen, and I take a step toward the door. "They're all in the study. It'll have to wait until tomorrow when Mom's at work. Is . . . is that okay? I don't know . . ." I can't bring myself to say, *I don't know how much time your parents have left.*

He bows his head. "I told you before. I will do whatever is asked of me."

"Good. Then I need you to stay up here and not make any noise, okay? I'll be back as soon as I can."

"As you wish."

"Thanks." I turn the handle and step into the hall, then look back over my shoulder. "I'm serious. Quiet as a church mouse."

He smirks, and it makes a little dimple in his left cheek. It's the first time I've seen him smile, and I get that static-spark feeling all over again. I close the door and hurry downstairs, swearing I'll never wear socks again.

$\mathcal{M}$om has the leftovers heated up and sitting on the table. "Sorry," I say, plopping down in my chair. "I have this big presentation in English tomorrow. I was just going over my notes."

"Anything I can help you with?" Mom asks. "I know I wasn't much of an English buff, but I remember a few things. What's it on?"

"*Wuthering Heights*."

Mom scrunches up her face. "Nope, sorry. Can't help you."

"I figured."

She laughs as she stabs a piece of chicken with her fork. "You could still read me your speech if you like. I'm an excellent listener."

"Maybe," I say. "If I get it done at a reasonable hour, but this may take an all-nighter."

"Well, don't stay up too late."

I place my hand against my chest, all fake indignation. "*Me?* I would never."

"Winter, I'm serious."

My hand drops to my side. "I know, Mom."

"You need your strength when you go out there—"

"Mom. I know."

She sips her wine, watching me over the rim of her glass. "So, how was your day?"

"Fine."

*BANG.* Something crashes to the floor above us.

Mom rises in her chair. "What the—"

I jump up, my napkin flying off my lap and landing on the butter dish. "Whoops. I, uh, I think I left my window open. The wind probably knocked something over." I giggle, a telltale sign I'm lying. *Crap.* "I'll just go close it."

Mom freezes in a half-sitting, half-standing position. "Need any help?"

"No, no, no. You eat. I'll just be a second."

I feel her eyes on me as I do my best to walk calmly out of the dining room. If it weren't for the creaky old floorboards, I'd be running as soon as I'm out of sight, but I can't let Mom know something's up. She has that spidey sense all Moms have when their kids are up to something, and for all the lessons he gave me, Dad never taught me exactly how he lied so well.

I climb the stairs and open the door to my room. Brightonshire stands on my faded yellow area rug, a textbook at his feet. He picks it up by the spine. The pages accordion out, loosening the folded-up pop quizzes that had been pushed into the cracks. The papers flutter down like snowflakes, scraping the floor.

"*What are you doing?*" I hiss, grabbing the textbook from him and placing it back on the desk. "What part of 'don't make any noise' did you not understand?"

The rest of the room is just as messy. Books open everywhere, more notes piled on the desk and floor. The closet doors are open, half of my clothes dangling precariously from their hangers while the rest lie in a pile beneath them.

"Did you go through my *clothes*?"

"I did not mean to disturb them. I was only curious. It is an oddly designed wardrobe."

"It's called a closet."

"Oh."

"Winter?" Mom calls from the base of the stairs. "Everything all right?"

I skid out into the hallway. "Yeah, just the wind like I thought. It knocked over some of my notes. I'll just clean it up and be right down, okay?"

"Well, hurry up," she says. "Your dinner's getting cold."

I slide back into my room and glance at the textbook Brightonshire was reading. American history, open to a chapter on the years leading up to the Second World War. Hitler stands behind a podium in a black-and-white glossy photo on one page, while a photo of kids playing with German marks takes up the other.

"You shouldn't be looking at this." Who knew how much history he could change if he went back to his time and started telling people about this country called Germany and a man who would try to take over the world in a hundred and fifty years? I mean, granted, it'd be nice if someone could have stopped Hitler before he even began, but as Dad used to say, changing one event in history, especially something as big as a world war, can lead to unspeakable damage. If not to the space-time continuum in general, then it could at least potentially lead to a big change, like someone warning Hitler about what *not* to do, and bing-bang-boom, suddenly things don't fall the way they were supposed to and we're all speaking German.

That's an exaggeration, of course, but it's why we don't mess with the past.

But Brightonshire's not paying me any attention. His hands roam over my bookcase, filled with everything from old picture books to required school reading to Dad's favorite John Grishams.

"These covers are remarkable," he says, pulling out one book after another. *To Kill a Mockingbird. Lord of the Flies. The Firm.* "And these." He pulls out my *Berenstain Bears* picture books. "The neighboring children would love these." He reads the first page, then holds the book out in front of him, shaking his head. "Though the writing is terribly informal."

I grab the books and shove them back where they belong. "Look, I get this world is new to you and all, but please try to behave yourself. At least until dinner's over."

"And these," he says, clearly not listening. He picks up a framed photograph of me, Mom, Dad, and Uncle Joe from when I was six and we went sledding on Christmas Day. His thumb caresses the edge of the photograph. He sets it down and picks up another—me and Meredith, seventh-grade field trip to the Statehouse. "What artist could have possibly painted these?"

"They're not paintings," I say, gentler this time. He doesn't mean to be annoying. I'd probably act the same way if I zipped through a future threshold and wound up surrounded by flying cars. "They're photos."

He looks up at me with a mixture of confusion and wonder in his eyes. "Photos?"

"Look, I'll explain every single thing in this room later if you'd like, but right now I have to get back to my mom before she thinks something's up, and the only way I can do that is if you *swear* you won't make any more noise."

It's a dangerous thing to promise him, but these are dangerous times, and I need to get back downstairs before Mom suspects anything.

He sighs and puts the picture frame back on top of the bookcase. "I will not be a bother. I swear it."

"Good. And don't read any more history books. Or science books. Or, you know what? Just stick to the *Berenstain Bears* and the books that say *classic* on the binding. I'll try to sneak you up some bread or something. I won't be able to get you anything else until the coast is clear."

He looks confused. "There is a coast nearby?"

"No." I sigh. "It's just an expression."

He shakes his head. "Does everyone in your time speak in such a fashion?"

"'Fraid so."

"It seems there is much I must learn."

That's what I'm worried about. If he's going to stay here until he finds out what happened to his parents and, by extension, my dad, it's inevitable he's going to pick up some things about our time. I can't exactly put my computer or my alarm clock or anything else in storage without Mom poking around or without putting myself in serious academic jeopardy. But the longer he stays here, the more he learns, the more I risk pulling apart the very fabric of time.

Brightonshire picks up the second-place ribbon from my sixth-grade science fair project on the potential of asteroid mining, revealing something colorful behind it. A Rubik's Cube. I grab the cube, swipe my sleeve across the dust, and swap it out for the ribbon. "Here," I say. "Play with this. You turn it like this, see? And you're supposed to make it so each face of the cube is one color. Like this side should be all blue, and this side should be all green, and so on. My friend Meredith beat it once, but I think she cheated."

He stares at it.

"Go on," I say, backing toward the door. Mom's bound to send a search party soon.

He twists it once and his eyes light up.

"There you go. I'll be back soon, okay?"

But he isn't listening, and suddenly my room is filled with the sound of the old Rubik's Cube squeaking with every turn and the wind whipping tree branches against my window.

⤜⤜⤜⤜

After dinner, I help Mom take the dishes to the sink and wait until she's fiddling with the dishwasher—plates clacking against one another and the water in the sink running—to stealthily tear off a chunk of French bread. I hide it behind my back and ask if there's anything else she needs me to do.

"I've got it, honey," she says. "You should work on your presentation."

"Okay. G'night, Mom." I turn away from her, keeping the bread close to my chest so she won't see it.

"Winter?"

I freeze. "Yeah?"

"Don't work too hard. You're looking a little . . ."

I glance back at her. "A little?"

She sighs. "Frazzled."

"I'm fine."

"If you say so. But just—just don't try to hide things from me. Okay?"

Sweat sprouts in the creases in my palms. "What do you mean?"

"I mean if things are getting to be too much for you, I can help. You just need to trust me." She doesn't say it, but it's written in the quiver of her lower lip, the shine in her eyes. *Like your father should have trusted me.*

I pause, wondering if I could tell her. If maybe she would know what to do. But no. Dad always made it clear that this was our fight, a fight no one else—not even Mom—could understand. And if there really is a plot to overthrow the council, letting Brightonshire into my world may be even more dangerous than I initially realized. I don't want to put her safety at risk. "Thanks, Mom. I will. But right now, I'm okay."

She stares at me and I don't know if I've convinced her, but she lets it go. "All right, then. Good night."

When I get back to my room, Brightonshire is swiveling around in my desk chair, the Rubik's Cube completed on his lap.

"Apparently that thing's easy for everyone except me," I say, closing the door behind me. "Awesome."

He reaches his hand out to catch himself on the desk. "This chair is pure genius! Who came up with this device? I must meet its maker."

"That might be a little hard," I say, "considering I think it was invented by Thomas Jefferson. Well, not that particular chair, but the original idea for it."

His eyebrows draw together, creating a dimple between them. "That rebel cur?"

"Easy there, Brightonshire. You're in America now, and we tend to think of him as a forefather."

He grits his teeth. "Apologies."

"Here." I hand him the bread. "It's not much, but it should tide you over until Mom goes to sleep and I can get you a real plate of food."

"Real food?" He frowns. "This bread is not real?"

"No, that's not . . ." I sigh. "It's just another saying. The bread is real, so eat up."

He takes a bite and closes his eyes. "Delicious. Did your mother make this?"

I nod. "She covers it in this herb butter before she bakes it. Puts every grocery store French bread to shame."

He finishes the bread and licks the crumbs from his fingers. I try not to notice how soft his lips look, an oddly feminine contrast to the hardness of the rest of him, like one of those rock stars from the eighties. My tongue darts out over my own suddenly dry lips.

"What are you expecting to find?" I ask him. "In the journals?"

"I'm not certain," he says. "Perhaps nothing at all, but it is the only place I can think to begin."

"We'll rifle through Dad's study tomorrow. Mom leaves for work at seven thirty sharp, and she won't be home until four thirty or so, which should give us plenty of time. I'll have to skip school," I say, more to myself than to him, "but what else is new?"

He clears his throat. "You still would hide my presence from your mother?"

"I don't have much of a choice. If she finds out what I've done, she'll just freak and tell Uncle Joe. And then we'll both be in serious trouble." My eyes flash to his. I hold them so he'll understand the importance of what I'm saying. "You *have* to stay hidden."

His features soften. "I will do anything you ask of me."

My breath hitches in my throat at the sincerity in his voice and the way his half-lidded eyes stare up at me, all thick, blond lashes and dark, slashing eyebrows. "Thank you."

He shrugs. "It is the least I can do in return for the kindness you have shown me this day."

I sit on the edge of my bed. "There's something else you could do."

His brow arches.

I point at the Rubik's Cube. "Teach me how you did that?"

# XVI

Two hours later, Brightonshire has taught me how to beat the cube I gave up on years ago, and I've explained (with as few tech-savvy words as possible so he won't be able to re-create anything) every single thing in my room to him as promised, from the reason my mattress is so soft to the electricity powering the overhead fan and the small TV in the corner. As soon as I turn the TV on, he's riveted. Even when I bring him a plate of leftovers, he only picks at it, scrolling through the channels as I showed him and commenting on the fashion, the way everyone talks, the predicaments they find themselves in. I make sure he keeps away from the educational programs and the news, hoping sitcoms will teach him just enough to understand why I dress and speak the way I do but not enough to actually change the course of history.

He likes *Three's Company*, but says it's entirely too suggestive for my feminine sensibilities. Part of me wants to tell him to *suggest this* and flip him the finger, but he probably wouldn't understand what I was doing anyway. And besides, it's kind of cute, especially when he lands on the home shopping channel and says, "Those overly shiny marbles are supposed to imitate diamonds? Has this woman never seen a real diamond?"

"It's cubic zirconia," I tell him as I sit on the edge of my bed, "and it's for people who can't afford or don't want to spend money on the real thing."

He clucks his tongue against the roof of his mouth. "Are the women of your day so accepting as to take fake diamonds from their suitors over real ones? I do believe that in my time a woman would spit in my face if I pulled such tomfoolery, and I would not blame her."

I spread out on my stomach, pushing my fingers through the holes in the afghan my grandmother knitted as I watch him. He sits in front of the TV like a child, knees pressed into his chest, arms wrapped around his legs. "Are you rich?" I ask him.

He looks at me for the first time since turning on the TV.

"Sorry, rude question," I say. "It's just—are you one of those people who can afford real diamonds?"

"What does that matter?"

I shrug. "It doesn't really. I'm just thinking that maybe if the option weren't available to you, you'd see the value in being able to give your, uh, 'suitor' something nice, even if it isn't the 'real thing.'"

He chuckles. "She would be my lady, not my suitor, and to answer your question, I am not a prince, nor am I a pauper."

Yeah, sure. That answered my question, all right. "Are you ever going to tell me anything about yourself, or are you going to make me call you *Brightonshire* the entire time you're here?"

He pushes his finger into the power button and the screen goes black. He turns away from it and puts one leg down, the other knee still up, his arm resting across it. A model pose, the kind that says *I know you want me* while sporting the new must-have jeans in Times Square. But he doesn't look smug, or like he's doing it on purpose to look sexy or something, like a guy from my time would. Instead, the pose looks natural. I can see him sitting in front of a fireplace like that. Or maybe on a grand sweeping porch surrounded by rolling green hills and a twilight-orange sky smudged with smoke.

"I am Henry Durant," he says, his accent lilting his words, "son of Augustus and Celia Durant, Baron and Baroness of Brightonshire."

"Baron? So you are rich."

"Not exactly," he says. "We have farmlands that sustain themselves and put coin in our pockets and the pockets of our tenants, that is true, but my parents are not interested in participating in the decorum and politics of the peerage. Their ventures are purely academic, and lie solely in the wood."

It feels weird, sitting here talking to someone about the wood who isn't a Parish or Uncle Joe. Foggy, like I know I'm in a dream and I'm just waiting to wake up. But it's kind of nice, too. For the first time in nearly two years, I don't have to pretend what I do isn't dangerous to protect my mom, and I don't have to follow Uncle Joe's orders. I can just be me. I don't even have that with Meredith anymore.

"And now, Madam, it is time you give me your name." Henry tips his head forward, studying me. His hair falls into his eyes and he pushes it back, the thick gold strands swallowing his fingers. "Or perchance you would have me guess?"

That could be fun. "Go for it."

He smiles. "Mary."

"No."

"Suzanna?"

I shake my head.

"Dorcas."

"Is that even a real name?"

"It's as real as Winter."

I gasp. "You cheated. You heard my mom say my name."

His eyes flash. "Careful, Madam. In my time, to call a man a cheat is to call into question the honor of the man himself."

"No offense," I say, holding my hands up, my fingers poking through the holes in the afghan. "It was a joke. I know you didn't actually cheat. You just . . . withheld information." I can't help myself. "To be a brat."

"I beg your pardon?"

"It's called sarcasm, Brightonshire," I say. "Ever heard of it?"

"Henry."

"Hmm?"

His smile is crooked, like the hangers still dangling in my closet. "Call me Henry."

"All right," I say, pulling my fingers out of the afghan and sitting up. "Henry."

"In my time, to use sarcasm is to be disrespectful of the company one keeps."

"Not here. Well, I guess sometimes it is here, too, but most people use sarcasm in a humorous way, or to lighten the mood."

He sits in the swivel chair, his posture rigidly straight. "Example?"

"Well, I could tell my best friend I hate her and she'll know it means I actually love her and don't know what I'd do without her. Or my mom could ask me how school was and I could say great and really mean terrible, and she'll know that by my tone and give me a hug or ask what's wrong. Don't people in your time do that?"

"I suppose so, on occasion. Although I must say, I have never heard anyone call me a—what was the word?"

"A brat."

"Ah yes, a *brat* before."

"Well, get used to it, Brightonsh—Henry. It's the only way you'll survive here." Not that he needs to survive for long. *Why am I telling him this anyway?* He's just going to go through the family archives, figure out whatever it is he needs to know, and then he'll be back in his time before he knows what hit him.

One or two days, tops.

Just before bed I show him where the bathroom is and explain how the toilet works—which, believe me, is something I never want to have to do again. I hand him my baggiest sweatpants and an Ohio State T-shirt that's a touch too big for me but will probably fit him like a second skin. While Henry changes, I go down to the garage and pull my old sleeping bag out of storage, careful not to make too much noise—Mom doesn't sleep well these days and it's easy to wake her. The sleeping bag's dusty and smells like bug spray mixed with mothballs, but it'll work. I've already set it up, wiping away the dust with a damp washcloth, when Henry tiptoes back to my room, zipping the drawstring back and forth on his pants.

Tight, loose. Tight, loose.

"*Miraculous,*" he says in a hushed whisper.

"Um, yeah. I guess."

He drops the drawstring and starts inspecting his shirt, which is ridiculously tight and shows off Every. Single. Ridge. Of. Muscle.

My cheeks warm and I stare at the space above his shoulder instead.

"I do miss having long sleeves," he says. "Tell me, do you not catch your death in such light fabric?"

"Well, we have this little thing called a furnace for the winter that keeps the house warm," I say, "but this time of year you don't really need it. If it gets cold at night, you just throw on another blanket, and if it gets cold during the day, you throw on a sweater. A sweater has longer sleeves," I add at the confusion in his eyes.

"Fascinating."

If anyone else had said it, I would have thought they were being sarcastic. But there's wonder in his voice, and I know he really is fascinated.

I point to the sleeping bag. "I set up a bed on the floor. I can take it if you want the actual bed, since you're a guest and all." What can I say? My mother raised me right.

He bows his head. "I could not do that. I will take the floor."

I'm about to say, *Suit yourself* and climb into bed, but as I turn away, I realize something.

I turn back. "Is it because I'm a girl?"

"Of course."

Okay, well, just to make things clear. "And you're a boy?"

He smirks. "I do believe so."

"Okay, so here's the thing. In my time, women are equal to men, which means I can sleep on the floor just as much as you can. I'd probably do it better, too," I say, teasing him.

"How, pray tell, would you 'do it better'?"

"I'd . . . sleep longer. And deeper."

"Ah."

"I'll tell you what," I say, grabbing my backpack from the corner of the room and rifling through the front pocket for my leftover vending-machine money. I pull out a quarter. "I'll flip you for it. Winner gets the bed. Heads or tails?"

He crosses his arms over his chest. "Heads."

I flip the coin in the air. It spirals end over end, lands in my palm and—

"Heads, it is." There, I'd done my part for womankind, making everything fair and equal. "The bed's all yours."

I start to move toward the sleeping bag, but there's a pressure on the backs of my knees and my legs fly out from under me. My head whips back and my neck presses into Henry's arm.

"*What are you doing?*" I hiss.

"Carrying you." He crosses the small room in one and a half steps and drops me on the bed. "I appreciate your character, Madam, but my conscience cannot allow me to let you sleep on the floor. I understand things are done differently in your time, but please, humor me."

"But I—"

"And remember," he says, peering down at me, "I am your guest, and you would not want me to feel uncomfortable. Correct?"

"I, um, yeah." I can't stop staring into his eyes. They're brighter now than when I first noticed them, when he was in the shade of the wood's canopy. Green like Easter basket grass. Like the neon-green crayon every kid whittles down to a nub because it makes Ariel's flippers or their Daytona race car pop off the page. "I guess."

"Good. I am glad to see not everything has changed in the past two centuries."

He pulls away from me and I snap back into myself. *Is this what Meredith goes through every time she's around a boy she likes?* Not that I like Henry, but he is the first boy who's ever slept over in my room. Okay, he's the first boy who's ever *been* in my room.

I hate it. It makes your tongue stick to the roof of your mouth and your mind go completely blank. It takes away every ounce of your control, and I've never liked not being in control. It could get you killed in my line of work, so whatever this is that's making me notice Henry's eye color and his accent, making my stomach do a little flip whenever he speaks, and making me forget that I don't even know if I can trust him, it needs to stop.

Now.

Henry slides into the sleeping bag and I turn out the lamp on my bedside table so I can't look at him anymore. Too bad it's almost a full moon and silver light pools through my wispy curtains, gliding across his skin and making his cheekbones appear even sharper, deepening the shadows beneath them.

I roll away and stare at the door instead.

"Good night, Winter," he says, his voice soft and warm, like candlelight. "And thank you."

One corner of my mouth lifts into a smile. "You're welcome."

I close my eyes but I don't sleep. Instead I think of all the ways this plan could go wrong. Of all the ways I could get caught—and that wouldn't even be the worst of my problems. This whole space-time continuum thing is extremely delicate. One wrong move and I could implode the universe as we know it, all because some guy wants to get his parents back and I think if I can help him do that, then maybe I can get my dad back, too.

And God help me—I'm a terrible person—but it feels worth it.

# XVII

In my dream, Dad stands on a pathway in the wood, next to a grouping of leaves turning black. The darkness oozes out of the leaves' pores. He watches it happen, his back to me, his entire body rigid like a corpse.

"Dad?"

I want to run to him, but every step forward keeps us at the same distance. I can see him, but I can't touch him.

He slowly turns his body toward me, his gaze sliding away from the leaves. "What have you done?" His voice is hollow, tinny. It doesn't sound like it should, and that scares me more than anything.

"I don't know," I say. Shadows move behind him even though the sun is high and the wood should be safe. "What's happening?"

"You shouldn't have let him through."

I have nothing to say to this. I know he's right.

"Two council members disappeared, and he thinks it has

something to do with what happened to you," I say instead. "I think he can help us."

"He doesn't belong here."

Tears spring to my eyes, but it isn't sadness taking over my body, making my fists curl and my heart hammer. "Too bad you're not making the decisions anymore, *Dad*. Maybe if you hadn't left us, none of this would be happening. Did you ever think of that?"

He doesn't answer.

I take a step forward, and another, but the distance between us remains the same. "Why'd you do it? Why did you walk off the path?"

He blinks, and then he starts to fade away. Not like Uncle Joe, not in sifts of sand that once made up his body, but like a ghost, growing more transparent until I can only see the faintest outline of his shoulders, his legs, the roundness of his skull.

"ANSWER ME!" I yell.

"Wake up." His voice carries on the wind.

Something beeps behind me.

"I can't . . ." I fall to my knees. Crumple in on myself. "I can't do this alone."

*Beepbeepbeep. Beepbeepbeep.*

"Winter." His hand rests on my cheek. His wedding ring glints in the sunlight. But when I look up at him, it's full dark, and worms wriggle out of his eyes.

*Wake up.*

⤙⤚

Henry shakes me. "You must awaken."

It takes me a moment to remember exactly who he is, why

120

he's here, and why I still hear the beeping from my dream. Another moment to realize it's my alarm clock, and that it's probably been going off for a while. If Mom comes in to check on me and sees Henry here, I'm dead. Stick me in a coffin and make me a tombstone that reads: *She had a boy in her room, so her mother killed her. Let it be a lesson to all.*

"This blasted machine of yours will not stop—"

I push him away and slam my palm down on the snooze button, then flip the off switch next to it. The clock reads 6:52. It's been going off for the past seven minutes. Thankfully, I hear the pipes clanging in the walls—Mom's taking a shower. She couldn't have heard it.

I let my head fall back on the pillow and groan. I stayed up way too late thinking about a job that should require little thought (patrol the wood, catch a traveler, send him back), and now my brain feels sticky, like it's peeling off my skull and jiggling back into place.

Henry picks up the clock and turns it over. "What is this infernal contraption?"

"It's an alarm clock," I say, my voice deep and sleep-scratchy. "It wakes you up."

He sets it back down. "Evidently not."

I stick my tongue out at him and he raises his eyebrows.

I wait until Mom's out of the shower, then slip into the bathroom with the tiny makeup bag she bought for me in middle school, its contents practically untouched. I work quickly, smothering my face in powder to make myself appear paler than I actually am, keeping my ears trained on Mom's movements.

When I get back to my room, the TV is on. Henry's watching *Saved by the Bell*.

"I think I am beginning to understand your vernacular," he tells me.

"Good." Although it really isn't. If I'd done my job right, he wouldn't need to understand my "vernacular." He'd be back in the eighteenth century, living his life as he was supposed to.

*Actually, he'd be dead.*

The thought makes my stomach roll. What am I saying? He *is* dead. I could take him to Brightonshire today and we could stare at his grave together. Just because he's sitting in my room, watching TV and wearing my T-shirt, does *not* mean he's a part of my world. He needs to go back, live his life, and die just like everyone else.

I try not to think about it long—it's too morbid for seven fifteen in the morning.

"For example," Henry says, "your breeches are *cool.*"

I smile. "Pants. Not breeches. And they're pajama pants, to be more accurate."

"Ah." He stares at my legs, and even though I know he's just interested in the fabric, I feel like I should cover myself. "Pah-jah-mahs." The word sounds strange on his tongue, but then again, so did *cool.*

"We'll work on it," I say.

I tell Henry to wait in my room and not make any noise, and then I slowly shuffle down the stairs. I grimace with every step, tenting my hand over my eyes as if the sunlight streaming in through the windows is physically painful. Mom's in the kitchen eating a bran muffin as she gathers papers into her briefcase. The second she sees me, her eyes widen.

"Winter? Are you all right?"

"I don't feel so good," I say, collapsing onto a stool at the island.

Mom frowns and places her hand on my forehead. "You don't feel like you have a fever." But I must do a good job of looking pathetic, because she pats my back and says, "Go to bed. I'll call the school and tell them you'll be home sick today."

"No, I can go—" I make a big show of trying to stand, my head lolling on my shoulders like it's in danger of falling off.

"Don't be ridiculous," Mom says, shooing me back down. "Do you want me to call Joe and see if he can patrol for you this morning?"

"No!" The last thing I need is for Joe to come poking around and find a traveler in our house saying things like *cool* and *electricity.*

Mom blinks.

"I mean, no, don't worry about it. I can call him. You don't want to be late for work."

She checks her watch. "Will you be all right here on your own? I have a full morning of lectures and some student meetings in the afternoon, but I could come home around lunch and make you some soup—"

"That's okay," I say, careful to keep my voice scratchy. "I think I'm just going to be sleeping all day anyway. I know where we keep the food if I get hungry."

"Are you sure?"

I nod.

"Okay," she says, popping the lid onto her thermos. "Get some sleep, baby."

"Thanks, Mom."

I take the stairs like a ninety-year-old, slow and steady. I'm proud of my performance—I haven't faked an illness since the fifth grade, and I wasn't certain I'd be able to pull it off. But Mom doesn't get too many opportunities to baby me these days, and she's probably just thrilled I consulted her on my decision to stay home at all, instead of toughing it out at school like I normally would. I text Mer to let her know I'm staying home sick and won't be able to pick her up. She responds with: *NOOOOO. You can't be sick!!! The football game's tonight and Trevor WILL BE THERE.*

Of course he'll be there. He's on the football team. I fight back a grin as I text back: *I'm pretty sick. I don't think I'll be able to make it.*

Mer: *BOO.*

Me: *Sorry.*

Mer: *U should at least try to make it to the bonfire since it's going to be right next door.*

Me: *What do you mean?*

Mer: *Brian Ferris is having a bonfire in his backyard. He's ur neighbor, right?*

I frown. Brian Ferris is even more of a loner than I am. I would have never guessed he'd invite the whole school over to his house for a bonfire. I'll have to keep an eye on it. Make sure no one goes near my backyard.

Me: *Yeah, he's my neighbor. I don't know if I'll make it, though.*

Mer: *Well, TRY. This may be your only shot at a date to homecoming.*

Me: *Ouch. Was that necessary?*

Mer: *The truth hurts.*

Mom leaves at seven thirty. I wipe the powder off my face

and change quickly for my morning patrol. I show Henry to Dad's study, reminding him to put everything back where he finds it. I bring him a cup of coffee and a strawberry Pop-Tart, which he claims is the greatest thing he's ever eaten.

I grab my jacket from the mudroom on the off chance that it'll finally feel like October outside, but no such luck. The air is already reminiscent of an August morning, despite it being only two weeks until Halloween, and humidity slicks my skin as I head into the wood.

⊰⊱

Whatever's causing the black leaves to spread from tree to tree, stinking of rot and pumping black ichor from seams in the bark like blood from an artery, it's getting worse.

I feel no travelers in my sector, but I walk the paths anyway, counting the infected trees. There's no way this is a coincidence; the timing is too perfect. It must be connected to Augustus and Celia's disappearance, and maybe even to Dad's disappearance as well, although that last one is admittedly a stretch, considering he disappeared nearly two years ago. But hope doesn't let me give up on the possibility, not when Henry found my father's name among his parents' things.

A clue. A connection. A possibility. It is all I need to spur me on. To believe.

I stop at a tree that is nothing but black leaves, its shape hunched and curled like an old woman's spine.

Uncle Joe appears next to my shoulder, silent as a ghost.

"It's dying, isn't it?" I ask, not taking my eyes off the tree.

"Yes."

"What is this? What's happening to it?"

"It appears to be the effects of dragon's bane," he replies, "an ancient, parasitic plant that used to grow in the wood. It would attach itself to a tree and suck the life out of it in order to grow. But this . . ." He shakes his head. "This is different. I've never seen such a widespread invasion without any visible dragon's bane nearby."

"You said, 'used to grow in the wood.' As in, it doesn't anymore?"

"It's not supposed to. Dragon's bane was the only known effective poison against our immortality. Most of our people just stayed away from it, but then, nearly five hundred years ago, an Old One named Varo used the plant as a weapon in an attempt to depose the council. Luckily, his plan was discovered before he could hurt anyone, and the council decreed all dragon's bane be destroyed, so no one could use it as a weapon again."

"But if it was all destroyed, how could it be back?"

"I don't know."

*They overheard a conversation they were not meant to hear. They couldn't be certain exactly who was speaking as they could not see their faces, but it became clear a plot to overthrow the council was brewing.*

It can't be a coincidence.

I try to make it sound like this isn't something I've been thinking about since last night as I ask, "But why would anyone want to depose the council?"

He sighs. "To understand that, you need to understand Varo. He was different from the rest of the council. The wood enraptured him. He spoke of nothing else, thought of nothing else. He would spend days, weeks, walking the paths. There was potential here, he said. Magic. Power beyond our wildest imaginings. All we had to do was reach out and take it."

"What happened to him?" I ask.

"The council was afraid of him. They said no one person should have power over the wood. It controls itself. To try to change that would be to throw the natural equilibrium of the world out of balance. But he refused to listen. He drew power from the wood. More magic than any council member should possess. He became addicted. He got it into his head that he could use his new power for good. Go back in time and right wrongs committed by others."

"But that's ridiculous. He'd be changing time based on his own bias and putting the entire human race in jeopardy."

He nods. "The council agreed with you, and they did the only thing they could. They kicked him out, stripped him of his title as a member of the council in an ancient ritual, and sent him through a threshold to a time and place where he could make little difference."

"Is it possible the same thing's happening again?"

He studies me, his eyes narrowed in that way he always gets when he thinks I'm up to something. My throat goes dry under his gaze but I refuse to swallow, lest he take it for the sign of guilt it so obviously would be.

"I suppose it's possible," he says, finally breaking eye contact. "Varo's supporters were never found." He stares at the tree a moment longer. "I'll take this information to the council, but we must be very careful whom we trust right now. If Varo's supporters really are up to their old tricks, anyone could be an enemy in disguise." He snaps his gaze to me. "*Anyone.*"

I ball my hands into fists to keep them from shaking. *He doesn't know about Henry. There's no way he could. Don't. Look. Guilty.*

"I understand."

He stares at me a moment longer, then nods as if the matter has been settled.

"By the way," I say before he can leave, "if Mom asks, you took over my patrol this morning."

"Why would I tell her such a thing?"

"Because I stayed home sick."

"You look fine to me."

I say the first lie that comes to mind. "I needed a break after what happened the other night."

His features soften at the reminder. "How are you doing?"

"Okay, I guess. Had a nightmare about Dad."

"Are you sure that's all that's wrong?"

*No, but there are too many wrong things in my life right now to count.* "I'm just tired."

"Maybe your mother's right. Maybe you should consider homeschooling."

"Yeah," I say. "Maybe."

# XVIII

enry is still in Dad's study when I get back.

I pause in the doorway, my back against the solid oak frame that was crafted hundreds of years ago. The walls are a deep navy color; the waist-high wainscoting the same dark oak as the door and bookcases. There's a fireplace against the wall across from me, framed by two long, slender windows that look out on the trees lining 315. They've started changing color overnight, catching up to our wood. Soon their leaves will fall, and snow will blanket the ground. If Dad were still here, he'd call me into the study to watch the deer at sunset. We could only see them from the front and side windows of the house; they never went into our wood. I can still see fourteen-year-old me standing at the window, a mug of hot chocolate in hand, green garland winding around the fireplace mantel, Dad standing behind me as we watched the deer glide through the snow.

It's been too long since I've been in here.

I clear my throat. Henry looks up from the desk, where he has three books of yellowed, crinkled parchment open. His hair is messy and flops to one side as if he's been running his hands through it all morning, and he's wearing his own clothes again.

"Have you ever heard of dragon's bane?" I ask him.

Henry scrunches up his face, thinking. "Not that I can recall."

I cross the room and sit in the reading chair in the corner, wedged between a window and a bookcase. "What about an Old One named Varo?"

"The Old One who wanted to overthrow the council?"

I nod.

"I do not know very much about him; only that he was once a respected elder, but his greed caused him to overreach, and he was ultimately banished from the wood," Henry says, a small smile playing across his lips. "My parents used it as a cautionary tale whenever I felt like challenging their authority. Why do you ask?"

I debate how much I should tell him. Uncle Joe's words ring in my ears—*anyone could be an enemy in disguise*—but the only reason I know as much as I do is because of Henry, and on the chance that he's right, that Dad is somehow connected to the disappearance of his parents, I have to trust him. And if Henry's lying to me, well . . . I'll deal with that when the time comes. But for now, I decide to lay it all out, explaining Varo's connection to dragon's bane and how his supporters were never found.

"Do you think it's possible one of this Varo guy's supporters is behind all of this?" I ask.

"I suppose anything's possible."

I gesture to the open books in front of him. "What did you find?"

"Old treatises," he says. "Journals dating back to the twelfth century. The most recent"—he holds up a book of soft brown leather—"being your grandfather's. I did not find your father's journal, nor yours."

"That's because I don't have one, and Dad didn't, either."

Henry frowns. "You are certain of this?"

"Very." He would've shown me if he'd kept a journal. He'd shown me Grandpa's and all the others, though I'd only been able to read the entries dating back to the late 1600s before all the *thee*'s and *thou*'s and weird cursive got too confusing. I'd always assumed I'd have better luck reading the medieval texts when I was older, but after Dad disappeared . . . Like I said, it's been too long since I've been in here. "I don't think he saw much of a point in it."

"There is very much a point in it," Henry says. "Did your father never tell you this is one of your duties, to keep a record of how the wood changes? How many travelers come through on a daily basis, where and when they come from, which thresholds are unusually active—"

"Okay, I get it," I say. "And yeah, I report those things to the council, but Dad never told me to keep a journal."

"Mayhap he was keeping one for the both of you?"

I shake my head. "No, he would've told me. He would have had me read it." But there's a niggling stab of doubt puncturing my heart. Maybe he was waiting until I was older, farther along in my lessons. Or maybe there were things he didn't want me to read. Things he wanted to keep secret.

Henry curses under his breath.

"What is it?" I ask. "What were you hoping to find?"

He shakes his head. "I am not entirely certain," he admits, "but I had hoped your father's journal would contain some clue as to what happened to him. I thought, perhaps, if I could make some sense of it, I would be able to deduce what happened to my parents."

"Trust me, I looked for every clue imaginable after he disappeared, but there was nothing. There *is* nothing."

"It is not logical," he says. "Every guardian since the signing of the Compact has kept a record of the travelers who have crossed into their territories. Why wouldn't your father?"

Maybe because he hated the wood? It was his dirty little secret that wasn't much of a secret at all. Mom tried to hide it from me on his worst days, telling me he was just in a bad mood, and then taking me out to see a movie or go shopping while Dad holed himself up in the study with a bottle of whiskey.

But there was one time she wasn't home, one time when I sat in here with him after an "incident" in the wood he refused to tell me about.

*Nothing we do actually means anything,* he said between sips, cradling the bottle. *Don't you get that? It's one big, fat joke. No, no, no. It's worse than that. It's a curse. I only wish I could go back in time and slug the sick son of a bitch responsible for it.*

I close my eyes. When I open them, I'm sixteen again, and Henry is the one sitting across from me. "I don't know what to tell you," I say. "I never saw my father with a journal."

"*You* never saw him with one," he says. "Is it possible your mother did?"

"I guess anything's possible."

Henry presses his steepled fingers against his lips, thinking. "Is it also possible that he might have hidden one?"

"Why would he do that?" I ask, even though I already know the answer.

"Perhaps he was protecting you from something?"

I don't have to respond. My silence says it all.

Henry leans forward. "Where would he have hidden it?"

# XIX

I take Henry to the attic. It is the only place I can think of where
something could be properly hidden in this house. It's a large
attic, but it doesn't feel that way, cluttered as it is with boxes and
dust and cobwebs. There are three lightbulbs that hang from the
ceiling, but I can only reach the first one before the boxes block
our path. I pull the cord and the bulb flickers on, revealing everything from a chest full of old paperback romances—which Mom
swears she'll give to charity one of these days—to Christmas decorations that haven't been put up since Dad disappeared. Farther
back, old furniture and paintings in giant frames stand covered
by drop cloths. They've always freaked me out. I used to think
it would be so easy for someone to hide back there, in the shadows, covered with a drop cloth. Waiting for the perfect moment
to let the fabric slip from their skeletal, ghostly body, curl their
bony fingers around the cord, and turn out the light.

"Where do you think he might have hidden it?" Henry asks,
dropping to one knee and wiping his palm across the dusty top
of an old VCR. He scrunches his face as he picks it up, inspects

it, and then unceremoniously drops it on the floor beside him. A plastic corner chips off and tumbles into the crack between the floorboards.

"Hey, careful with that. How's my mom supposed to show old, embarrassing home movies of me if it's broken?" I pause. "Actually, drop it harder next time."

But Henry isn't listening. He's found the chest of paperback romances, and his eyes are practically popping out of his skull as he takes in the bodice-ripping covers. "These, uh—" He clears his throat. "That is to say, books have certainly changed a bit since my time."

I push the chest aside. "If Dad hid anything up here—and that's a big *if*—he wouldn't have put it near the front, where Mom or I could have found it. So, come on. Help me dig a tunnel."

It takes the better part of an hour to make it to the second lightbulb, in the middle of the attic. We've gone back several decades, each section represented by very specific items: my old Barbie dolls and Easy-Bake oven in boxes along with old photo albums and my first pair of hiking boots; prom dresses with shoulder pads I can't believe Mom ever wore; a Nintendo and an Atari sitting side by side; Star Wars action figures from when Dad was a kid.

"We should start looking here," I say, as Dad's childhood toys start to morph into 1950s furniture and creepy porcelain dolls. No one would ever come back this far, which makes it a pretty good hiding place.

Henry scratches his neck. "There is much to go through."

"My family's lived in this house since 1794," I say. "A lot of junk can be left behind in that amount of time. I guess no one's ever wanted to take the initiative to clean it out."

He nods. "There are times walking through my home when I do not know if I truly live in the eighteenth century, or if I have gone back to medieval times, or perhaps the Dark Ages as far as some of the privies are concerned. You are fortunate." He meets my gaze. "At least you have a connection to these artifacts. I have no real connection to the suits of armor in the halls or the portraits of the people who used to live in the manor before my parents took up residence. At times, I feel as though I am an intruder in a life that belonged to someone else."

"What happened to them? The family who lived there before your parents?"

Henry removes the drop cloth from an antique dresser and begins rifling through the drawers. "I am not certain. I'm told the family was bankrupt and could not care for their land or their tenants. My parents offered them a more-than-fair price for the property, and they jumped at the chance to be free of the land and the responsibility. Now, several hundred years later, my parents are the baron and baroness, the land is fertile, the tenants are well fed, and Augustus and Celia are able to use their magic so that no one wonders why it is the baron and baroness have never aged, or why the baroness never appeared to be with child before their son was born."

He opens the bottom drawer and pulls out a leather-bound book with thin pages. My heart skips a beat as he opens it. He shakes his head, turning it around to show me the words *King James Bible* on the first page. He places it back in the drawer and moves on to a side table.

"What kind of magic do they do?" I ask. Other than my coin and the wonders of the wood itself, the only true form of magic I've ever seen has been via Uncle Joe. I mean, I'd always assumed the council members possessed similar powers, but it's odd to hear it actually said aloud. To learn these little pieces about the people who have so much control over my life and yet give me so little information about their own.

"My mother is a healer," he says, a line between his brows creasing as he pushes a stack of old papers and magazines aside, "and my father is a bit of a mind reader. He cannot pick your thoughts from your brain, but he can read people very well. He knows when they are lying, when they are being manipulative or manipulated, and he can tell if a person is good and trustworthy at his very core." He laughs. "Growing up, it made sneaking broken vases and stolen cigars past him very difficult. I imagine it was because of his intuition that my parents learned of the conspiracy in the first place."

I pull the drop cloth from an old dressing table. There's still a hairbrush with an opal handle and silver combs lying on its surface. I pick up an old makeup jar and twist open the top. It smells like roses.

Whenever I came up here to help Mom gather decorations or put away some boxes, I should have asked more questions. About our family, about how every single person, guardian or spouse, dealt with the responsibility of the wood. I should have used every opportunity I had to better prepare myself for the day Dad wouldn't be here to help me anymore.

I can't say for certain that I would know what to do now if I had, but that's not the point. The point is this: Dad's gone, and it doesn't matter that I was just a kid who didn't realize he could be taken away from me in the time between going to bed one night and opening my eyes the next morning.

I should have asked.

Mom calls to check up on me at lunchtime. I promise her I'm taking care of myself, and that I'm actually feeling a little better, which is a complete lie—I feel a million times worse than when I woke up this morning. I want to ask her if Dad kept a journal, if he kept more secrets from me than I realized, but that would only make her suspicious. I'll ask her when she gets home, as if it's just a random thought I had while lying around sick instead of the important, potentially life-altering question it really is. Mom tells me a faculty meeting popped up at the last minute, but that she'll be home with all the ingredients for her famous chicken soup by six thirty.

After we hang up, I make Henry a sandwich and tell him he can stay in the attic if he likes, but only until six, at which point he'll need to hide himself in my room and dart into the closet if anyone other than me comes barging through my bedroom door.

I need to clear my head. I take a quick shower, hot water gliding over my skin, loosening the ever-present knots in my shoulders and along my spine. I'm too wired to stand still long enough to dry my hair, so I don't even bother with it before entering the wood.

The leaves are so brilliant with the afternoon sun reflecting off them, a cathedral of red and gold diamonds stretching above my head as far as I can see, that I can do nothing but stop and stare for a moment. It is not the first time I've seen this sight, but it's beautiful and tragic all at the same time. Beautiful because the leaves are crystallized fire, undulating in the breeze; tragic because they are fleeting. Beautiful because they're here; tragic because Dad isn't.

A branch lies across the path. I kick it away. It rolls five feet ahead of me and stops. I kick it again.

I will not turn into my dad, laughing off my job on my best days, drinking until I lose consciousness on my worst. Of course, that was only near the end, and I wonder—if he did have a journal, would I be able to go through it now and pick out the entry where everything changed? The day when my father began to drink more than he should have? The day he started to pull away from us? From the wood? It had happened so gradually, but there had to be an inciting moment.

Happy people don't just hit the bottle for no reason.

I'm getting closer to knowing what happened to him—I can feel it deep in my guardian bones—and, for the first time, I'm not sure I want to know.

I find only one traveler in my sector: St. Petersburg, 1917. He's well dressed in a military uniform, with gold braids that fall from his shoulders and shiny gold buttons on his coat. He has a brown beard and kind blue eyes and I fear he may be a Romanov, or tied to them somehow. I want to warn him what's coming, but I don't. I can't. So I send the man back to St. Petersburg and, possibly, to his death at the hands of a revolution.

Sometimes, this job really sucks.

I don't keep track of the time—I just walk and walk, until finally my stomach twinges and I realize the light is dimming. I head back toward my threshold, wondering if I should start keeping a journal like the guardians before me. Wondering why I never questioned Dad about it, why it never struck me as odd that we had all this archived material we could access, but we weren't leaving anything new behind for the next generation.

Boot steps, soft as rain patter, echo off the trees. I whip my head toward the sound. My first thought is of Uncle Joe. I don't feel any travelers, and as far as I know, guardians have never left their own sectors to enter someone else's. But the person who appears in front of me, gliding through the trees, a long, black cloak billowing around his legs, isn't Uncle Joe. His collar is turned up so I can't see his face, but a cloud of birch-white hair covers his head.

My instincts tell me something is wrong, but I have a job to do, so I call out to him. "Sir?"

He stops, then slowly turns, revealing an ancient face like withered stone and pale amethyst eyes. And that's when I realize he isn't standing on a path.

He's *inside* the wood.

We stare at each other, the old man as transfixed by me as I am by him.

My voice fails me. I clear my throat and try again. "Wh-who are you?"

He doesn't answer. Instead, he cocks his head at me, then claps his hands together. Thick tendrils of obsidian smoke curl out from his palms. He whispers something in the language of the Old Ones, but I'm too far away to make it out. The smoke turns into a pillar, tangling itself in the branches above us, choking out the last golden rays of sunset.

The old man meets my gaze and utters one clear word.

*"Tierl'asi."*

Shadows peel themselves from the bark of the trees surrounding me, amorphous blobs that turn into vaguely human shapes with bloated heads and rows of gleaming white teeth.

Sentinels.

The path buckles under my feet. The trees twist and sway,

their branches bending and reaching for me. It's just like my nightmare. The wood has turned from day to night in a matter of seconds, but this isn't a dream. This is real.

I run.

Shadows swim past me as the path dips and bucks beneath me, so that one moment I'm slamming my foot too hard against the ground, sending shooting pains up my shins, and then the next I'm falling, *down, down, down* to meet the path. I grip my coin between my fingers.

*Joe*, I scream in my thoughts. *I need you!*

The wood creaks and groans around me, a starving thing hungry for blood. A branch cuts across the path. I veer out of the way just in time, so that it gets caught in the edge of my shirt, slicing away a piece of fabric instead of my skin.

I glance over my shoulder, but I can't see anything past the wall of shadows bearing down on me. I force my eyes forward and—

Smack into a tree.

No, not a tree. A person. I stumble back, reaching for my knife.

"Win, it's me." Uncle Joe grabs me by the shoulders, his eyes widening as he takes in the scene behind me. "My God," he whispers. "It's him."

"Who?" I try to turn back, but Joe pushes me ahead of him, screaming at me to run. He follows behind me, whispering spells in his ancient language. The smoke that had curled over the wood's canopy shatters like a mirror, raining down on us in chips of glass. I hit the ground, covering my head, but the glass turns to black dust and covers the ground like snow.

The sunlight returns. The Sentinels scream, a piercing sound that echoes off the trees as they disappear into hollowed-out logs and dark cubbyholes. The darkness. This is what the French traveler was talking about. This was why he didn't want to be in the shadows. They can't cross over into the sunlight. Even now, when the sun is faded and low on the horizon, it's enough to keep us safe. I lean my hands on my knees and take deep, shuddering breaths.

"Who the hell was that?" I wheeze.

"Varo," Uncle Joe says. "He's back."

"What do you mean he's back? I thought he was banished!"

"He was." Uncle Joe rubs his hand over his mouth, his head shaking back and forth like he can't make sense of it. "He must have found some way to return."

"Is he behind what's happening in the wood?"

"I don't know," Joe says. "But I'm going to find out."

"What can I do to help?"

"You can go home and wait until I have more information."

My jaw drops. "That's it? Go home and be a good little girl?"

"For starters, yes. The sun's going down, and I'll be damned if anything happens to you."

"Fine. But you better let me know the minute you hear anything." I don't like the idea of Joe facing this alone, not when we have no clue who this guy's supporters are or why he's back. Not when people keep disappearing and the wood is being poisoned with the one thing that can kill the Old Ones.

He nods. "Now, get home."

"Be careful," I say to his already fading form. I can't lose him, too.

His smile turns to dust, ripped away by the wind. "Always."

⁙⁖

Mom pulls into the driveway as I exit the wood. She's watching the faint line of orange on the horizon being smudged out by the darkness, and then her eyes find mine. Her whole body folds in, and though I can't hear the sigh from here, I know it's a big one.

She doesn't need to know what happened in the wood. One more near-death experience for me would likely be one too many for her to handle. At best, she would have a complete nervous breakdown, and probably end up in a hospital from exhaustion or malnutrition by Christmas. At worst, she'd kidnap me and try to take me somewhere the wood can't reach me, even though such a place doesn't exist. So, I meet her on the driveway after doing my stretches with the brightest, nothing-bad-happened-while-you-were-gone smile I can muster. She grabs a box full of papers from the backseat.

"Sorry I'm late," Mom says, placing the box on top of the trunk and reaching in for another. "I tried to get here before sunset, but there was traffic—"

"Mom. You're allowed to have a life, you know. You don't have to be here every time the sun goes down."

She stops. "Yes, I do."

I don't argue with her.

"What are you doing out here anyway? I thought you were going to call your uncle."

"Oh, I, uh, I *was*, but then I took a nap after lunch, and felt a lot better. I must have just overdone it last night."

Mom looks skeptical. "Oh?"

"Yeah. I mean, it's like you're always telling me. I need to slow down before my body does it for me. I guess this was just one of those days." It's the you–told–me–so card I've been keeping in my back pocket, and I feel like a terrible daughter telling such a blatant lie, but it works.

"Well, you should still take it easy," she says, mollified. "What do you say to a mother-daughter movie night?"

I grab the box on top of the trunk and try to think fast. Normally, I'd be all for a movie night, but I don't want to leave Henry all alone in my room for God knows how long while he gets into God knows what. "Um, yeah, that sounds good, but I kind of promised Meredith I'd go to this bonfire thing tonight if I was feeling better."

Really? Was that really the first thing I thought of? Were there really no other options?

"You were too sick to go to school, but you want to go to a bonfire?"

"I don't *want* to go, but a bonfire next door with a bunch of drunk teenagers means a lot of foot traffic near the threshold."

Mom looks off into the distance at Brian's house. "You couldn't just watch them from the house?"

Yeah, that was my original thought, before my fear of Mom finding Henry overrode my aversion to high school parties. "It'd be easier to keep an eye on them at the party. Besides, I know you really want me to socialize more outside of school. You know, be a normal teenager."

Mom softens, and I have to fight the urge to wince. I'm so going to be paying out the you-know-what in karma for this.

"What time is this bonfire?"

"I'm not sure," I say. "After the football game."

"Are you going to that, too?"

"Not if I can help it."

Mom arches a brow.

"I mean—I think I'm going to lie down after dinner and get a little more rest first," I say. "Just to make sure I feel up to going out."

"All right, but you owe me a mother-daughter movie night."

"Deal."

# XXI

Henry is sitting at my desk, flipping through *Lord of the Flies*, when I slip into my room. He looks up at me, his brow furrowed. "These children are heathens."

"That's kind of the point," I say. "Any luck in the attic?"

Henry sighs and sets the book on his lap. "Unfortunately, no, but I have not given up hope."

"Still, we should come up with a backup plan, just in case. Even if we find a journal—which I highly doubt we will—there's no guarantee there'll be anything useful in it."

"I'll take that under advisement." His tone is light, but I can tell by the set of his shoulders, the hardness of his jaw as he grits his teeth, that he's worried. I want to comfort him, to put my arm around him and tell him everything will be all right. But I don't know him well enough to touch him, and the truth is, I don't know if everything will be all right, and while sometimes it feels like all I do anymore is lie, I don't want to lie to him.

"Henry, something happened. In the wood."

He bolts out of the chair and crosses the room to me. "Are you all right?"

"Yes, I'm fine, but"—I take a deep breath—"Varo's back."

"Varo? The Old One who was banished?"

I nod. "I saw him. In the wood. Uncle Joe confirmed it was him. And whatever he's up to, he didn't like that I saw him." I tell Henry how he clapped his hands together and changed day into night. How the wood turned on me. "If Joe hadn't shown up when he did, I don't know what would have happened."

Henry pales. "If he's the one behind all of this . . . If he tried to hurt you just for seeing him . . ." He swallows. "What did he do to my parents?"

"Hey."

He doesn't look at me.

Oh, to hell with not knowing him well enough. Tentatively, I reach for him, wrapping my arms around his shoulders and holding him against me. His body is tense at first, resistant, but I don't let go. "We don't know what happened to your parents, but there's no reason right now to think the worst."

Of course, I had the same thought. If they truly did disappear for knowing too much, the chance that Varo would let them live, given his track record, is slim. But I can't let Henry lose hope yet. Partly because I couldn't stand to see the same hollow look in his bright green eyes that I see in Mom's every day, and partly because I can't get the image of Dad's name on Henry's parents' desk out of my head. If Dad's somehow connected to all of this, I *have* to find out how, and I'm afraid that if I lose Henry now, I never will.

"Jumping to conclusions isn't going to help us," I continue, "and it certainly isn't going to help them. We just need to stay the course, okay?"

He takes a deep breath and, finally, nods. "You're right," he agrees. "Of course you're right." But the blood still hasn't returned to his cheeks.

I let go of him and take a step back, worrying my bottom lip between my teeth. "So, I know this is going to be the last thing you want to do right now, but we have to leave."

His eyes widen. "Why? Is Varo coming? Are you in danger?"

I wave off his alarm. "No, nothing like that. There's this bonfire at my neighbor's house tonight. All the kids from my school are going to be there, and it's kind of a security risk. I need to be there to keep an eye on them, and I need to get you out of the house so Mom doesn't find you while I'm gone. I know it's awful of me to ask you to go to a party instead of spending the night doing more to find your parents, but—"

"Winter." He cups my chin with his hand, forcing me to meet his gaze. "I knew when I came here that I would be impeding your life and your responsibilities. I did not lie when I told you I would do whatever was asked of me. If we need to go, we'll go."

I sigh. "Thank you."

I glance down at what I'm wearing. The shirt is black and the jeans are mud-splattered. It doesn't really scream school pride. I flip through my closet, looking for anything in the purple or gold family. The closest I get is a lavender T-shirt I haven't worn since eighth grade stuffed in the back of my closet, which looks small enough now to show off my belly button and half my rib cage—*no, thank you*—or a dark-blue sweater that maybe, in the right lighting and if viewed by a partially blind person, could pass for purple.

I open the door, sweater and a fresh pair of jeans in hand, but Mom's in her bedroom, changing into sweats, her door wide open. She'll see me go into the bathroom to change, and then she'll definitely know something's up.

I close the door and slump against it. "Crap."

When I open my eyes, Henry's standing right in front of me. I jump. "Jeez, make noise when you walk, will you?"

He frowns. "I thought you wanted me to be quiet when your mother is home."

*Okay, he has me there.* "You're right, sorry. I'm just a little stressed. I wasn't exactly planning on taking you out into modern society while you're here, let alone sneaking you past my mom to do it."

He shrugs. "You were able to sneak me in. It cannot be much different."

"Yeah, well, my mom wasn't four feet down the hall last time."

I press my ear against the door. I can still hear Mom moving around her bedroom. That's the good and bad thing about living in a two-hundred-plus-year-old house: I can hear exactly where she is, but she can hear exactly where I am, too.

I sigh and spin my finger. "Turn around."

He stares at me.

I hold up the sweater. "I need to change."

He blushes and turns around, pressing himself into the far corner of the room. He mumbles an apology and cracks his knuckles, his head ducked low as I slip out of my shirt.

It's a weird feeling, standing in the same room as a boy with your bra exposed and the cold air seeping through the cracks around the window sprouting goose bumps on your flesh. I'm extra-aware of my skin, my too-loud heart. I fling the black top into my hamper and tug the sweater over my head. My hair crackles with static, and I'm pretty sure I smeared deodorant on the fabric, but at least it's on.

Next come the jeans, skinny ones that get caught around my ankles when I try to pull them off. I hop on one leg, trying to get them off, and tumble into the side of my bed.

"Are you well?" Henry asks, his voice muffled by the wall.

"Yep. Fine. Just keep staring at the wall, Brightonshire."

He laughs, a low sound that reminds me of a purr. And even though I'm completely mortified, it makes me smile, knowing I can make him laugh like that even when his world is crashing down around him.

I pull on the ankle without mercy until it finally gives, then wiggle into the fresh pair of jeans, thankfully *not* of the skinny variety. "Okay. Ready."

Henry turns, but he still won't look at me.

"No, really," I say. "Fully clothed now."

His eyes inch up to meet mine and the air crackles between us. His irises are darker than before, laser-focused. My skin prickles. Something pulls in my stomach, the same something that leads me into the wood during the day and back to the house when the sun sets. An instinct too strong to be ignored.

He looks away and the feeling fades. "Will I be—Am I dressed appropriately?"

Good point. Sure, *I'm* used to his clothes—I've practically taken a graduate-level course in fashion history in my time in the wood—but everyone else will be staring at him, which means attention. Which means gossip. Which means *not good.*

"I'll grab some of my dad's old clothes after dinner. I'm going to need you to stay up here for another hour or so. Will you be all right?"

"Of course," he replies, returning to the desk and picking up his book. "I must discover what happens to these horrible children."

I smirk. "I'll sneak you up some food when I get the chance."

He waves me out the door, his face disappearing behind the old, yellowed pages. My heart tugs at the sight. I know he's just putting on a brave face—I can't imagine how much more worried he is about his parents now that he knows a psychopath is on the loose—but it reminds me of my dad, of the lessons he instilled in me. There's a quiet strength in a person who can go on and do what needs to be done even when all hope seems lost. And yeah, maybe I still don't know enough about Henry to totally trust him, but now that I'm learning the kind of person he is, it's getting harder to keep my guard up.

My phone buzzes in my pocket as I sit down at the dinner table.

Mer: *U coming 2nite?*

Me (while doing my best to hide my frustration from Mom): *Yep.*

Mer: *!!!!!!!*

Mom sets a bowl of chicken soup and a basket of fresh-baked bread in front of me. My phone buzzes again.

Mer: *I know u have a ridiculous aversion to makeup, but please wear some tonight. I'm getting u a date to the dance if it kills me.*

I roll my eyes and stuff my phone back in my pocket. Finding a date to the dance is the least of my worries. I can't be too annoyed with her, though. It wouldn't be fair. She doesn't know what my life entails. She doesn't know the last thing I need is a boyfriend. Or a makeup lesson.

"Are you sure you're feeling up to going out tonight?" Mom asks as she dips her spoon into her soup bowl.

I nod. "I don't really have a choice, but since it's next door, I can come right home if I start to feel sick again."

"All right," Mom says. "Just don't overdo it."

I take a few sips of my soup, then place my spoon back on the table. "Mom?"

She glances at me as she rips off a piece of bread. "Yes?"

Deep breaths. "Did Dad ever keep a journal?"

"Why do you ask?"

Okay, not the reaction I was expecting. "Well, I was just thinking—"

"Seems you did a lot of that today."

"Yeah, well, when you have nothing else to do . . ." I clear my throat. "So, anyway, I was thinking about all the journals in Dad's office. They go back hundreds of years, and they're obviously important since we've taken such good care of them. So . . . why didn't Dad have one?"

Mom rubs her hand across her brow. "I really don't want to get into this right now. I've had a long day."

I know I should stop. Mom doesn't like to talk about Dad, especially anything concerning him and the wood. But I need to know. "Mom." I set my hand on top of hers. "It's important."

She hesitates. "He did keep one," she says, "a long time ago. When we were first married, he used to take it with him everywhere he went. But then, as the years went by, I began to see it less and less, and then I never saw it again."

"Do you remember the last time you saw him with it?"

She shakes her head. "You were young, a toddler maybe, when I started to see it less, but the last time? It must have been right around when you started your lessons."

"Do you know why he stopped writing in it?"

"No, I don't."

"But—"

She slams her hand on the table. "You *saw* how he was, Winter. Why do you think he stopped writing in it?"

I stare at her, speechless.

She picks up her bowl and dumps it in the kitchen sink. Her fingers curl around the counter, her shoulders shaking.

"Mom." My voice comes out croaky and awful. "I didn't mean to—"

"I know." She wipes the back of her hand underneath her eyes. "Just—just go upstairs, okay? I need a second."

I swallow. "Mom—"

"Winter, *please.*"

I get up from the table. I grab the rest of the bread from the basket, but she doesn't notice. I head up to my room, quietly closing the door behind me.

# XXII

While Mom's busy doing the dishes, I grab a pair of Dad's old jeans and a green cable-knit sweater from her closet, pushing the hangers together to hide the gaps they leave behind. Mer texts me as I shut Mom's door quietly behind me, the clothes draped over my arm.

*I'm here*, she says. *Where r u?*

*Be there soon*, I text back, leaning against the faded blue wallpaper. *Getting ready.*

When I open the door, I find Henry sitting on the edge of my bed, flipping through a scrapbook of this last summer that Mer made for me as a back-to-school gift. He stops at a picture of me at her parents' Fourth of July party. I'm wearing shorts and a vintage polka-dot halter top. My skin is tan and bare and everywhere. He pushes his hair back, his lips parting as he stares at Summer Me. A rush of breath flows from his mouth in a gentle *whoosh*. It reminds me of this archaeologist friend of Mom's I saw at an ancient pottery exhibit on campus, the way he stared at the artifacts like they were too beautiful to really exist.

I clear my throat.

Henry jumps, knocking the scrapbook to the floor. He clutches his hand to his chest. "You frightened me."

I grin, but it's a fragile thing. My palms are too sweaty and my stomach too queasy for it to be anything more than ephemeral. "Here," I say, handing him the clothes. "These will help you fit in."

He takes the jeans and rubs his thumbs along the denim. "These are breeches?"

I nod. "Hopefully they're long enough." I think they should be; he's about the same height as my dad was. The sweater is more concerning. Henry has a small, tapered waist like Dad, but his chest is wide and his shoulders could carry dinner trays. Something tells me he does a lot more manual labor than I would have expected of a baron's son.

"They are much too wide in the leg."

"That's how they're supposed to be."

"Do men of your time not find them cumbersome? Does it not impede their trade?"

"Well, men of my time who are your age don't usually have a trade yet. They just go to school and sit at desks all day and, I don't know, talk about sports and boobs over fried cheese sticks at lunch."

"Boobs?"

"Never mind. The point is, this is what we wear in my time, and if I'm going to take you to a bonfire where you'll be surrounded by a horde of teenagers who can smell 'different' from a mile away, you're going to wear what I tell you to wear. Got it?"

He smirks. "As you wish, my lady. I am here to serve."

Now if only all men saw it that way.

He stares at me. I stare back at him. He spins his finger as I did earlier and says, "Turn."

"Oh." Heat rushes to my cheeks as I turn my back on him. "Right."

There's a lot of fumbling noises, followed by curses muttered under his breath. I catch his shadow on the wall from my desk lamp as he struggles to tug on the sweater, and I have to bite my lip to keep from laughing. But when his shadow starts to work on getting his pants off, the laughter dies in my throat and I shut my eyes tight, my heart beating faster.

"Do not turn," he says after another minute of jostling. "I have managed to don the shirt, but I . . ." He exhales, stumbling over his words. "I cannot seem to, uh—that is, what is to be done about the metal triangle?"

"The metal triangle? The—oh!" The zipper. "Um." I grab the muddy jeans I wore earlier from the top of my hamper, then take a couple steps back while keeping my eyes squarely on the wall. I angle my hands toward him so he can see the jeans over my shoulder. His hair brushes my neck as he leans forward, and his scent, that earthy campfire smell, envelops me.

I demonstrate how the zipper works on my pair, which is followed by the sound of the zipper on his jeans zipping up and down, up and down. Just like the drawstring.

Zip, zip. Zip, zip.

"Got it?" I ask, still staring at the wall.

"I believe so," he whispers back.

"Can I see?"

He doesn't say yes, but he doesn't say no, either. I slowly turn on my heel, and—

All my breath leaves my body.

The sweater's snug on him in the chest, but the sleeves and hem are long enough, and, God help me, I like the way it looks, clinging to him like that. A large would just swallow him up. And the jeans fit him in the leg but they're a touch too baggy in the waist—not really a big deal since that's how a lot of guys wear them anyway, but where you might typically see the top band of a boy's underwear from too-baggy jeans, there's skin.

A pretty thick slice of it.

My cheeks warm and I press my hand to the side of my face, looking away. "Underwear," I say. "You need underwear. And a belt." God, I'm an idiot.

"Underwear?"

"You know. Undergarments? Clothes you wear under your clothes?"

He blushes again. I catch our reflection in the full-length mirror on my closet door, and there we are, the two of us looking like boiled lobsters. "I assumed people of your time did not wear them. Have I made a mistake?"

"No!" I say quickly. "It was my mistake." The water in the kitchen sink is still running, and I can hear the clatter of dishes being set on top of one another. "You just sit tight and I'll be right back."

I try not to think about the fact that I'm going to be digging through my dad's underwear drawer as I sneak back into Mom's room, but I'm in luck. There's a brand-new, unopened package of boxer briefs that she must have bought for him before—well, before. I grab one of Dad's old belts, then tiptoe back to my room.

Ripping open the package, I hurl the underwear and belt at Henry, describing how the underwear goes on just like pants and the belt threads through the loops around his hips, and then I dial Meredith's number.

She picks up on the first ring. "Winter? Where are you?"

"Sorry, I'll be there as soon as I can. I had to—"

"These are amazing," Henry says to my back. "How is it the fabric can stretch so without breaking?" I hear a snap that I can only assume is the underwear band smacking his flesh.

I take another step away from him and bury my head in the corner. "I'm, um, picking up a family friend. His parents are in town on a, uh, business trip, and he had nothing to do, so I invited him. I mean, who wants to be alone on a Friday night, right?" There's that nervous laugh. I really need to get that under control.

"Okay, I guess I'll see—wait. Did you say 'he'?"

Of course that would be the part Mer would get hung up on. "Um, yeah?"

"You dog!"

"It's not like that—"

"You just take your time," she says, her voice dripping with suggestion. "I'm busy stalking Johnny anyway. I think he might actually ask me out tonight."

"Johnny Fletcher? The tailback?"

"No, Johnny Carmichael. The wide receiver."

"What happened to the tailback?"

"One date, last week. I told you, remember? He was the one who licked my face like a dog bowl? I told him to lose my number? None of this ringing a bell?"

"Oh, yeah, sorry." Actually it's not, but it wouldn't be the first time I'd tuned out her boy rants. "I'll get there as soon as I can, okay?"

"Take your time, honey. Take. Your. Time."

"It's not like that."

"Don't worry," she says. "I won't tell Trevor you're actually interested in this guy. It's good to keep your options open. Besides, he might ask you out sooner if he thinks someone's moving in on his territory."

"Which 'he'?"

"Does it matter?"

"Whatever. See you soon."

I hang up, turn around, and practically smack into Henry's chest.

"Does this look better?" he asks.

It does. The jeans still hang low on his hips, but only about a quarter of an inch of black underwear is peeking out of the top now that the belt has secured them to his hips. I don't think I'd be able to steal a pair of Dad's old shoes without Mom noticing, but Henry's shoes look expensive anyway, all soft leather and silver buckles. Someone will probably think they're haute couture, snatched off a runway in Milan or something. With his shoulder-length blond hair and chiseled features, he looks like he stepped out of a perfume ad holding a bottle of Eau de Prince Charming.

Suddenly, an image pops into my head, of the girls from my school with fake orange tans and dragon nails fawning all over him, and a stab of jealousy pricks my stomach. Which is ridiculous. What do I have to be jealous about? So what if other girls find him attractive? It doesn't matter. It's not like he's going to date them or anything. Soon he'll be back home in the eighteenth century, hopefully with his parents alive and well by his side, and then he can be hounded by girls from his own time.

Which is so not any better.

"Very nice," I tell him, though the words are hard to get out now that my throat's as dry as the Sahara. "I guess there's nothing to do now but . . . leave."

As if that's going to be easy.

I tug on a pair of flat leather boots as Henry buckles his own shoes. Mom must be really upset, because the vacuum's rolling across the hardwood in the family room now—I can hear the suction of the hose attachment inhaling the dust on the baseboards. She only cleans when she wants to take her mind off something. I must be in the running for the Worst Daughter Ever Award tonight. First, I make her cry, and now I'm sneaking a boy out of my room. A boy I brought home from the wood like some kind of lost puppy. A boy who slept on my floor last night. A boy who I skipped school to be with today.

Wait, that isn't right. I didn't skip school today to be *with* him. I skipped school on official guardian business, which is really very admirable of me. The fact that I had to lie about it and act sick is irrelevant, as is the fact that I spent approximately half the time checking Henry out when he wasn't looking.

I tiptoe to the door and open it slowly so it won't creak. I glance back at Henry. "Follow me, and don't make any noise. Step where I step and stop where I stop. Got it?"

He nods.

I exhale. "Here goes nothing."

# XXIII

The vacuum covers our footsteps as we creep down the staircase at half-past ten and into the kitchen. I press myself against the wall and motion for Henry to do the same, then peer around the corner of the doorway into the living room. Mom's back is to us. I motion Henry to move first. He slides past the door like a shadow, sneaking into the mudroom.

I take a step forward just as the vacuum cuts off.

"You're heading out?"

I've never understood the expression "my heart stopped" before. I understand the one about feeling like someone's punched you in the gut—that's how I felt when Uncle Joe told me Dad was gone. All the air flew out of my lungs and my stomach contracted in on itself and I thought I would never breathe again. My heart kept beating, and it felt like a traitor.

But my heart stops now. It comes to a grinding, painful halt as I freeze midstep. For the briefest and scariest of seconds, I wonder if it will start back up again, or if this is how I'll go. Literally dying of fright because my mom caught me sneaking a boy out of the house. But then my heart flips, like a pancake, and kicks itself back into rhythm.

I put my foot down and meet her gaze. Her eyes are red and puffy, but she's trying hard to look like she hasn't been crying. "Yeah," I say. "But I'll be right next door, so just text me if you need anything."

She gives me a soft laugh. "You sound like the parent."

I swallow. "Mom, I'm really sorry—"

She holds up her hand, cutting me off. "It's all right. You didn't do anything wrong."

I feel awful leaving her like this, but I don't have much of a choice. "Okay. I guess I'll be going then."

"Have fun." Mom wraps me in a hug and she's practically in the kitchen. She has to see Henry there. I'm *screwed, screwed, screwed.*

"Tell Meredith I said hi." She pats my cheek and turns to the dining table, scraping crumbs into her hand.

"O-okay."

I head into the mudroom, but Henry isn't there. I pivot on my heel, hissing his name.

"Winter?" Mom calls. "Did you say something?"

I wince. "I said, 'See you later.'"

"See you."

I glance out the window in the door just as Henry peers around a tree off the back porch. I exhale.

This boy is going to be the death of me.

I head through the mudroom door, closing it behind me. My boots clack against the wooden boards, and then mush down overgrown grass.

"I apologize," Henry says once I reach him. "I know you

wanted me to stay close, but I did not want your mother to find me."

"Yeah, good thinking," I admit. I check the porch and kitchen windows over my shoulder, but Mom isn't watching me. "Okay, let's go."

⟶⟶⟩⟨⟵

The night is thick and warm with the day's fading heat. There are no stars, no moon, just heavy black clouds that block out their light. The bonfire is already raging. My classmates dance to the music pulsating out of Brian's parents' outdoor surround system. They undulate in front of the fire like pagan worshippers, red Solo cups sloshing beer onto the grass. I know from Meredith's text that our school won the game 59–0, and that most of the people here were already drunk before they came, passing water bottles filled with vodka between them in the stands.

Henry pulls back at the sight of them all. I slide my palm across his, interlacing our fingers. He looks down at my hand as if it is a magical thing, as if he's afraid to look away and find it was never real to begin with.

"It's okay," I tell him. "You're going to be fine. Just let me do the talking."

His gaze meets mine. The orange light of the flames is just close enough to spark against his eyes, like gemstones. "In my time," he says quietly, "we would not hold hands in public like this unless we were engaged."

"Does it make you uncomfortable?"

He shakes his head, a small smile tilting his lips. "Quite the contrary."

"Well, then," I say, "I won't tell anyone if you don't."

"Of course not," he replies. "We will be in enough trouble as it is if anyone discovers what we've done without adding this to our list of transgressions."

"Don't remind me."

I don't know how he managed to keep Mom from seeing him. It was a close call, too close for comfort. I may be forced to tell her whether I want to or not, but that's for future Winter to worry about. Present Winter has managed to sneak a boy out of her room for the night, keeping her mother oblivious, and therefore, safe.

Meredith is surrounded by boys, although Johnny the wide receiver is nowhere to be found. None of the football players are. They must still be showering or performing Maori war dances in the locker room, or whatever it is football players do after winning a big game. She spots us and raises her cup. "Win! You made it!"

She starts toward us, and I pull Henry back.

"Okay, here's the thing about Meredith," I quickly whisper. "She's probably going to come across as rude by your time's standards—heck, she can be rude by *my* time's standards, but she means well, so—"

"Winter," he says, stopping me, and I don't know why, but my name sounds so amazing on his lips in that moment. Exotic and full and rich, like chocolate melting on his tongue. It sends electric pulses through my veins. "Any friend of yours is a friend of mine."

Meredith lunges for me, wrapping me in a tight hug. "Win, it was amazing! You should have been there. Johnny caught three touchdown passes, and I ran onto the field after the game and he bent me back and kissed me just like in that World War Two picture you like so much." She notices Henry and gives him a big smile. "Hi! You must be Win's friend. I'm Meredith."

Henry takes Meredith's hand and turns it to kiss her knuckles. "Henry Durant," he says. "*Enchanté*."

Her eyes widen. "Whoa. You're hot." She leans toward me and whisper-shouts, "He's *hot*, Win."

"Oh no," Henry says. "I'm quite comfortable, actually."

Mer giggles. "Win says you're visiting from out of town?"

Henry stands rigid, his hands behind his back. It's a pose he seems accustomed to; one I imagine he's used in countless ballrooms throughout his life. "Yes, I suppose you could say that."

"So, where are you from?" she asks. "Somewhere close, I hope."

I say the first thing that comes to mind. "New York."

Henry and Meredith both stare at me.

"He's from New York," I say again.

Mer scrunches up her face. "You don't sound like you're from New York." Her eyes brighten, like she's just realized something. "You're from England, aren't you?"

Henry glances at me, uncertain. I nod, and he replies, "Yes, from Brightonshire."

"When did you move to New York?"

"I, uh, well . . . that is to say . . ." Henry stumbles over his response, but thankfully more cars arrive, honking as they pull into the front yard and tearing Mer's attention away from him. Boys wearing letterman jackets lean out the windows, shouting our school's fight song. I haven't seen Brian anywhere yet. His parents must be out of town—that's the only way this could be happening. I wince as one of the cars runs over his mom's prize hydrangea bushes.

The football players have arrived.

# XXIV

Henry and I fade into the background, watching, listening. For the most part, the party stays centralized around the bonfire and outdoor surround system pumping out a litany of rap music. At one point, a group of friends decide to play a drunk version of hide-and-seek, making my adrenaline spike, but they stick close to Brian's house, never straying too far from the keg. Even the couples who disappear into the trees on the edge of Brian's property aren't a threat. As long as they don't enter the wood through the threshold, they'll stay in this world, where the only monsters they'll have to fear are spiders, poison ivy, and their own surging hormones.

I sneak glances at Henry every few seconds. His jaw is tense and his arms are crossed over his chest—defensive to the max. I can't imagine what it must be like for him, an eighteenth-century aristocrat surrounded by guys doing keg stands and scantily clad girls air-humping to the music, but he doesn't complain or ask to leave. He understands the importance of us being here.

"Hey, Parish!"

Trevor finds me in the crowd and makes his way over.

I exhale. "Crap."

"Is something the matter?" Henry asks.

I shake my head, but Trevor's already too close for me to explain who he is to Henry without Trevor overhearing. Still, Henry notices Trevor making his way toward me and the concern I'm trying to blink out of my eyes. And then, so subtly I could almost believe it was an accident, Henry moves his body so he's half blocking me. It's a possessive stance that reminds me of a gorilla documentary I watched once, when a silverback beat his fists against his chest at another male approaching. Trevor frowns at him, and then Henry moves away from me just enough for Trevor to spot our entwined hands.

Still, Trevor doesn't give up. He gets that all-American smile on his face, the one all cute quarterbacks seem to have, complete with dimples and flashing white teeth. "Hey, Winter," he says, reaching out for a hug. Weird, considering we've never hugged before, not even during that awkward week in sixth grade. Still, it happens so fast I don't know how to stop it. Henry doesn't let go of my hand, so it's more of a half hug that feels as awkward as it sounds. "Glad you could make it. Who's your friend?"

"Henry," I say. "Henry, this is Trevor."

They shake hands, their eyes narrowed.

"Is he your date?" Trevor asks me without taking his eyes off Henry.

"Um . . ." I don't know how to answer that, but it doesn't matter because Henry answers for me.

"Yes," he says. "I am."

I'm pretty sure they didn't use the word "date" in Henry's time, which means he either discerned the meaning of the word through Trevor's body language, or he learned a lot more than I thought he would from watching TV for a few hours.

Trevor slides his hands into his pockets, his shoulders an unformed shrug. "Well, then. Have fun. Maybe you can save a dance for me later, Win?"

"Um, I don't think we're going to be here that long."

"All right. Well, find me if you change your mind."

"Not likely," I mumble, but he doesn't hear me over the music.

Henry tugs on my sleeve. "Winter. Look." He nods toward my backyard.

Someone is walking toward the wood. He's too far away to make out his face, but he cups his hands around a lighter, igniting a white cylinder way too fat to be a cigarette.

*Shit.*

I run after him, Henry right behind me. I try to call out to the guy—"Hey! You can't be over here!"—but he either doesn't hear me or doesn't care. He strolls languidly up the path and past the rock with my parents' initials, heading straight for the threshold, completely unaware that he is walking into death's arms. He can't hear the whispers fluttering through the trees, the monsters eagerly awaiting his sacrifice.

"Wait up!" I yell.

He stops. Glances back at me. A small ring of light smolders as he inhales. And then, just like that—

He's gone.

I keep running.

"What are you doing?" Henry shouts at my back.

"I have to go in after him!"

"Winter, wait." He grabs hold of my arm.

"Let go!"

He yanks me to a stop. "You cannot follow him without a proper plan."

"I do have a plan," I bite back. "I'm going to go in there and grab him before he goes too far."

Henry swears under his breath. He fumbles with something in his pocket. "I'm coming with you."

"Don't be ridic—"

He pulls out his flask, unscrewing the top and taking a long swig. "You cannot stop me."

"Henry—"

"Winter." He takes my hand. "I will not let you go in there alone."

I try to think of something I can say, something I can do, to make sure he doesn't follow me into the wood, but I'm running out of time. "Fine, but you can't leave my side."

"Never."

I turn toward my threshold. "Stay close."

The trees creak and sway as I approach. Shadows skitter from branch to branch. Henry can't see them from out here—no one but a guardian can—but he seems to sense the predators watching us from above, the cackles of laughter and smacking of lips.

Henry's right—I do need a plan. My mind races for something. *Anything.* If I'm going to break one of the most important rules of the wood—don't go in after dark—putting my life at risk as well as Henry's, I need to do more than just wing it. But I've never really thought about what I would do in a worst-case scenario like this. In all my training, I always hoped I would be able to stop someone from entering the wood through my threshold before they even got close to it, especially at night, because anything less than that was unforgivable.

"I should be able to feel where he is as soon we enter," I say. "There's no telling how far he's gone, so we'll have to be careful. Watch your footing; the paths will try to kill you just like everything else in there." I glance back at him. "We only have a shot at surviving if we're fast, so as soon we get in there, I need you to run, and don't stop running until we're safe again. Got it?"

He nods.

I take a deep breath. "Here goes nothing."

Henry takes my hand and, together, we step into the wood.

# XXV

I can't see anything, not even my hands held out in front of me. This is worse than the darkness that had just begun to creep in at sunset. Worse than the illusion of night Varo created this afternoon. The wood is alive around us, shrieks whipping past our ears, slimy things slithering across our boots, leathery wings catching in my hair. Something knocks into me, pushing me to the ground. My hands fly out, my arms sinking to my elbows in mud that smells like raw sewage. My heart slams against my rib cage.

I'm no longer holding Henry's hand.

"Henry!" I call.

"I'm here." Henry's hands splay against my back in the darkness. He lifts me up and says it again, his breath a circle of warmth on the nape of my neck: "I'm here."

We try to run, holding on to each other's hands so tightly, I fear our knuckles might burst through our skin, but it's no use. The mud is too thick.

We are prey ripe for the killing.

I do the only thing I can think of, palming my coin and crying out, "*Sahabri'el!*" I don't know if my fireflies will hear me, or if they'll even still be my friends here in the darkness, but it's a chance we have to take. The glyphs glow white and it's enough light to see Henry stumbling in the muck next to me. Enough light to see the monsters that were once inked over my Latin conjugations oscillating around us. Bloated heads and glowing eyes, needle teeth and jagged talons. The creatures of my worst nightmares.

I force myself to breathe instead of scream.

I don't know why they don't just kill us and get it over with, and then I realize—they're toying with us. They know they have hours before the sun comes up. They can play with their food and eat it, too. And as I scan the darkness, searching, searching, searching for the light of my fireflies, I start to think they're right.

*We're going to die in here.*

It's so loud, the wind roaring through the trees and the screeching and clicking and growling of the monsters around us, I can't hear myself think. My foot catches on something, and I stumble forward again. Henry wrenches me upright before I can fall, but it's no use. I stop fighting. Instead, I reach for Henry, wrapping my arms around him and burrowing my face into his shoulder.

"I'm so sorry," I whisper.

"Shh," he murmurs. "We're going to make it."

I shake my head. "Henry—"

A laugh escapes his lips. "Here they come."

And then, miraculously, a cloud of sapphire blue envelops us, twisting around us like a cyclone. Thousands of wings buzz in our ears, their light radiating warmth. The monsters lunge.

White-blue arcs zap them back. Some monsters run away. Others try to barrel into us again and again, but the fireflies absorb the impact every time. Tears prick my eyes as I watch them defend us, their glorious light sparking like star fire. The last monsters peel away from us, shrinking back into the night. They don't go far—they haven't completely given up—but it's enough.

We're safe for now.

My words are no more than a breath on my lips. "I can't believe it worked."

Henry pushes my hair behind my ear and smiles down at me. "You continue to amaze me at every turn, Winter Parish."

His eyes travel down my face, resting on my lips. We don't say anything, and even though we have only just escaped certain death, all I can think is *Is he going to kiss me?* And *I've never kissed a boy before.* And *Will I be good at it?*

He leans forward. My eyes flutter closed as I inhale that familiar scent. Black tea and cinnamon, the campfire smell just barely clinging to his hair now that he's wearing new clothes. His lips are an inch from mine, and I wonder if they'll feel as soft as they look.

My eyes snap open. "The traveler."

Henry freezes, a question in his eyes.

I can't believe I forgot, even for just that fraction of a second. "Stoner Guy," I explain, even though Henry has no idea what a stoner is. "We have to find him."

Henry's eyes widen. In the midst of our shared relief, he forgot, too.

"Do you think he's still alive?"

"There's only one way to find out."

I start forward, but I can't see much through our light shield.

I move my palm over my eyes and say, "Open." The fireflies slide away, creating a hole the size of a hand mirror to peer through.

The paths are still muddy, and our progress is slow going. Every step deeper into the wood is a bad sign for Stoner Guy, but I don't give up. We walk.

And walk.

Trudging through the ever-thickening mud.

Almost right past him.

At first, all I see is a shoe. And then a knee. An arm. A swatch of torso. And a face, eyes closed, blood dripping from a wound over his brow. The rest of him is covered in vines and thick roots, slowly pulling him beneath a tree. Into the earth.

I grip my knife and start hacking at the vines. The wounded vines writhe back in pain, but the others snap at me, trying to clamp onto my wrists. The fireflies zap them back, and a few of my friends even break away from the pack, burning the vines until they can't hold on to Stoner Guy any longer.

The tree roots are not as easily intimidated. They grip onto Stoner Guy harder. Henry grabs the one around the boy's neck, pulling it away from his windpipe. I try to slice through the roots, but they're too thick for my tiny blade.

"We're going to have to pull him out somehow," I say.

Henry glances around, his eyes brightening. "I have an idea." He gestures to the logs lining the path. "Do they move? We could use them as leverage."

It's worth a shot. I've never been able to get close to the edge of the path to follow Dad, but this is different. This *has* to be different. *I'm not trying to leave*, I scream-think the words. *I'm just trying to save this traveler.*

I scramble on my hands and knees across the muck, half the fireflies following me and the other half staying behind with Henry. My fingers reach for the nearest log, but my body freezes several inches from the edge of the path.

*Please.*

My arm burns, but I keep stretching.

*I need it.*

I grit my teeth and will myself forward.

*I am the daughter of Jack Parish,* I think. *Granddaughter of Edward Parish. I am the guardian of this wood, and I need to use these logs to save this traveler.*

But it doesn't work. Whatever authority I have in this wood, it stops at the rules instituted by the Old Ones over a thousand years ago.

"I can't reach them," I shout over the creaking of the tree roots, tightening their hold on the boy.

"Let me try," Henry says. "Take my spot."

"I don't think—"

He meets my gaze, the veins in his neck bulging as he struggles to keep one of the roots from crushing Stoner Guy's windpipe. "Old Ones can walk off the paths."

"But you're not an Old One."

"The elixir makes me more like them than you think."

I want to ask him what the hell he means by that, but there's no time. Stoner Guy inches closer to the edge of the path, the base of the tree opening up to swallow him whole. Cursing under my breath, I take Henry's place, pulling at the root around Stoner Guy's neck. Henry must have been working on loosening the hold the root had on the guy's neck while I was trying to reach the log, because with just a little more prying, I'm able to angle Stoner Guy's head enough to slide the root off him. The root tries to grab hold again, but my fireflies close around us, keeping it away.

I hear a grunt and watch in disbelief as Henry tears four logs from the muck, his foot scraping the edge of the path without a hint of resistance. He throws the logs back to me, and we get to work placing them in strategic locations around Stoner Guy's body, threading them through multiple roots and angling them so Henry can press down on two logs with each hand.

"On the count of three, pull him out. Ready?"

I nod.

"One. Two. Three!"

Henry bears down with all his weight on the logs. The roots barely move an inch, but between the leverage Henry is creating and the scorch marks the fireflies are searing onto their ropelike flesh, loosening their hold even more, it's enough. I grab Stoner Guy by the shoulders and heave him out, my feet slipping in the mud. He crashes down on top of me, rolling over my wrist at an awkward angle that has me gasping in pain.

Henry lets go of the logs. With nothing left to fight against, the roots crack against the tree trunk, burrowing back down into the soil.

"Is he breathing?" Henry asks me.

I lay my head on the boy's chest. His heart is beating, and a gentle whoosh of air fills his lungs.

"Yes."

Henry moves around to the boy's other side, and together we pull him to his feet.

"We should leave," Henry says. "I do not trust this place."

"Wait. Do you hear that?"

Henry stops. We stand silent, the buzzing of the fireflies around our ears the only sound. And then—

"Chanting," Henry says.

"Not just any chanting," I murmur. "It's *Hersei*."

The language of the Old Ones.

We don't have to go far to find the source of the chanting, thank God; dragging Stoner Guy through the mud is so not how I wanted to spend my night.

Standing in a clearing off the path, shrouded in a purple mist that rises from a central campfire of the same color, are four figures wearing long, black cloaks, the hoods pulled low over their faces. Another figure stands in the center of them, his hood thrown back, his hair the color of freshly fallen snow.

Varo.

We crouch down behind a bush, the fireflies creating a protective wall behind us. I worry their light may be too bright, but Varo's supporters are all focused on him, and Varo is staring into the amethyst flames. Overhead, Sentinels flit from tree to tree, although I can't tell if the reason they don't attack is because of the mist the other monsters refuse to penetrate or because they are completely under Varo's control.

Varo raises his hands and the chanting cuts off.

"Septimus."

One of the cloaked figures steps forward. The hood covers his face, but there is only one Septimus I know of on the council, and he's Alban's right-hand man.

*How deep does this go?*

"Have they been found?" Varo asks.

"Not yet," Septimus answers. "Forgive me, but are you certain they are still alive?"

Varo's lip curls. "If they weren't, the wood would not be dying now, would it?"

"Sir?"

"Celia must have leached the dragon's bane from their blood and infected the wood instead. It's the only answer for what's happening here," Varo growls.

Henry sucks in a breath at the mention of his mother's name.

"We must find them," Varo continues. "They know too much."

"Of course. You have my word." Septimus bows his head, then folds himself back into the circle.

Another follower steps forward. "And what of the attack on the council?"

"It is imminent," Varo replies. "You only need wait for my signal."

*An attack on the council? I have to let Uncle Joe know about this.*

I glance at Henry. Messaging Joe now will mean revealing Henry's and my deception, but this is bigger than both of us, or what might happen to us. And I'm sure Joe will understand when I explain everything.

*Won't he?*

It doesn't matter. I grip my coin in my palm. *Joe. Varo's having*

*a meeting in the wood. He's talking about attacking the council. You
have to see this.*

"Winter," Henry hisses, gesturing to Stoner Guy. It takes me
a moment to realize what's wrong.

Stoner Guy's waking up.

"Let's go," I whisper.

I reposition his arm over my shoulder and brace my legs to
stand. Henry does the same, but the movement must jostle Stoner
Guy too much, because—

He groans. Loudly.

Varo's eyes whip toward the sound. Henry and I freeze.

"Someone's here," one of Varo's followers says.

In unison, the others turn their hooded gazes toward our
hiding spot.

"Go, go," I say, pushing to my feet.

The fireflies surround us once more. We stumble through the
mud, moving as fast as we can, but Stoner Guy's dragging feet
slow us down. His head rolls from side to side, his red-rimmed
eyes opening and closing again.

"You're going to have to wake up now!" I yell at him.

He doesn't respond.

"Winter," Henry says. "They're coming."

I glance over Stoner Guy's shoulder. I can't see anything
through the bright blue light surrounding us, but I can hear them
all crashing through the muck and asking Varo what they
should do.

"Bring them to me," Varo shouts, his voice echoing off the
trees. "Alive."

I pat Stoner Guy's face. "Wake up!"

His eyes open, then narrow against the light.

"Can you run?" I ask him.

"What's happening?" he asks, the words thick in his cotton mouth.

"We're being chased." A tree cracks in half, plummeting to the ground. It misses us by inches. I feel the wind it creates brush the nape of my neck. "You need to run."

Stoner Guy reaches for the fireflies. "Trippy."

"The boy is clearly addled," Henry shouts.

Stoner Guy's jaw drops. "I am not. I can run."

"Then do it!" I yell.

His steps are slow at first. He can't seem to understand what's grabbing at his ankles, sucking his feet down, but it's better than him dragging his legs. Henry and I keep running with him supported between us. We take a curve in the path.

Lightning cracks around us, scorching holes in the trees. I can hear Varo's followers getting closer, muttering *Hersei* under their breath, and I'm not sure if it's the wood rebelling against our presence or them, but it doesn't matter. The smell of burning wood spurs Stoner Guy on. He rips his arms from around our shoulders and pumps his feet through the mud, picking up speed.

We take another bend onto the main path leading to my threshold. I can see my house through the trees. And I don't know if they'll follow us, or if they'll come back later now that they know for sure who I am, where I live, but what other choice do we have?

*You can't escape me forever, little one*, a dark, hollow voice echoes through my head.

"Did you hear that?" I ask Henry.

He shakes his head.

My coin warms against my wrist. Varo is using it to communicate with me.

*You and I need to talk,* he says. *I would like to get the guardians on my side. I think you may be the answer.*

I grip the coin and think back: *Not on your life, pal.*

Varo laughs. *I assure you, you'll feel differently once you know everything. Matters such as these are not always as they seem.*

*Matters such as these?* I reply, my lungs burning for air. *You mean overthrowing the council? Killing those who stand in your way?*

*To speak when knowing only one side of the story is the height of foolishness.*

Varo's followers crash through the wood behind us. The path roils, hitching up and down, making us stumble. The trees move in closer, their roots and vines reaching for us. A last-ditch effort.

*Maybe,* I reply. *But I'm done listening to you.*

The fireflies peel away, creating a shield behind us as we barrel through my threshold. The air is alive again with the sounds of the human world. Cars speeding past on 315 and music thumping on the breeze.

Varo's supporters do not follow.

Henry stares at the wood, grinning despite the fact we almost died.

"Henry?" I ask, gasping for breath.

"Did you hear what he said about my parents? They're alive." He turns to me, his eyes wide, and wraps his arms around me, picking me up off the ground. "My parents are alive!"

Stoner Guy, oblivious, plops down on the grass and leans his back against my parents' rock. "That has got to be the weirdest shit I've ever smoked."

⤷⤷⤷⥲⥲

Stoner Guy blends back into the crowd seamlessly, thinking the whole thing was just a really bad trip. Henry checked him for any broken bones or suspicious bruising, but other than the dried-up cut on his forehead, he seemed fine. We're lucky. If it had been anyone else, I'm not sure how I would have explained what he'd experienced.

We find Mer sitting on the back porch steps, scrolling through her phone and looking generally annoyed.

"There you guys are," she says. "I've been texting you for only, like, the past hour." Her gaze darts between us, a suggestive gleam in her eye as she takes in the mud on our clothes and the red patch on Henry's cheek that's sure to turn into a bruise but currently looks like a really weird place for a hickey. "Where exactly *were* you guys?"

"Nowhere you're thinking," I tell her.

She slides her phone back into her clutch. "Can we leave now? This party blows."

"What happened to Johnny?"

Mer rolls her eyes. "He's making out with Trixie Malone."

I scan the party. There are still too many drunk idiots here I need to stay and watch. "Maybe we should stick around and find someone for you to make out with, then. To get back at him."

Meredith grins. "Thanks for trying to cheer me up, Win, but this party's about two minutes away from getting busted."

"How do you know?"

"I may have called in an anonymous complaint."

I blink. "What? Why?"

She rolls her eyes. "I found Brian freaking out over the mess everyone was making of his house. I thought it was the least I could do. Besides, Johnny and Trixie can't keep making out if they're detained for underage drinking." She grins. "So, yeah. We probably shouldn't be here when the cops show up."

I arch a brow at her slightly sadistic smile. "Good thinking. Do you need a ride home?"

"Actually, I was hoping I could crash at your place."

There are about a million reasons why that is *not* a good idea. "I don't know if my mom—"

"*Please*, Win. I'm already way past curfew, and my parents would flip if they found out I was at a party."

"Where do they think you are?"

"Duh. Sleeping over at your place."

I close my eyes and take three deep breaths.

Mer leans closer. "Is that a yes?"

I blow out a frustrated breath. "Fine, but you're crashing on the couch."

"Why?"

"Because I said so."

She crosses her arms over her chest.

"And because I don't want to wake Mom up," I add. "She had a rough night."

*Thanks to me.*

"Hey, whatever keeps my parents in the dark is fine by me."

Sirens wail in the distance.

Mer grabs my arm and starts tugging me toward my house. "I believe that's our cue to go."

# XXVII

Half an hour later, Mer's set up on the couch, checking her various social media timelines. Henry and I pretend to say good-bye at the door before sneaking upstairs. Mom's bedroom door is open and a flickering blue light floods the hallway. I motion for Henry to wait at the top of the stairs, and then I tiptoe into her room.

Mom's curled up on her side on top of the covers, still wearing the same clothes she had on earlier. Dad's picture is propped up against the pillow across from her.

"Mom?" I whisper, but her chest rises and falls slowly, unchanging. I grab one of Grandma's quilts from the basket next to her bed and lay it on top of her. I think about turning off the TV, but decide against it. She hates waking up in the dark.

I sneak back out into the hallway, closing the door behind me.

In the bathroom light, I get my first real glimpse of the damage Henry sustained before the fireflies came to rescue us. The red mark on his cheek is starting to turn purple and there's a gash on the back of his hand. If he has any other injuries, they're covered by the mud caking his arms. My own wrist is still sore, but I can move it well enough, so I don't think it's broken. I lead Henry to the sink and turn the faucet to warm.

"Put your hands under the water and keep them there," I tell him.

He does as I ask without saying a word while I rifle through the cabinets for the first-aid kit and a bottle of hydrogen peroxide. I uncap the bottle and turn off the water. "This may sting a little."

He winces as the hydrogen peroxide bubbles white around his cut, but he doesn't show any other sign of pain. When that's done, I cover the wound with Neosporin, then wrap his hand in gauze.

"There. All better."

Henry trails his fingers down my cheek. The gauze scratches my jaw. "Thank you," he whispers.

"For what?"

The smile he gives me makes my heart squeeze. "If it weren't for you," he says, "I would not know my parents are alive. We still have to worry about Varo finding them, of course—"

"Not if we find them first." I close the first-aid kit and put it back under the sink. "Do you know where they might have gone?"

He shakes his head. "They could have traveled through any threshold, into any time or place."

I nod, thinking. "Okay then, tomorrow morning, we'll hit the books again. Find out everything we can about Varo and dragon's bane. Whatever will give us an advantage over him."

Henry shrugs. "It's a start."

Now that his cut has been taken care of, I take in the mud on his arms, his cheek, the side of his neck. "Do you want to take a shower?"

"A what?"

I smile. "Trust me, you're going to love it."

I explain how the shower works, which bottles to use on his hair and which on his body. How to squeeze the body wash onto the loofah and rub it in with his hands so it gets nice and foamy. I grab the same sweatpants and shirt he slept in last night and lay them on the counter, and then I turn on the water and remind him which way to turn the knob if it gets too hot or too cold.

I'm just as muddy, but my shower will have to wait. I run a washcloth under the sink faucet and take it into my bedroom along with a dry towel. I do my best to wash the mud from my skin, then change into my pajamas.

I lay on my bed with my chem notes in front of me, trying to study for the test on Monday, but I can't stop reliving what happened in the wood. Images flash through my mind. Holding Henry, certain we were going to die. My fireflies coming to our rescue. Varo's followers chanting around the fire like a cult. Varo infiltrating my mind.

*Matters such as these are not always as they seem.*

My coin warms on my wrist, and for a moment I think I've somehow summoned him to speak to me again, but then Joe's voice breaks through my thoughts.

*Winter.*

*Joe?*

*Come outside,* he says. *I need to see you're all right.*

I glance at the wall, through which I can hear the pipes groaning and water plopping against the tub like rain.

I sigh. *Be right there.*

I creep down the staircase, hugging the wall to avoid the creaky steps. Mer's already passed out, her arm flung over her eyes and her neck tipped back for maximum snorage. Through the kitchen window I catch Joe pacing the backyard, his hands on his hips, his movements jerky and uncertain. I tiptoe through the mudroom and out onto the porch, softly snicking the back door closed behind me.

He exhales as soon as he sees me, as if he's been holding his breath this entire time. "Thank God you're all right."

Uncle Joe's never been very affectionate. He's more the tough love, teach-you-how-to-fight-like-a-badass kind of uncle. But he hugs me now. Holds on to me like it's the only way he can tell for sure I'm really here.

"Where were you?" I ask, my words muffled by his shirt.

He holds me a second longer, then takes a deep breath and steps away. "Headquarters. I tried to get there as soon as I could, but you were already gone."

As soon as he could? Exactly how long does it take someone who can teleport to show up when you call them?

"What happened?" he asks. "What were you doing in the wood after dark?"

I tell him about the party, about Stoner Guy and Varo's followers. I don't mention Henry, or what Varo said to me. I tell myself it's because it doesn't matter what that black-magic freak has to say for himself, but, really, it's because I don't want Uncle Joe knowing he infiltrated my mind so easily.

Or that, even though I know I'm playing right into Varo's hands, he piqued my curiosity.

*Matters such as these . . .*

Uncle Joe takes everything in without interrupting, although his jaw tenses and his hands clench into fists when I tell him about the wood attacking us.

When I finish, he closes his eyes, thinking. "All right, first things first. Does the traveler need to be taken care of?"

I shake my head. "He was on some sort of drug. He thinks the whole thing was just a bad trip."

"You're lucky."

"I know."

He starts pacing again. "You'll need to be more careful. Varo undoubtedly knows who you are now if he didn't before, and everything you've seen has made you a threat."

"What should I do?"

"Ideally, you'll stay out of the wood until this whole thing blows over."

"Yeah, well, I can't exactly do that, can I?"

"You'll have to keep a low profile, then," he says. "Don't wander as much. Stay close to your threshold and only go in deeper if you feel a traveler. And then you do your job and get out, understand?"

"Yes," I say, even though I have no intention of doing any such thing, not when Henry's parents are out there somewhere. Possibly waiting for someone to rescue them. "Do I need to worry about Varo coming after me now that he knows where I live?"

Joe glances up at Mom's bedroom window. Both of us would die before we let anyone touch her. "I don't think so. He's hiding out, biding his time. Any sort of trouble could come to a guardian in the wood, but crossing through a threshold to attack a guardian would raise too many red flags."

"He didn't sound like he was biding his time for much longer," I say. "He's going to attack the council soon."

"We'll be ready."

"What can I do to help?"

His lips twitch into a sad smile. "Truthfully?"

I nod.

"Stay out of it."

"Excuse me?" I am so not the stay-out-of-it girl.

"I won't be able to concentrate on what I need to do if I have to worry about your safety." He grabs me by the shoulders. Forces me to look at him. "Promise me."

I exhale. "Fine. I promise."

So maybe Dad did teach me how to lie a little.

"By the way," I tell him, "Septimus is one of them."

"That doesn't bode well. He has a lot of power on the council." He releases a breath. "I'll see what else I can find out."

"You'll let me know what you learn?"

He arches a brow. "Only if it's something you need to know. Like I said, I won't compromise your safety."

I sigh. "Fair enough."

Joe insists on watching me go back inside the house before he leaves. I guess he thinks if he doesn't, I'm liable to go running off into the wood like some sort of crazy person. I feel his eyes on me as I walk up the porch and open the door. I turn back around to wave—Joe nods once, satisfied—and that's when I notice it.

The mud coating the hem of his pants.

# XXVIII

I tell myself, as I head back upstairs, that there's probably a really good reason Joe's pants were muddy. He did say he went into the wood looking for me. Surely the mud's just from that. But when you combine that with how long he took to come find me, it creates one horrible, nauseating question:

*Is the reason Uncle Joe took so long to find me tonight, the reason he had mud on his pants, because he's one of Varo's followers?*

I stop on the staircase and lean my forehead against the wall. I'm being ridiculous. *Why would Uncle Joe choose to follow Varo? Why would anyone?*

*Matters such as these are not always as they seem.*

The bathroom light is still on, but the shower is no longer running. I hurry into my room and lie on the bed, pretending to pore over my chem book. Henry tiptoes in a moment later and closes the door behind him, water dripping from his hair onto his shoulders. He lays Dad's muddy clothes on top of my dresser. I'll have to wash them and get them back in Mom's closet before she notices they're missing.

"Forget everything I have ever said." Henry sinks into my desk chair, his long legs stretching out in front of him, arms languidly dangling at his sides. "That was the most miraculous phenomenon I have ever experienced."

I force a smile. "Better than drawstring pants, huh?"

He nods.

"Better than TV?"

"Very much so." He leans his head back against the top of the chair and shakes his head, his eyes closed. "The men of your time are geniuses."

"I'm going to assume you meant men and women."

He smirks. "Of course. My apologies."

"Your time wasn't so bad, either."

"Yes, but water that pours from the wall already heated? Light that comes from wires instead of flame? A box where you can watch a play without leaving the comfort of your home and sitting in a stuffy theater? Poor taste in fashion aside, I could become quite accustomed to this life."

I sit up. "Henry, you know you can't tell anyone about anything you've seen here, right? You can't try to invent these things for yourself, in your time, or tell people about everything you've seen—"

"I have told you before, Winter."

"I know, I just—I need to say it, and I need to hear you say you understand. It's my job."

He nods. "I understand. When I return to my time, I will act as though I have no idea of the wonders that await future generations."

"Good."

He doesn't take his eyes off me. They're heavy, weighing me

down. My throat goes dry and my palms itch, so I fluff the pillow behind me, breaking the connection.

"Ready for bed?"

I don't realize until it's too late that my comment would have been a lot more innocent last night, before we'd almost kissed. Now, Henry continues to watch me, his relaxed body suddenly rigid, and I know he's thinking of our almost-kiss, too. "Because I can turn off the light," I say, "and I can get in my bed, and you can get in yours. And we can sleep."

*Great. Way to make it clear, loser.*

"All right." He crawls into his sleeping bag and I turn off the light. I slip under the covers, waiting for my eyes to adjust to the darkness. It's late, and the strips of moonlight pouring through my window don't gild him like they did last night. Instead, they climb up the wall, and it's easier to talk to him when I can't see his cheekbones lined in silver.

"Henry?"

"Yes?"

"We'll find your parents," I say. "I promise."

"Do not promise something that may be out of your grasp, Winter. It will make a liar of you. Instead, promise you will work hard to help me find my parents, or promise you will not send me back until we have exhausted our resources here. Those are promises you could keep."

I don't say anything. I lie in the dark, turning his words over as I watch the shadows of tree branches rattle in the moonlight.

"Henry?"

"Yes?"

"We'll find your parents."

# XXIX

I wake with a buzzing beneath my skin. A million bees nesting in my muscles, boring their way through flesh. The sun is a low orange ball in the corner of my window, painting the trees copper on one side, black on the other. I feel the pull from deep behind my belly button, the string connecting me to my threshold. It tugs, loosens, tugs again. Harder this time. More insistent.

There's a traveler in my wood.

Henry's still asleep on the floor, his arms crossed under his head. The bruise looks worse today, and small traces of blood have seeped through the bandage on his hand. I make a mental note to get him some aspirin for the pain when he wakes.

I shield myself behind the open closet door and pull on a pair of jeans and a black sweater. There's frost on the window—the heat wave has officially broken—so I grab a black knit hat and gloves from the winter box in the linen closet.

Mom is in the kitchen making herself an egg-white omelet with green peppers and low-fat cheese when I come down the stairs. "Hi, honey. I didn't expect to see you up so early. Want some breakfast?"

"Can't." I power walk into the mudroom, stomping my feet into my boots and lacing them up the front as quickly as my sleep-addled fingers will allow. The laces miss a couple loops, but it's good enough to keep them on my feet and that's all that matters.

Mom appears in the doorway with a mug of coffee. "Should I ask why Meredith is sleeping on our couch?"

I wince. I completely forgot about Mer. "She got dumped by her boyfriend last night and didn't want to go home."

"Do her parents know she's here?"

"Yep." Because that's where she told them she would be all along. But Mom doesn't need to know that.

"Here." Mom hands me the coffee as I stand. "At least wake yourself up a little before you go in."

I take the mug. The coffee is lukewarm, and I tip it back like a college student downing a shot.

The buzzing under my skin feels like a jackhammer now, though I don't know if it's because there's more than one traveler or if it's from the caffeine. I lean my head against the wall and hand back the mug. "Thanks."

"Be careful out there."

I throw on my jacket, placing my hand on the door to the back porch before I remember.

"Mom?"

She turns.

"Let me take care of the laundry today, okay?"

Her brow arches. "Why the sudden need to be domestic? Is

there something hidden in your laundry you don't want me to find?"

Just Dad's old clothes splattered with mud. Oh, and a boy in my room who'll have nowhere to hide if you barge in there looking for dirty socks.

"I wish. I just know you have all those papers to grade and I thought I'd help out."

She smiles. "Well, I'd be a dummy to turn down an offer like that."

It's not enough to feel safe, but it's all I can do. I say a silent prayer that Mom won't find Henry while I'm gone, then I turn the knob and head out into the cool morning air.

Frosted grass glitters in the sunlight like snow. I watch my breath curl out in front of me and dissipate. The windows in the houses across the street are dark, their owners sleeping in like normal people should on a Saturday morning. I rub my gloved hands across my eyes and step through my threshold.

In the light of day, there is no evidence that Henry and I nearly died in here last night. The path is solid again, and no creepy guys in black cloaks stalk the trees. Still, I'm extra vigilant as I start forward, constantly scanning the wood for signs of Varo or his supporters. The invisible string pulls me a tenth of a mile before the main walkway from my threshold forks into six different, log-lined paths, all weaving their way through skinny, twisted trees and fat sturdy ones. The leaves block out the sky in a blanket of bright fire-truck red, pumpkin orange, highlighter yellow. The sun reaches higher in the sky, its light bouncing off the leaves as if they're coated in lacquer.

I step onto the third branched-off path to my right, and the wood changes.

The leaves are wilted black tar. The trunks are gray, long strips of bark peeling off, revealing yellow-green sores that pucker and ooze. Even the ground is infected with the sickness, damp and spongy, like walking through a pile of raked leaves instead of packed earth. I crouch down and place my hand against the dirt. It's warm. A weak pulse flickers against my palm, and the wind whispers through the trees in a voice only I can hear.

*Help us, Winter. Save us—*

I pull my hand back with a gasp, tears pricking my eyes. "You're dying."

The wind knifes through my jacket. An affirmation.

I walk on, leaving my handprint behind me. I move through the wood, taking a bend in the path, following my instinct as I always do. It is such a familiar feeling that I don't even have to think about it; my feet practically move of their own accord. I can think about other things during this time—homework that's due, the boy currently sleeping in my room—without losing focus of where I need to go.

Or, at least, I *usually* can. I'm not sure when the buzzing starts to subside, when the thread of instinct leading me to the traveler begins to fade. I only know that now it feels weak and feathery, like a heart struggling to beat. I come to another fork in the path and, for the first time in almost two years, I'm not sure which way to go.

I close my eyes and try to focus on the tugging sensation behind my belly button and the itch on the soles of my feet.

*Left. I think.*

I take the path to the left, but it doesn't help. I'm running blind.

My pulse pounds in my ears. I close my eyes again, but there's nothing. I focus on my breathing, just like Dad taught me to do—*So you won't lose your head*, he used to say, *a guardian without a head won't do anyone much good*—and I keep moving forward. The temperature continues to drop the farther I go, and the diffused light is only growing dimmer, as if a storm cloud is blocking out the sun.

"Where are you?" I shout. I say it again and again. My words echo back to me off the trees. And then, finally, something screams back. I'm not sure what it says, but the sound turns the blood in my veins to sludge.

The scream is low and muffled, full of anguish and lost hope. And then it turns into a soft moan, followed by a whimper that flutters through the trees like hummingbird wings. Cursing, I turn on my heel and run toward the sound, pumping my legs harder, willing them to go faster, faster, *faster*.

The wind is stronger here, howling through the gaps in the trees, shredding through my clothes and slicing my skin. My boots grow heavy on my feet and my breath rushes out of me in a white puff, and still I run, until I make it to a small, shaded clearing that is dark as night and I see him, a bloody mass on the ground, his clothes lying in tattered ribbons around him. He is surrounded by shadows that undulate and swim through the air, the dirt beneath them turning to ice.

Sentinels. *They freeze their victims, keeping the meat fresh so they can take their time skinning them alive.*

Most of his flesh is gone. The copper scent of blood mixes with the smell of the wood. His muscles look like slabs of beef held together by spaghetti. I palm my coin out of habit and think *Joe, get your ass here. Now.*

I start forward, but bile rises up my throat. I crouch on the ground and vomit until there's nothing left. I don't think the traveler could possibly still be alive, but then his head, all exposed muscle and bone, tilts in my direction, shards of ice along his neck creaking and breaking as he mouths the words, "Help me."

I rub my sleeve across my mouth and run forward, waving my arms and shrieking at the shadows as if they're birds that can be scared away. "Go! Get out of here!"

But the shadows don't leave. Their laughter sounds like ice breaking.

I pull my knife on them. "Get away from him," I say, trying to sound brave even as I take a step back.

The shadows slither closer, darker in the spaces where their bodies overlap. They reach for me with twiglike fingers, their whispers clogging my ears. *Fresh meat*, they wheeze. *So nice to eat.* I take another step back and trip into a patch of sunlight. The shadow fingers pull back quick, as if they've been burned.

I'm safe here, in this circle of light, even as the Sentinels slink around the edges of it as if searching for a weakness, a shadow bridge they can swim through to get to me, but I can't stay. The shadows are already returning to the traveler. They take another strip of skin from his hip, and I don't think. I step into the darkness. "Hey!"

They turn to me. They move faster than my eyes can track them. The back of my hand burns suddenly; I jump back into the circle of light, hoping some of them will follow me and die, or get hurt enough to back off, or *something*, but they stay in the darkness.

My hand bleeds where a slice of skin has been peeled off.

"Winter!" Uncle Joe's voice echoes off the trees. I glance behind me. A scowl wrinkles his otherwise unmarred face as he storms down the path, a black leather duster blowing out behind him.

He steps in front of me, shielding my body with his. He holds up his hand, curling his fist around an orb of white light as if it were a baseball. Strips of light break through the gaps between his fingers. "Be gone, demons."

The light shoots from his palm and the shadows break apart. They burrow into the ground, into black nooks in the trees and beneath fallen logs. Their high-pitched screams tinkle through the air like falling glass.

I stand, my legs wobbling beneath me. I take a step forward, but Uncle Joe's hand grips my shoulder.

"Stay back," he says.

"Th-there's a traveler in there," I say, pointing to the flayed body on the ground. The sun has returned to the clearing, though the mottled shade of the canopy still shrouds the boy. My teeth are chattering like maracas and I can't stop shaking. Too much adrenaline coursing through my veins. Too much, *too much*—I don't know what to do with it all.

"I'll get him," Joe says, stepping out of the sunlight. He crouches next to the body and places his ear against the lattice-work of muscles and veins stretching over his chest. Joe pulls back with a sigh and shakes his head.

"No." The word tumbles out of my mouth.

I was too late. I didn't save him.

I don't even know where he came from, or how old he was. The only thing I know for certain is this: He wasn't supposed to die here. He might have been fated to die ten seconds after he walked back through the threshold into his own time, or ten years after, or fifty. But it should have been in his time, in his world. Not now. Not here.

I'm the reason he's dead. If I had found him first, if I had listened more closely, if I had been better, stronger, faster—

Joe wipes a tear from my cheek. I watch the droplet run down his finger.

"I did this," I say.

"No," he says, "you didn't."

I look up at him, guilt sparking into anger. "Yes, I did. It's my job to get these travelers home safely. I'm responsible for what happens to them in here."

"Winter—"

"I have to patrol." I take off through the trees, even though I know it's no use. There's no one else in my sector—no one I can feel anyway. Maybe there are some I can't feel because they're no longer alive, because they've been flayed to death, too.

"Winter, stop," Uncle Joe shouts, his footsteps crunching branches behind me. "It isn't safe."

"Just leave me alone," I yell back, glancing over my shoulder, but I can barely see him through the wall of tears blinding me.

"Winter!"

I crumple to the ground, sobs racking my body. Uncle Joe stops next to me and wraps an arm around my shoulder. He smells like cigarettes and worn leather.

"What if there's someone else?" I ask him.

"There isn't."

"How do you know?"

He sighs. "Frankly, I don't. What I do know is you promised me last night you'd be careful and not go traipsing around the wood without a reason, and you're going to keep that promise."

Last night. It all comes rushing back to me. I want to ask him why he had mud on his pants. Why he took so long to come find me. I want to ask him straight out if he's one of Varo's followers, but I don't.

Because I'm weaker than I let on. Because I can't lose him, too.

So I say nothing. I just let him lead me back the way I came, where the main path from my threshold forks, where the air is warm and has long since burned off the morning frost. Where the leaves look normal—or as normal as they've ever looked for being made of magic and other secret things—and the ground is solid beneath my feet.

⟴

I feel sick when I finally leave the wood, Joe disappearing behind me. Bile claws up my throat, *pushing pushing pushing* until I can't keep it in anymore. I bend over Dad's rock—my rock—where his and Mom's initials have been scraped in, and dry heave over the damp grass. My stomach convulses, over and over again. I can't breathe. I start to panic, tell myself I need to stop, that there's nothing left.

But that's the problem. There's nothing left—it's being taken away from me, one thing at a time.

My home, my wood, *my life* has been invaded. When Dad first told me about the wood, I didn't know there would be heroes and villains in this story. I thought it was just this: the guardians, the council, the wood. Constantly working together to protect the delicate fabric of time. Never deviating from what has been, what is now, what will be.

I force myself to stop dry heaving, to erase the image of the boy without his skin from my mind, to breathe. I wipe my sleeve across my mouth and stumble toward the back porch. My head swims—I should have done my stretches—and when I twist the knob and lean against the door, I practically fall through.

Henry and Mer are sitting at the kitchen island.

Along with my mom.

"Young lady," she says, her voice slick with venom and disappointment. "You have a lot of explaining to do."

# XXX

om tells Mer to wait in the kitchen and pulls Henry and me into the study, closing the door behind her.

"Explain yourself," she whispers, her nostrils flaring.

I look at Henry.

He looks at me.

"Your mother found me this morning," he explains. "I had to tell her where I was from. I had no other choice."

I figured as much. I take a deep breath but before I can say anything, Mom starts pacing.

"What possessed you to do this?" she asks. "I mean, who in their right mind would do something like this? And then to hide it from me!"

"Mom, please," I say, "try to calm down."

She whirls on me. "Don't you dare tell me to calm down. You had a boy sleeping in your room last night."

"It wasn't like that—"

"Like what?"

I huff out a breath. "Like we were doing things we shouldn't be doing."

"Well, what do you expect me to think when you hide it from me, Winter?"

I know I'm in the wrong here, that I should be nothing but apologetic, but my anger snaps like a live wire. "What? You don't trust me?"

"Don't even get me started on trust," she says. "When a mother finds a boy in her daughter's room, it's going to be a long time before she can even *think* about trusting her again."

"I'm really sorry I kept it a secret from you, but I had to."

Her brow arches. "Oh really?"

"Yes," I say. "Really. What we're doing . . . It's dangerous, and I didn't want to put you at risk."

"Oh, well, that just makes me feel *so much better.*"

"I promise I'll tell you everything," I say, glancing at the door. "But it has to do with you-know-what, and I don't feel comfortable talking about it while Mer's still here."

"To hell with it, and to hell with that place," Mom says, gesturing toward the window and the trees that watch us through them. "I'm sick of it running our lives!"

"Well, we don't have much of a choice, do we?"

Mom glares at me.

I glare back.

She rubs her temples with her fingers. "Okay, here's what we're going to do. I'm going to take Meredith home. When I get back, you better be ready to give me the whole story, and with a little less attitude. Got it?"

"Yes, ma'am," I say through gritted teeth.

Mom gives Henry one more look, the kind of look that says, *If you even* think *about looking at my daughter the wrong way, I will cut your eyes out of your face*, before striding through the door.

"I think that went rather well, don't you?" Henry asks.

I sigh.

❧

I make a pot of coffee. Henry takes it with cream and sugar. I take it black.

We sit at the kitchen island and I tell him about the shadows, the boy without his skin, the section of the wood that once smelled like fresh grass and sunshine and now smells like a corpse. Henry listens, his knuckles white around the handle of the ceramic mug.

"Is the council doing anything to stop this?" he asks.

"Joe says he was at headquarters last night, and that he's going to see what else he can find out, but he wouldn't tell me if anyone other than him is looking into it." *Because he doesn't want me getting too involved? Or because it isn't true?*

"What now?"

Exhaling, I run my hands through my hair and shake my head. "We stick to the plan. Search for anything related to Varo or dragon's bane. If no one from the council will tell us what to expect, we'll just have to figure it out for ourselves."

Joe said Varo was banished nearly five hundred years ago, so we start in the sixteenth-century texts. It doesn't take long to find information on him, but it isn't anything we don't already know. Respected elder turned power-hungry rebel; tried to take over the council; wound up banished. Followers never discovered.

"Do you think they knew he'd come back?" I ask. "His followers? Do you think they've just been biding their time?"

Henry nibbles on his bottom lip as he flips through a journal. "It seems that way. There were more of them than I expected." He glances up at me. Hesitates. "You know this means no one on the council can be above suspicion."

I cock my head, not entirely sure where he's going with this. "I know."

"Not even . . ." He takes a deep breath. "Not even people you trust."

My eyes narrow. "What are you implying?" I already know, of course, but I want to hear him say it.

"Winter." He says my name so differently from the way he said it last night. Next to the fire, it was a benediction. Now, it's a confession whispered in a dark box, full of fear and guilt and a touch of insolence. "How well do you know Joe?"

It is the question I've been asking myself since last night. The question that keeps popping up as if from out of nowhere, making me feel equal parts paranoid and guilt-ridden.

My voice is a sharp, jagged blade, meant to hurt me just as much as him. "I would be very careful if I were you, Brightonshire," I say. "You are only here because I chose to trust you."

"Winter—"

"I have known Joe my entire life. I've only known you for three days. If I can't trust him, then I certainly can't trust you." They're the right words, but I hate how uncertain they sound to my own ears. As if I'm trying to convince myself as well as Henry.

He holds up his hands in surrender. "I'm sorry," he says. "Truly, I am, but you must see that the only chance we have of discovering what happened to our parents is if we hold everyone, every single person on the council, to the same level of suspicion."

"Everyone? Including your parents?"

His gaze darkens. "Careful, Madam."

"Oh, so you can question my family, but I can't question yours?"

I stand and head for the door, but Henry's hand bracelets my wrist, stopping me. "You're right," he says, begrudgingly. "Please, forgive me."

I stare at him, and he stares back. Neither of us flinches, or blinks, or looks away.

"No," I say, my breath catching in my too-dry throat. "You're right. No one can be above suspicion."

He doesn't say anything. Just keeps holding my wrist.

Mom slams the front door closed behind her, then walks into the study, purse swinging violently at her side. "All right," she says. "Tell me everything."

# XXXI

We sit in the study, Henry and me on the couch, Mom in Dad's old reading chair. It feels right to discuss this here, where so many important discussions have taken place. The first time I learned about the wood; the first time Mom and I discussed whether we should have a small, family-only memorial service for Dad; the first time Mom had begged me to pack a suitcase and go into hiding with her, which led to the first time Mom tried to convince me to enroll in homeschooling so I wouldn't have to work so hard to balance everything. She'd been afraid the pressure was going to be too much for me, that I'd put myself in either the same kind of depression that took hold of Dad, or that I'd lose focus in the wood one day and put myself in an early grave.

Our memorial service was just the two of us and Uncle Joe, planting a ring of tulips around the rock bearing my parents' initials. Mom carried tulips on her wedding day, and she'd wanted to plant something that would come back every year, just as she hoped Dad would come back to us one day. That he'd stumble out of the wood just like the green stalks sprout out of the thawing winter soil; nothing one day, there the next.

The argument regarding my education happened later that night, when Mom had a panic attack and tried to convince me to leave with her. Instead, I convinced her to stay. I can still see the flash of betrayal in her eyes. I don't know why homeschooling was the next thing to pop into her head; I imagine it was just one of many thoughts she'd had all day. She'd wanted to win that argument, too, but I couldn't let her. It may have been selfish, but at the time, being at school was therapeutic. Dad wasn't imprinted on its white walls or linoleum floors or dented lockers like he was imprinted on everything at home. It wasn't until later that school stopped being a place of refuge for me and started being a place of normalcy, but its importance in my life didn't change.

Now, Mom stares out the window, thinking. I told her about my first encounter with Henry in the wood, and my second, and my third. I told her—with Henry's help—about his parents, and his belief that their disappearance may be connected to Dad. I told her about the council, about Varo, and why I chose to keep everything a secret from her, to protect her from any harm that could come from her knowing too much, a plan that was now blown to hell ("Language, Winter," Mom reprimanded me). I was even honest about how many nights Henry had stayed in my room ("But it was all innocent, *I swear*") and about how I faked being sick so I could stay home with him and pore through the journals. I left out a couple things: the disease spreading through the wood, my run-in with the Sentinels, the fact that I saw a boy flayed to death right in front of me. These are things she would want to know, but I can't help myself. I still want to protect her as much as I can, even if it's just protecting her from the confirmation of her greatest fears.

Finally, she looks at me, her shoulders hunched forward a little, as if the weight of my revelations is a heavy yoke to bear. "And you didn't once think of telling me any of this? You didn't once think I might understand?"

"I just wanted to—"

"Protect me, I know." She scoffs, but not at me. At the idea, maybe, or the situation. "Did you know that when we were first married, your father and I would sit at the dinner table every night, and he would tell me everything that had happened in the wood? Every person he encountered, every boring council meeting, every fight with a combatant traveler? We were husband and wife—he couldn't hide the bruises from me any more than I could hide my concern from him. So he told me everything. It was only when you were old enough to understand our conversations that we started hiding things. It was a team effort, at first. But the less we talked at the dinner table, the less we talked overall, and eventually he stopped telling me anything. Sometimes I think if we had kept talking, if I could have heard the resignation in his voice sooner, if I could have found the courage to tell him he'd had enough, that alcohol wouldn't solve his problems— but what did I know? I wasn't a guardian. I couldn't tell him how to do his job any more than he could tell me how to do mine."

"Mom—"

"But you never saw any of that," she continues. "Silence and lies are all you've ever known, and so, of course, when you became a guardian, you adopted your father's habits. I don't blame you, I really don't. However, that does not give you the right to sneak a boy—work-related or not—into this house, or to have him sleep in your room without my knowledge, or to lie to me to get out of going to school when you know perfectly well I would have understood you needed to stay home to work."

The real reason I faked sick—the one I shoved deep into the back of my mind—is a hot coal in my stomach, radiating guilt and shame. "Okay," I say, "maybe I faked being sick because I was afraid if I told you the real reason I wanted to stay home, you'd use it against me the next time you brought up homeschooling."

Mom arches a brow. "Maybe?"

"Okay, definitely, but the rest of it was to protect you, and I won't apologize for that."

Henry yanks on my sleeve. "*Winter.*"

I hold up a hand, shushing him. "But I *will* apologize for how I went about it. I shouldn't have kept it a secret from you. I'm really sorry."

Mom watches me, tapping her fingers against the edge of the armrest.

"If it makes you feel any better," I add, "I felt terrible the whole time I was doing it."

"The whole time?" Mom asks.

"Well, most of the time. A solid eighty percent."

Mom laughs. "Oh, you are your father's daughter, all right. Speaking of which." She turns to Henry, the light in her eyes dimming. "Do you really think my husband's disappearance is connected to the disappearance of your parents?"

"Yes, Mrs. Parish," he says. "I do."

Mom sighs. "I want it to be clear that I don't condone what

you two have done. The thought of a stranger sneaking around my house the past two days doesn't exactly sit well with me, especially when that stranger is a teenage boy who's been sleeping in my daughter's bedroom. But *if* what you're saying is true, if there really is a conspiracy happening within the council, and if it could lead us to discover what exactly happened to Jack, or if we could maybe even find him . . ." She shakes her head; she won't go down that road. She clears her throat and starts again. "What I'm trying to say is, Henry can stay here, but he will not be staying in your room. Is that understood?"

Henry nods. "Perfectly."

"And just so we're clear," Mom says, turning to me, "your apology is accepted, but you are still in serious trouble, and once this is over, you will have to make up for it."

"What? You mean, like, you're going to ground me?" The idea is so preposterous, I can't stop the chuckle underlining my words. I'm a homebody. When I'm not at school or in the wood, I'm in my room. She has nothing to ground me from.

"I mean, like," Mom says, "giving you dishwashing duties, and cleaning duties, and laundry duties, for as long as I see fit."

My mouth drops. "I don't have time for that. I barely have time to balance my schoolwork with my guardian duties as it is!"

"If you have enough time to go to a normal school and still perform your duties, then you have enough time to help me around the house," she says. "Of course, if you want to revisit the homeschooling option again, I'd be more than happy to—"

"No, it's fine," I say quickly. "I can handle it."

"Good. Now then, I'll get out of your way so you two can get to work, but I'll be leaving the door open, understand?"

We both nod.

I hold up a hand, telling Henry to wait in the study. I stop Mom in the hallway.

"I really am sorry," I tell her.

She brushes a strand of hair off my face. "I know," she says, "but it doesn't change the fact that something special has been lost between us. It's going to be a long time before I can trust you again."

"I know," I say, "but I'll do everything I can to gain your trust back. I promise."

She taps my cheek, then turns and heads into the kitchen. I walk back into the study and bury myself in old journals and treatises, my eyes straining for any mention of Varo or dragon's bane.

# XXXII

We look for hours, neither of us coming up with anything. We go back further, taking journals and documents written prior to the sixteenth century out of their protective, temperature-controlled glass cases, and begin flipping through them gently with white-gloved fingers. After a while, the words start to blur on the page, and I have to rub my eyes every few seconds for them to focus.

The next time I glance up at the clock, it's after noon. I'm about to suggest we get some lunch when Henry says, "Winter." He's sitting hunched over Dad's desk, with the lamp pulled to the center, creating a spotlight over a treatise he's reading.

"What is it?" I ask, setting my book aside. "Did you find something? Is it Varo?"

He shakes his head. "Something else."

I cross the room to him. He angles the book so I can see. I trace the words with my fingertips. The text is written in Old English, familiar and, at the same time, not at all. The handwriting doesn't help; it's beautiful, all giant loops and delicate swirls, but many of the letters look different from how I'm used to seeing them. It would probably take me all day to translate one page. Henry seems to be doing better, if the number of pages he's already read is any indication, but he's rubbing his temples as if it's given him a headache.

It's not the text, however, that catches my eye. It's a sketch on the page next to it, depicting a tree with black leaves and pustules on the bark. I gasp and pull the page closer. "That looks like—"

"—what's happening to the wood," Henry finishes.

A plant grows beneath the tree, one I've never seen before. There's a circle drawn around it, and a line that shoots out from it, connecting it to a bigger circle, inside of which is a sketch of the plant up close, as if it's being viewed through a microscope. It's the devil's version of baby's breath; white stalks with red veins and tiny black flowers. "Dragon's bane," I whisper, remembering what Uncle Joe said about how it was used as a weapon by Varo in the past.

Henry tugs the book back toward him, his fingers underlining the passage beneath the sketch. "'A parasitic organism that attaches itself to the root system of a larger organism, most often a tree, dragon's bane is the only substance in the known world with the ability to end an immortal life. While ingesting or infecting the blood with any part of the plant could lead to death, the most toxic component is the flower. Merely one small petal taken into the body by means of digestion or through the blood will cause certain death.'" Henry's fists tighten as he reads, until the veins on his arms threaten to pop.

I lay my hand on his shoulder. "Remember what Varo said. Your parents are alive. The dragon's bane didn't kill them."

He exhales, loosening his fists slightly. "Thank God for that."

"What I don't understand," I say, angling the book toward me, "is how the disease is spreading. This makes it seem like every infected tree should have dragon's bane attached to it, but I haven't seen any at all."

Henry chews on his bottom lip, thinking. "Varo said my mother must have leached it out of herself and my father and somehow transferred the poison to the wood. So perhaps it is traveling through the trees as it would travel through a body. Not with a plant attached, slowly extracting its host's essence, but with the poison itself flooding the root systems as it would a person's veins. If that were the case . . ." His brow furrows. "There would have to be a source. Wherever the infection began would, logically speaking, be worse off than any other part of the wood."

"So if we can find where the infection began—"

"We find my parents' last known location before their disappearance."

*And I'll be one step closer to finding out Dad's connection to all of this.*

I smile. "Well, then. I think we have a source to find."

⊱✦⊰

Henry wants to head right into the wood, but I convince him to eat first. I don't know what we'll find, and the last thing I want to do is weaken our defenses from starvation.

I make grilled cheese sandwiches and tomato soup for lunch while Mom and Henry discuss the socioeconomic impact of tenant farming in the late eighteenth century. Mom still eyes him with distrust, but her suspicion and paranoia begin to give way to more important things, like the pursuit of knowledge and lively debate. By the time I've plated the sandwiches and ladled out the soup, she's staring at Henry like he's the most significant archaeological treasure she's ever unearthed.

I've just finished my sandwich and started on my soup when my phone rings. It's Meredith. Mom looks up at me and I show her the screen. She nods.

"Hey. What's up?"

"*What's up?* You had a boy sleep in your room last night and all you have to say to me is 'what's up?'"

"Um . . . yeah?"

"WINTER. I NEED MORE INFORMATION THAN THAT."

I pull the phone away from my ear. "Mer, stop shouting."

"What did you two do? Did he kiss you, grope you, make you a woman? Did your mom kill you? Are you talking to me from beyond the grave?"

I hold up my finger and slide out of my seat. I wait until I'm in the back hallway to whisper, "Mer, nothing happened."

"Look, you can pull that crap on your mom all you want— if you're lucky, she might even believe you—but I know a boy doesn't stay in your room overnight with absolutely nothing happening."

"Do you know that from personal experience?"

"Nooooo," Mer says, drawing out the word. "Unlike some best friends I know, I would actually tell you if something that amazing happened to me. Now, come on, spill. Did he at least kiss you?"

"I really can't talk about this now."

"Is your mom there?"

"Yeah."

"Okay, fine. We'll talk about it when you come over tonight."

"What?"

She sighs, low and purposely dramatic, like she's trying to hide the hurt behind the sound, but I've known my friend too long not to hear it. "I know last night was crazy, but I didn't think you'd forget."

I press my forehead against the wall. "The ACTs."

"Mmm-hmm."

"I'm supposed to help you study."

"Mmm-hmm."

I don't know what to do. Every second not spent searching for the truth of what happened to Dad and Henry's parents feels like a betrayal. But then I think of all the times I've ditched Mer over the past six years—first for lessons, then for patrols. She was understanding, but there was only so much even the most understanding person could take.

Besides, Mer's right. Her entire future is riding on these test scores.

"Do you think your mom will still let you come over?" she asks.

"I don't know, I'll have to ask. Hold on." I put my hand over the mouthpiece and walk into the dining room. "Can I go to Mer's tonight? I was supposed to help her study."

Mom pauses. "No," she says, "but she can come here."

I'm not sure if she says this because she doesn't want to be alone with Henry, or because she doesn't trust that I'm actually going to be where I say I am. Probably a little of both.

I uncover the mouthpiece. "Why don't you come over for dinner? I'm not sure what Mom's making, but it's bound to be good."

Meredith makes a *hmmm* sound and says, "I would die for some of your mom's cooking. I haven't been over to your house for dinner in ages."

I don't think the comment was meant to make me feel guilty, but it does all the same.

I ask, "Um, how does seven sound?" That'll give Henry and me time to do a sweep of the wood first.

"Great," she says. "See you soon."

"Hey, Mer?"

"Yeah?"

"I'm sorry I forgot."

"I know, Win. It's okay. With your dad and all—" She cuts herself off. "I just mean, I know you've been going through a lot."

"Yeah."

"You can talk to me about it, you know. If you want."

"Yeah," I say. "I know."

"Okay." Her tone brightens. "See you at seven?"

"Yeah, see you."

I finish eating, then take our empty plates and bowls to the sink, rinsing them out and stacking them in the dishwasher without Mom having to ask me to. It's a small thing, I know, and probably something I should have started doing more often anyway, whether I was in trouble or not, but all I can do is hope that a million small things will, eventually, add up to one big thing—gaining Mom's trust back.

I turn and lean against the counter. I catch Henry's eye and cock my head at the window, where the trees of this world blur into the trees of another. "You ready?"

He nods, rubbing a napkin over his lips. He takes the flask with the elixir from his belt and drinks. The liquid sloshing around inside makes the flask sound considerably less full than it did when he first showed it to me, and I wonder how much he has left.

I glance at the clock. Five hours, thirty-two minutes to sundown.

Mom says, "Be careful."

I say, "Always."

# XXXIII

The wood is quiet. I try not to think about what I saw just hours before, but every time I blink, he's there, the traveler without his skin, the shadows hovering over him. His body is imprinted on the backs of my eyelids like the flash from a camera.

The path gives way to the same mushy consistency from earlier as we walk, and the trees have begun shedding their black leaves. They sizzle when they hit the ground, emitting a black smoke that smells like sulfur and leaving behind a boiling puddle of black tar. We search the base of every tree, but there are no traces of dragon's bane.

The wind picks up the farther we go, and the stench of rot intensifies. A good sign we're heading in the right direction. I pull my coat close and Henry does the same. Dad's clothes are in the wash, and Henry's back to wearing his eighteenth-century clothing. If Uncle Joe finds us together, I'll act like Henry's just another traveler I've found, like I've never seen him before this moment.

We meander along the paths, taking various twists and turns. Doubling back when it's clear by the relative health of the trees that we're going the wrong way. We follow the sickness like bread crumbs.

"Winter," Henry says after several hours have passed and I have already begun to give up hope. "Look."

Glittering beneath a buckled root, half-covered by the blackened foliage, is a delicate gold necklace with a sapphire pendant.

"It's my mother's," Henry whispers, awestruck. He reaches his hand out to grab it—

"No." I grab his hand, pulling it back. "It's off the path. You can't get it."

Henry's brow arches. "Remember when I said the elixir makes me more like the Old Ones than you think?"

Yes, but grabbing logs from the edge of the path is a far cry from actually walking *off* the path. "Henry . . ."

He steps over a log, his feet crunching the grass and fallen leaves on the other side, and my heart jumps into my throat. I squeeze my eyes shut.

He chuckles. "Winter," he says, his breath tickling my ear. "I'm all right."

I open my eyes. He's already back on the path, holding the necklace. He flips it over, inspecting it.

I try to tease him, saying, "You're *not* a typical traveler, are you?" but the words are thick as sludge in my tightened throat.

He stares at the necklace in wonder. "They were here."

We look for another sign of them, but there's nothing. Just the necklace.

"At least we know we're on the right path," I say. "Let's keep going."

I lead Henry into the deepest section of the wood, near the border of my territory. There are fewer thresholds here. The plaques above them bear older names, some in languages I've never seen. There are Xs crossing out the names like the other thresholds that have permanently closed, and suddenly I'm ten again, witnessing one close for the first time.

It has been two months since my lessons officially began. I have been in the wood a total of three times and watched Dad return a traveler twice. When I enter the wood now, the strange blue lightning bugs snuggle up near my face, the wind generated by their wings a gentle vibration against my cheeks.

Dad says, "Looks like they've taken a shine to you." But he frowns when he says it, and I feel like I've done something wrong.

We walk deeper into the wood. My boots squeak and crunch with every step. Dad's boots make no noise at all. He tells me this is something I must learn. To be silent when others are not. To listen when others ignore.

Green stalks sprout from muddy ground on either side of the path. Spring is coming, and just like with every season, the wood has its own idea of how it should look. The green is neon, so bright it hurts my eyes, and the air smells cloyingly fresh, like dryer sheets.

"How much time?" he asks.

I close my eyes and concentrate. It would be easier if Dad let me wear a watch, but that was covered in lesson one. I wore my favorite Betty Boop watch in the wood that first day. The hands, which were perfectly normal-looking before passing through our threshold, spun like a pinwheel on a windy day. It made me dizzy.

When we left the wood, the hands stopped spinning and wouldn't start again. Mom took the watch to three different jewelers and none of them could figure out what was wrong with it.

"That was her favorite watch," I overheard Mom telling Dad as I sat hidden at the top of the stairs. "You should have warned her."

"She needs to see it for herself," Dad said. "She needs to *know*."

Now, I listen to my instincts and say, "Forty-six minutes?"

"Forty-three minutes, sixteen seconds." He gives me a smile that is becoming all too rare. "But you're getting closer."

He leads me to a threshold. I know it's ancient Egyptian, but I don't know what it says. I've only just added hieroglyphics and hieratic script to my lessons.

"Thebes," Dad answers my unasked question. "Forty-one BC."

He takes a red Sharpie from his pocket and draws a big *X* over the name.

"What are you doing?"

"This one's closed. It helps me to keep track of them."

I remember him telling me about this on the morning of my birthday, a mug of cranberry cider warming my hands, but this is the first time I've actually seen it.

"It feels pretty good to knock another one out," he says. "Don't you think?"

"I guess."

"Maybe someday they'll all be crossed out, and we won't be stuck here anymore. We could move somewhere warm. Florida maybe, or one of the Carolinas. We could live by the beach and eat fresh seafood every night. You'd like that, wouldn't you?"

I smile, even though we both know it'll never happen. "Yeah. Sounds nice, Dad."

He puts the Sharpie in his pocket and slaps his hands together. His head tilts to the side. Listening. Always listening. "We've got company."

⟜⟝⟞

The memory fades in my mind like a ghost. I walk up to a threshold, run my fingers along the $X$ that has crossed out London, 1066. It is dark, almost brown. Nothing at all like the Sharpie Dad used.

"Sheep's blood," Henry says.

"How do you know?"

He shifts on the balls of his feet. "The journals. There's a special ritual the guardian is required to observe when a threshold permanently closes. Didn't your—"

"No," I snap. "My dad never told me." I shake my head at the $X$ and murmur, "There are a lot of things he never told me."

What made him such a pessimist? Was Grandpa like that? Were the other guardians before him? Or was Dad the exception? Maybe—*No, don't think it*. But it's too late; the thought swims through my head, burns like disappointment followed swiftly by guilt.

I don't know for sure that using a red Sharpie instead of sheep's blood made any difference—the thresholds are still closed after all—but I can't help thinking that maybe Dad's the reason all of this is happening. Maybe if he had done his job right instead of half-assed all the time, we wouldn't be in this mess. Maybe Varo wouldn't have found our defenses so weak.

I stare at the threshold a moment longer, then take a step back. "Come on. We don't have much time."

The wood changes as we go deeper. First, all the trees are bare. The trunks are black with disease, twisted and hunched. And then they're covered in a thin sheet of ice that skitters across the path. The ice cracks wherever we step, until we walk farther and the ice has thickened—quarter of an inch, half an inch—and it no longer cracks. We slide our feet forward without picking them up to keep traction, and then we step through a curtain of snow, and the ice is covered in a fresh, powdery blanket. There is nothing but white on the path where we stand and darkness just beyond, where the trees have moved closer together, huddling for warmth. Their black branches create a cathedral over us, blocking out the sun, but that is not what makes the path ahead so dark.

A meadow of dragon's bane shrouds the path with its white stalks and red veins and pitch-black flowers, stretching beyond the logs and into the trees. The source of the sickness.

Henry walks to the edge of the toxic meadow and drops to one knee. "This must be where they were almost . . ." He swallows the awful word.

"Wherever they disappeared to," I say, "do you think they would have gone far?"

He shakes his head. "I don't know."

Tinkling laughter echoes through the trees above us.

Henry stands. "Did you hear that?"

I nod.

Shadows pulse between the trees. They're swift, in the corner of your eye and then gone before you turn your head. They watch us, the small flakes of sunlight that manage to break through the canopy the only thing keeping them at bay. I could almost convince myself they aren't really there had I not already seen them and the destruction they cause firsthand.

"We should go," I say, reaching for his hand.

"Wait." His lips are cracked and bleeding. His breath leaves ice crystals on the top edge of his coat. "There's something written on that tree there. Do you see it?"

I squint my eyes, but it's too dark. "I don't see anyth— Henry!"

He steps off the path again, and I pull out my pocketknife instinctively, not that it'll be any help against the shadows. He stops at a tree, wiping away the fresh layer of snow dotting the ice. He blows onto the ice and wipes a circle with his sleeve.

"It looks like a code—"

A shadow circles him.

"Henry, look out!"

Henry stares at the tree a moment longer. The Sentinel dives. There's a sharp intake of breath, and then Henry runs, stumbling back onto the path. A line of blood mars his neck.

"Nicked it on a tree branch," he explains, pressing his hand against it,

"No, you didn't." The slice looks exactly the same as the one on my hand. "What you actually did was almost get yourself killed."

"Maybe," he says, "but I think I know where my parents are."

My eyes widen. "Where?"

A twig snaps somewhere off the path.

"Was that you?" I ask Henry, even though I already know the answer.

"No," he whispers.

We listen to the silence, the clouds of our breath intertwining, and then—

Footsteps crunching the snow.

"We need to leave." I reach for Henry's hand just as the tiny bit of sun that had been bleeding through the sky overhead blinks out.

# XXXIV

"Henry!"

I reach for him, try to find his hand, but there's just empty space. I spin in a circle, hands outstretched, knowing he has to be nearby—he was standing next to me just a second ago—

*No, no, no, there can't be nothing. He has to be here somewhere.*

"Winter!"

He sounds far away, on another path, his voice echoing off the trees. Wind that burns across my cheeks like ice roars past me—*fresh meat, so nice to eat*—but the Sentinels don't touch me.

They're going after Henry.

I stumble forward. I have no idea if I'm going the right way. My eyes don't adjust to the darkness because there's nothing to adjust *to*. It is the pure absence of light.

*Winter Parish.* Varo's voice seeps into my brain. Deep like canyon echoes. Crackling like old, crinkled paper. *Have you thought over my proposal?*

Somewhere far, far ahead of me, Henry screams, a guttural sound that mangles my heart. I grip my coin and call the fireflies, ordering them to his side. I think of the skinless traveler. Wonder how long it took for him to get that way. They were supposed to take their time, the Sentinels, but what if Varo ordered them to be quick?

"Hold on, Henry!" I shout into the void. "Help is coming!"

Varo tsks. *You have a bit of the rebel in you, Winter Parish*, he says. *Inviting a traveler through your threshold. Feeding him, housing him. Giving him access to our history.*

I whip my head toward the sound of Varo's voice, even though I know he could be standing anywhere. A football field away or right next to me. "How do you know that?"

He chuckles. *Your thoughts are not as protected as you like to think.*

Henry screams again. There's some force behind it, as if he's fighting back. Or maybe I'm just imagining that. Hoping—praying—they haven't hurt him yet. My eyes scan the darkness.

*Come on, Henry. Where are you?*

Varo laughs again. *Your friends are on their way, do not worry. Although, you should know I am wise to your trick now. I could stop them dead long before they got here if I wanted to.*

"Then why don't you?" I spit back at him through clenched teeth.

*Because this is merely a reminder*, he replies. *There are going to be sides to take, and now that I have shown you a glimpse of the power I wield in this place, you must realize the council is going to lose. Anyone who stands in the way of that will be destroyed, but there will still be a place for the guardians. Your duties will not really change, so what does it matter who's running the council?*

"It matters if the person running things implodes the space-time continuum."

*Says the girl who's allowed a traveler to spend the past several days in the future,* he snaps. *I have not changed my position since last night. I want the guardians on my side, and I believe you are the best person for that job.*

A cloud of blue light appears, cutting through the trees several paths away from me. They gather around Henry so fast I can't see him, can't tell if he's hurt, but the height of their shield tells me he's standing, so he has to be okay. He *has* to.

*You're running out of time,* Varo continues. *Do not wait much longer to make your decision.*

The branches overhead creak as they peel back, exposing the sun once more. The Sentinels scream and vanish into the dark, hollow spaces in the nearest tree bark. Varo suddenly appears in front of me, so close I can see the red veins spreading like spiderwebs from his violet eyes.

"Next time," he says, his chapped lips cracking as he speaks, "I will not hold the Sentinels back. Remember that." He wraps his cloak around him. It spins, spins, spins, then turns to black smoke that mixes with my breath in the frigid air before disappearing altogether, leaving behind an acrid smell, like tobacco mixed with sulfur.

I turn on my heel and run to Henry. The fireflies break apart to encompass us both as I draw near, and even though we don't need them anymore, I can't imagine calling them off. Not when Varo could change his mind and come after us again. I'll keep them with us until we're out of the wood.

Henry's skin is flushed from the heat of the fireflies, his hair wet where ice chips have melted, but aside from several thin, clawlike scratches on the backs of his hands and behind his ears, he's unharmed.

I let go of the breath I've been holding and wrap my arms around him. "Thank God you're okay."

"And you?" he asks, holding me tight against him with one arm and threading his other hand through my hair, cradling my head. "Are you injured?"

"No," I say. "I'm fine."

We stand there like that for another moment, releasing our relief and our fear and other unnameable things between us, holding on too tightly to possibly lose each other again. But I can feel the sun going down, and we have a long walk home, so I give him one more quick squeeze, then step out of the circle of his arms.

"We need to go."

He nods, lacing his fingers through mine as we start down the path. I can tell something's wrong with Henry. He won't look at me, and he's clenching his teeth so hard, a muscle in his jaw twitches.

My brow furrows. "Are you sure you're all right?"

He shakes his head. "I should have never come here," he murmurs. "My presence has caused you nothing but distress."

"Hey." I pull him to a stop. Force him to meet my gaze. "You aren't responsible for what's happening here. I'd be dealing with it if you were here or not, except I'd be completely lost. I wouldn't know what to do, what to think. You being here, helping piece this all together—it's what's keeping me together right now."

He stares back at me, doubt and uncertainty roiling like a storm cloud in his eyes.

"And you said you think you know where your parents are now, right?" I ask him.

"They left a code," Henry says. "Written on the tree. WP1675-131:2:3:7."

"What does that mean?"

"It's one of the journals. William Parish, 1675. Page one thirty-one, paragraph two, sentence three, word seven. It's a secret language my parents have been using for years. We just need to figure out what the word is to discover where they've gone, and then . . . and then I'm not sure what we should do. They might be somewhere we can't follow."

"Then we'll take it to the council."

"Is that wise?" he asks. "We still do not know who can be trusted."

"No, it isn't wise," I agree. "But it may be our only option. Only Old Ones can cross thresholds. If we tried, we could get stuck in another time. Forever."

He chews on his bottom lip, thinking. "You're right."

"Henry?"

"Yes?"

"We're one step closer to finding your parents." I smile. "Be happy. It's almost over."

"I fear you are wrong," he says. "I fear it is only beginning."

# XXXV

om has a roast in the oven when we get back. Henry sniffs the air appreciatively. Mom promises she'll make him up a plate and sneak it to him. We both decide it's a better idea all around if Henry doesn't eat dinner with us—Mer would be seriously confused if Mom let a boy who spent the previous night in my room eat dinner with us as if it were a perfectly normal thing to do, and it would probably lead to Mer asking some very uncomfortable questions later. Henry doesn't mind, though. As soon as he gets his shoes off in the mudroom, he disappears into the study to look for William Parish's journal, then takes it upstairs to my room to read. Mom agreed he can stay up there while Mer's here, but he'll be sleeping on the couch tonight.

Mer arrives shortly after. Her eyes widen as I answer the door. "So, are you grounded for the rest of your life?" she whispers.

"Not grounded so much as indentured."

"Lucky. If my parents found a boy in my room, I'd be shipped off to a convent faster than you can say *chastity belt*."

"Come on," I say, leading her into the family room. "Let's get to work."

An hour of studying and a cross-examination about what Henry and I did and did not do last night later, Mom calls us into the dining room for dinner. Mer digs into the roast beef and twice-baked potatoes like it's her last meal. She talks to Mom about school, and Mom talks to her about work and tries, once again, to sway her toward studying archaeology when she gets into Ohio State.

"They're not going to take me," Mer says. "My grades are too low and my practice ACT scores have been *way* below average."

"Well, that's why Winter's helping you. Isn't that right, Win?"

"Hmm? Oh. Yeah." I've been zoning out all night, thinking about the wood, about what would have happened to Henry if the fireflies hadn't gotten to him in time, or if Varo had made good on his threat to stop them. *Can I even trust going back into the wood again now that my greatest ally, the sun, can be stripped from me at any moment? Now that Varo has invaded my thoughts twice?*

I think of Dad, too. I know it isn't safe to hope, but I can't help wondering . . . Have Henry's parents discovered something new about Dad's disappearance? And if they're still alive, just in another place and time, does that mean there's a chance Dad's still alive, too? Will they be able to help me find him if he is?

And I think of Joe. A week ago—heck, a *day* ago—I would have called for him when Varo took the sun away from me. Would have told him everything that's happened and would've trusted him to handle it. But Henry's right—we don't know whose side anyone is on, and until we do, until this all comes to a head and Varo's supporters are forced to reveal themselves, Joe has to be just as much a suspect as anyone else.

I try to force those thoughts from my mind, knowing it's unhealthy to think so long and so hard about things that are out of my control, but I just end up thinking of the boy in my room. The way his fingers brushed my cheek last night, his lips inches from mine. The way he looks at me, like I'm strong and smart and independent and *mesmerizing*. The way he moves, graceful yet with purpose, a blend between his aristocratic upbringing and the days he spends working alongside the tenant farmers in his fields.

"I like working with my hands," he told Mom this afternoon while I rummaged through the fridge for butter and cheese. "Besides, it's my land. What kind of caretaker would I be if I just ignored it and let everyone else handle it?"

He's brilliant and responsible and amazing, and there's this part of me, deep down, that whispers every time I look at him: *What if?* It's a dangerous start to a question. What if things could be different? What if he could—I don't know—move here, to this century, with his family? If his parents can really live in any time period they choose, then why can't Henry? Sure, he isn't an Old One, and if Henry doesn't live out his life in the eighteenth century, it could have serious ramifications, but should that really stand in the way of true love? If fairy tales are to be believed, I should be able to have my prince and keep the space-time continuum from imploding, too.

*Get over it, Win,* I tell myself. *He's leaving whether you want him to or not. You've known that since the very beginning.*

But I'm not ready to let him go. *God, how selfish is that?*

We've accomplished what Henry came here to do. We've tracked his parents, and we have every reason to believe they're alive, and that they have information about Dad. And I'm so happy about that, happier than I've been in twenty months and six—almost seven—days, but imagining Henry not being here anymore . . .

It's like imagining another piece of myself being lost to the wood forever.

❧

"So, are you in love with him?"

"Mer!"

"She can't hear me," Meredith whispers as she turns the page of her Algebra II book.

I glance at Mom in the dining room, grading papers with a red pen in one hand, massaging her temples with the other.

"You don't have to say anything anyway," Mer says, stretching her legs out behind her. "It's written all over your face."

I squirm from her all-knowing stare. "It is not."

"Please. So, when's lover boy going back to New York?"

I push off my stomach and sit up, leaning my back against the couch. "Tomorrow, probably."

"Will he be back to visit?"

My throat goes dry. "No."

She nods. "So that explains the sleepover."

"We haven't been doing anything. We just talk."

She taps her pen against the glossy page, leaving behind blue spots that, if they shifted an inch to the left, could really screw up the answers to some work problems. "Sometimes talking can be more dangerous than anything else," she murmurs.

I study her. "Is that why you're a serial dater?"

She shrugs. "If you don't get to know a guy, he can't break your heart. He can hurt your pride by breaking up with you, or make you feel like an idiot when he turns out to be a total ass, but he can't make you fall in love with him. Not if he's just one frog in the long line of amphibians you have to kiss before you find your Prince Charming."

"You know, there's just one little problem with your theory. You'll have to actually get to know a guy to find out if he's your Prince Charming or not."

"Well, then," she says, sitting up. "Enlighten me. How's this whole getting-to-know-Henry thing working out for you?"

"It sucks."

"Gee, don't make it sound too appealing."

I exhale. "It sucks because I really like him. A lot. And he's leaving. And I'm never going to see him again."

"And you call me dramatic. There's always college, you know. You could track down where he's going and—"

"No."

She rolls her eyes. "Are you kidding? With your grades you could get in anywhere, and you wouldn't be the first girl to chase a guy to college."

"Just drop it, okay?"

"Okay." She picks up her textbook and ACT practice book. "I have to hit the road anyway. I'm meeting Johnny at the movies in half an hour."

"Johnny the wide receiver?"

She shakes her head. "The tailback. Weird kissing aside, he's . . . I don't know. Nice. And he thinks Trixie Malone looks like a carp."

I walk her to the door. "You know, Mer, you might actually want to try to get to know this one. Just to mix things up a little."

"I will, if you promise not to give up on Henry so easily. If you think he's the one, you can make it work. A lot of couples have made it through worse things than long-distance relationships."

"Like who?"

"Heathcliff and Catherine?"

"You haven't finished the book yet, have you?"

She snaps her fingers. "Edward and Vivian."

I blink.

"You know," she says, "from *Pretty Woman*?"

"Better, although I don't know how I feel about being compared to a prostitute."

"She's not any old prostitute. She's Julia Roberts, for God's sake."

"Okay, okay. I'll see what I can do," I say, even though it's a lie. There's nothing I can do. The typical long-distance relationship has never had to deal with the whole he-lives-in-a-different-century, she-has-a-magical-forest-to-protect angle.

"Pinkie promise?"

I link my pinkie around hers. "Yeah, whatever. Now go talk to Johnny and see if he's your Prince Charming already."

She starts through the door.

"Hey, Mer?"

She glances at me over her shoulder.

I take a deep breath. "I'm sorry I haven't been around much lately. I can't really explain it, but my life is pretty complicated."

"Clearly. I mean, you have gorgeous British men sleeping over in your room. I'd kill for my life to be that complicated."

"Man, not *men*," I correct her. "Anyway, I'm going to try to do better."

Mer turns around, taking my hand and giving me a small smile. "Win, you don't have to explain anything to me, or promise me anything. We're sisters, and we'll always be sisters. Even if we went years without talking or seeing each other, that would never change."

I arch a brow. "We better not go years without doing either of those things."

Mer laughs. "You know what I mean. We're cool, so you don't have to worry. Okay?"

I swallow against the sudden dryness in my throat. "Okay."

"Now, I'm going to go kiss that frog and see if he's my prince. Wish me luck."

I smile. "Good luck!"

I watch her go, feeling the differences between us more keenly than usual. If only I could be her, and Henry could be Johnny, and we could get to know each other over bad action movies and overly buttered popcorn. He could drive me home and kiss me good night and I could write his name with little doodle hearts in my notebook during class.

Now that sounds like real magic.

# XXXVI

I do the dishes after Mer leaves, rinsing and drying them as fast as possible. I can feel my time with Henry slipping away from me, and I want to spend every second I can with him before he leaves. It's an odd sensation, one I wasn't expecting at all. Just a couple days ago, I couldn't wait to get rid of him. And now . . .

Now the thought of Henry leaving makes my soul ache.

"Door open while you're up there together, Winter," Mom tells me without looking up from her work while I dry my hands with a dish towel.

"Yes, ma'am."

I fix Henry a plate of Oreo cookies for dessert and pour two glasses of milk, one for each of us. Balancing the plate on one of the glasses, I head upstairs.

Henry is so intent on his book—his eyes furiously scanning the page, his thumb grazing his bottom lip—that he doesn't seem to hear my bedroom door squeak open, or my footsteps as I walk in. I carefully set the plate and glasses on my dresser and creep forward. His jaw drops at something on the page, and then—

"Boo!" I yell.

He jumps out of his seat, his hand going to his side as if reaching for a weapon. I bend over laughing.

He takes a deep breath. "Scaring people is not a very becoming attribute in a young lady."

"Whatever," I say between barely hushed giggles. "You should've seen your face."

He gives me a half smile. "I will make you pay for this when you least expect it."

I stop laughing. His smile falters. And neither of us says it, but we know we're both thinking it: He won't have the chance to pay me back. These are probably our last hours together.

I clear my throat. "Do you know where your parents are?"

He closes his book and nods. "Brussels."

"Great. That's, um, great." *Yeah, you already said that, Miss Honor Roll. Let's try to think of some other adjectives for next time, shall we?*

"Though I'm not certain what time period," he admits.

"I think there's only one Brussels threshold, but the council will know for sure. I'll take you to headquarters as soon as the sun comes up."

"Thank you."

"Are you worried?" I ask. "About what the council will do to you once you've told them who you are?"

"I am more concerned about what will happen to my parents if I do not act quickly," he says. "As long as I find them alive, I can withstand any punishment the council may give me. Why? Are you afraid?"

I'm afraid of a lot of things. I'm afraid of what's happening to the wood, afraid of Varo. Afraid of the hope growing in my chest when I think about the fact that Henry's parents are alive and that maybe, just maybe, if they're alive, then my dad could be alive, too. Hidden somewhere, like Brussels, or medieval Japan, or ancient Greece. She hasn't said it, but I know Mom's holding on to that hope, too, and that scares me even more. I don't know how she'll handle it if Dad's beyond saving, or, perhaps even worse, if he never had anything to do with this in the first place. If his name on Henry's parents' desk was just a coincidence. If we will still be left wondering what happened to him. If we will always be stuck in this limbo where we can never truly move forward or backward, but just reside in this vacuous hole of a place where nothing feels like it'll ever be right again.

I'm afraid of saying good-bye to Henry. Afraid that he may be the only person who will ever truly understand the wood and my destiny, and that I'll never be able to find another friend, another person, like him. But afraid of what the council will do to me when they discover I helped him find his parents?

"No," I say. "I'm not afraid."

His finger taps the cover of *Lord of the Flies*, and he looks up at me from beneath short, blond lashes that catch the light and shimmer, like fine-spun gold. "I do not know what my parents have been doing to stop Varo, but I assure you they are not the type to simply run and hide when they know something must be done. I will work with them to stop him in any way I can. You will not"—he clears his throat—"*I* will not let you be alone in this, Winter."

I nod. I don't trust myself to speak when all I want to do is cry.

He takes a step forward. "I want to thank you. For helping me. I could not have done this without you. No," he says as I shrug and try to wave his compliment away. "It's true. I will not let you be modest. I had the elixir, yes, but I never could have made it through the wood without you guiding me, or guarding me against those dark monstrosities. Receiving the message my parents left behind for me, knowing they are safe—or, if not that, at least knowing where to look for them next—I cannot properly describe the relief that comes with that knowledge."

I clear my throat. "Well, that is my job, you know. Guide and guard. It's in my handbook."

"That may be, but it is most certainly not your job to give a traveler like me a chance, to listen to him when he says he needs help, to shelter him and feed him and clothe him, or to show him there are marvelous things in this world that he can keep close to him all the days of his life."

"Like TV?"

He closes the distance between us, his hands tentatively, shyly, brushing my arms. "Like you. You have something in you, Winter, that shines brighter than candle flame. You have opened up my world. You have shown me that the right person can make a poor fool like me happier than he ever thought possible." He fingers twine through mine. His eyes darken and his voice scratches on something in his throat. "Frankly, I do not know what I will do without you."

I know what I *should* say. I should say that's ridiculous, that we barely know each other and we couldn't possibly feel this strong a connection after just a couple days. I should say that love-at-first-sight crap is manufactured by Hollywood and the greeting-card companies to make young, impressionable girls want to see every single romantic comedy and beg their boyfriends to buy them Valentine's Day cards and, someday, to plan the perfect wedding, the kind that fairy tales themselves couldn't even compete with.

I should say I'm the kind of girl who has never believed in any of it. I was raised to be pragmatic, even before Dad disappeared and I realized the world isn't this magical place, even though magic exists and I see it every day. It's a hard world, where people can be taken from you in an instant and it's better to keep your heart closed, to just do your job and keep your feet moving and never, *ever*, question things, because questions can lead to unhappiness and suspicion and guilt and all those other emotions that make up the tears in your eyes when you can't fall asleep at night.

But I'm not that girl anymore. Henry has shown me there is something magical in the little things—the electrical charge that shoots down my back when skin touches skin; the indescribable connection I felt to him the second his eyes met mine that day in the wood, before I even knew who he was or what he wanted or that I was the only person in the world who could give it to him; the way I want him to kiss me so badly it hurts, an ache so deep inside that it has me leaning forward on my toes, my fingers squeezing his, my lips a breath from his lips, and then—

And then he kisses me. His bottom lip dances against mine, and it's like a glass of iced tea on the hottest summer day. My muscles relax and my mind clears and there's just this: Henry's arms tightening around me, his lips soft as rose petals, his body hard and strong against mine. He could wrap me up like a blanket and make me disappear and it would be the best gift anyone has ever given me. To have a guardian of my very own.

The want, *the need*, is so great, it smothers me.

I push away from him. "Stop. I can't do this."

He places his hand against his heart. "Forgive me. I thought—"

"You thought wrong. I—I don't want this." My voice breaks on the words, but I inhale sharply and imagine the air in my lungs as pure steel. "You're my friend, Henry. That's all. Whatever you think you feel between the two of us, I don't feel the same way."

He takes a step back, and suddenly the room's too cold. He looks down at the rug beneath our feet, his hair shielding his face from me. My hands reach for him but I pull them back. This is the way it has to be. What would telling him the truth accomplish?

It would only hurt more to have to say good-bye knowing that what we had was more than business, more than friendship, more than teenage hormones, or any other explanation science could come up with to explain why I've never wanted anything so badly as I want to keep him here next to me.

"Forgive me," he says again.

"You're a nice guy, Henry—"

"I should head downstairs," he says. "Your mother will come looking for me soon if I do not."

He heads for the door. I grab his hand, stopping him.

"Don't," I say, and the words rush up my throat, sliding across my tongue—*I want you to stay, I feel something too, please don't leave me tomorrow*—but instead I say, "Don't be mad. I don't want to fight on our last night together."

He deflates. "I am not angry, Winter," he says, "but I cannot say in all good conscience that I am not disappointed. That is not your fault, though. I misread the situation."

I gesture to the Oreo plate. "I brought you dessert."

"I find I am not very hungry."

I nod, the pain in my chest too sharp, too heavy, too impossible to breathe or think around. "Okay. Good night, Henry."

He bows. "Good night, Miss Parish."

He slips out the door, and I crumble onto my bed, crying silently so no one will hear.

⊱────≻

I can't sleep. I creep downstairs and peek into the family room. Henry lies on the couch, his arm bent behind his head, his lips slightly parted. His eyes are closed and his breathing is even. I grab a glass of water from the kitchen and take it into the study.

I sit at my father's desk, my hands trailing over the dark oak and the leather ink blotter, and I wonder how much he gave up for the wood before it finally took his life. He and Mom met when she was in college, and from all their stories, it was as if he'd never loved anyone before her, but what if? What if he'd fallen in love with someone who would never understand his destiny, who would never believe her if he told her what he really did day after day, who would send him to a mental institution for even thinking such a thing was possible? Did he know what it was like to give up happiness in exchange for duty? I close my eyes and try to imagine what he would say to me, but it's Henry's voice that comes through instead.

*I did not find your father's journal.*

I get up from my chair and cross to the bookcases. There are forty-six journals in all, dating back to the early 1200s, that have been kept and restored, as well as a handful of books and treatises on the wood and the workings of the council. I pull them out, one by one, and stack them on the floor. I don't know what I expect to find this time that I haven't found before. Dad's journal that I've never once seen in my life hidden behind another book?

But there's nothing. The bookcases are empty, and the shelves are smooth. No latches, no doors, no hollow spaces. I lean against the fireplace, cold stone seeping the warmth from my skin, and look around at the mess I made for nothing.

It's all been for nothing.

I look up at the ceiling, knocking the back of my head against the mantel. "Where is it, Dad? Huh? Didn't you think you owed it to me to let me in on your secrets? Didn't you—?"

My elbow scrapes against a sharp point in the middle of the fireplace. I suck in a breath. It's a shallow cut, the kind that sends a million nerve endings into overdrive. A thin line of red bubbles to the surface. I rub my fingers against the sharp stone—someone should really sand it down—and it moves.

It *moves*. Just a little to the right. I dig my fingertips into the grooves and wiggle it forward. The stone is half the length of my forearm, and it takes a solid heave to pry it loose from the stones surrounding it. It smacks into my stomach, pushing the breath from my lungs. I lay it down gently on the carpet and look inside the hole it left behind. My fingers shake.

A journal. A fat, dusty, leather-bound journal.

I pull it out, and right there on the front are Dad's initials: *JP, 1989–*

I take it to the desk, open to the first page, and start reading.

⊱⊱⊱≻⊰

June 10, 1989
8:35 a.m.

This is it, graduation day. Everyone else I know is going through a mixture of emotions—excitement for summer vacation, anxiety over moving away and all the decisions that will come with starting college in the fall. What will they major in, where will they live? Will they like their roommates, will they like their professors? Will college really be any different from high school? Will the ones who could coast by in their classes actually have to put effort into their chosen degrees? How will our valedictorian—who told everyone who would listen that she's starting summer classes at Yale next week—handle the change from the little pond to the big one? Will she still be the big fish, or will she drive herself crazy trying to compete with thousands of other students just like her?

But graduation day is not the first step to my future. It is the last step of my past. Dad officially retires today. He's on his last patrol as I write this, and this afternoon, directly following my graduation ceremony, I will conduct the afternoon patrol by myself.

Dad tells me not to worry, that he'll ease me into the role of primary guardian, and even then, I won't be on my own. His body won't let him ignore the wood completely, not until he's dead and buried. And then there's Joe, of course, my permanent link to the council. Still, it's a lonely feeling, knowing this is all my life will ever be.

Dreaming of anything else is pointless.

June 10, 1989
9:05 p.m.

Sent two travelers back this afternoon. A kid from 1964 Chicago, and a woman from 1602 London.

Now that the sun's finally down, we're going out to eat to "celebrate."

What a joke.

June 17, 1989
10:45 p.m.

Joe took me to my first meeting as the primary guardian. That's the one thing Dad says he's most excited about, never having to make the journey to their headquarters again. I had only been to one meeting before, when I was ten and Dad had to observe some archaic ritual in which the council recognized I would begin my training as a guardian. It was a lot more exciting back

*then, before I realized what this destiny really*
*was.*

*A prison sentence.*

*Three travelers today. San Francisco, 1911.*
*Johannesburg, 2026. Tenochtitlán, 1456.*

Although it doesn't sound like it from these first entries, I know Dad and Uncle Joe became best friends before too long, and by the time Dad got married and Mom was pregnant with me, he and Joe were like brothers. There were picture albums full of the three of them together in front of Christmas trees or around the kitchen table, taking me to the zoo when I was a toddler or dropping me off for my first day of school. Wherever Dad and Mom went, Uncle Joe followed.

Dad's relationship with the wood, it turns out, was always a conflicted one, but the journal entries get less hostile the older he gets. Although he doesn't directly say it, I think Mom is the reason for this.

Things start to take a turn again on the night before my tenth birthday. Dad writes about how he's going to tell me about the wood in the morning, starting me on a path that is centuries in the making, but he's conflicted about it. *How can I, in all good conscience,* he writes, *subject my daughter to the same fate that has tied me to this place all these years? How can I take away from her the dream that she can be anything she wants to be when she grows up? How can I shackle her to this place for the rest of her life?*

But he doesn't have a choice. I've been shackled since birth, just like every Parish before me.

It's four in the morning by the time I've skimmed through the entries and made it to Dad's last year. These entries are harder to read. The pen strokes are darker, as if he tried to punch the ink through the paper, and in the margins are sideways notes scribbled like afterthoughts: *What's the point? Is this really all there is? All there will ever be?*

His anger is palpable on every page—toward the wood; the travelers; the council; even the sun, for rising every morning—and I flip back through the entries, making up a sick game to figure out when exactly that anger turned to hatred. When exactly he started drinking too much. When exactly he started fading away from us. Wondering if he really disappeared because he stepped off the path, or because there just wasn't enough will left inside him to exist.

I give up looking—procrastinating, really—and finally turn to the last pages. The first entry in this section is dated a week before he disappeared.

> *It seems my disillusionment with the wood has begun to affect Joe, of all people. He keeps making odd comments he wants me to think are offhand, but Joe is too deliberate for his words to be anything but calculated. It started with a simple agreement with me one day, when I drunkenly wondered aloud what the point of it all was, why my daughter had to suffer the same fate as the rest of the imprisoned Parish line. Why she*

*couldn't have more. And now it has progressed to
Joe openly questioning the council, saying he
believes it's time for a change.*

*He has something up his sleeve. I'm not sure
what it is, but I'm going to find out.*

My eyes shift to the last entry my dad ever wrote, and suddenly I don't want to read it. I want to hold on to this moment where a part of him is still alive. I want to run my fingers over his handwriting and imagine he's upstairs sleeping, and I've crept down here to read his secret, most private thoughts, and he'll kill me in the morning if he finds out, but I'll smile when he does, because he'll be *alive.*

My eyes burn and I think: *no more.*

I read my father's final entry.

*Joe is talking like a madman. He wants to
overthrow the council, start a war all for some
new world order. He says he's been seeking out
Varo's old supporters, and now he wants to start
getting the guardians on his side. He wants me
to be his right-hand man in this, but what he's
talking about . . . I hate the wood with every
fiber of my being. I hate what it has done to my
family. I hate that I will never know what it's
like to travel, to have a normal job, to be the*

master of my own life, and I hate that I have
sentenced my daughter to the same fate.

But what Joe is suggesting is anarchy, and it will
lead to the end of the world as we know it.

I have to stop him.

# XXXVII

"Get up."

Henry looks at me blearily, his eyes half-closed and a string of drool on his lips. His eyes widen and he brushes his hand across his mouth. "What is it? What's wrong?"

"Nothing's wrong," I say, my voice flat. "The sun's coming up. Time to go."

"Is that all you have to say to me?"

I nod. "Get dressed, and take your elixir."

I turn for the door, but he pushes up off the couch and his hand circles my arm. "Wait. What happened?"

"I told you. Nothing happened."

"You do not look like yourself. You look like—"

"A ghost?"

"I was going to say a woman possessed, but *ghost* works as well. You look empty, Winter."

"Maybe because I am."

"Tell me what happened. Trust me, for once—"

"I don't need to trust anyone. I don't *need* anyone. I—" I'm about to say I can handle this on my own, but it would be giving away too much, and I need to keep everything locked down, bottled tight. "You can get dressed in my room. Meet me back down here in five minutes."

He's in the kitchen in two. We tug on our boots in the mudroom, dried mud flaking off the soles. I stuff a flashlight into my coat pocket and open the door to the back porch. "After you."

He stares at me a moment too long, but I keep my eyes shuttered, my face vacant. I am a robot, unfeeling, unmerciful.

He clears his throat and moves forward. I follow him onto the porch, sunlight just breaking over the horizon, turning the navy-blue sky pink along the eastern lip, and stop short.

All the leaves are black. Even Henry, who should not be able to see past the glamour that makes the wood look like all the normal trees surrounding it, sucks in a breath. Which means the glamour is fading. Anyone passing by on 315 will see the dead, withered branches, the oozing black pus.

But that isn't the worst of it. The sickness is spreading beyond the wood. The trees along our driveway have been infected, black tar rolling down the tips of the lowest leaves, droplets sizzling onto the pavement.

Poisoning our world.

"Come on," I say, taking a step forward. "We have to stop this before it's too late."

Henry links his fingers through mine, stopping me.

"Tell me what's going on first," he says. "I am not leaving until you do."

I gesture to the leaves and snap, "We don't have time for this."

He sits on the porch steps. "Then we do not have time for

me to sit here and watch the sunrise either but, well, would you look at that? That seems to be precisely what I am doing."

"Henry."

"Winter."

"Fine. You win." I spread my arms open wide. "Joe's the reason all of this is happening."

Henry's jaw drops. "*What?* How do you know that?"

"I found Dad's journal," I say, tears stinging my eyes. But I refuse to cry. I can break when this is all over, but not now. Not when there are still so many questions swirling through my head and only one person who can answer them. "The last thing Dad wrote was that he had to stop Joe, and I think . . . I think Joe may have made Dad disappear."

I don't know how I didn't realize it before. Joe was the one who told us he was gone, and we didn't question it. We asked how, but we believed him when he said Dad walked off the path, even though no guardian had ever done such a thing before. Even though I could never do it myself.

Henry's voice is low and too controlled. "You were going to confront Joe by yourself, weren't you?"

I stare at the ground.

"Winter."

I sigh. "That was the plan."

He stands, his whole body quivering like an arrow strung too tight on a bow. "And pray, tell me, are you addled, or merely suicidal?"

"*He killed my father, Henry.*" My stomach churns as I remember Uncle Joe standing in the kitchen, saying Dad walked off the path. I know now that wasn't true. He was *pushed*—it's the only thing that makes sense. No guardian could walk off the path on their own, but they could be forced off. Joe must have found out Dad knew too much, and Joe silenced him for it.

"That does not mean you must face him alone." Henry takes my hands in his. "Please, let me help you. Let my parents help you. Let the council. Together, we might be able to stop him. But you, on your own—you would not stand a chance."

"I'm glad you have so much faith in me."

"This is serious, Winter. This man is deranged and he will not let you stand in his way—"

"You think I don't know that?"

"Winter, please. I understand what you are feeling right now."

"How? How could you understand? Has your father been murdered?"

His lips twist into a sardonic smile. "Not that I know of, but when my parents disappeared, I feared the worst. I became drunk on whiskey and set off for the nearest threshold, consequences be damned. It was only when I was standing at the mouth of the wood that I realized I could not help them if I got myself killed, and I returned home to come up with a better plan. Now I am telling you the same thing. You must have a clear head about this. You cannot avenge your father if you're dead."

There's logic in what he's saying, but I can't take it in. I need to find Joe. I need to know exactly what happened to my father and make Joe pay for it, and I can't let Henry get in the way of that.

I swallow back the lump in my throat. "You're right. I know you're right. Do you—do you really think the council would help us?"

He exhales. "It's all we have."

I nod. "Okay. Let's go."

We step through the threshold as the first rays of pure, golden sunlight splinter the sky, but its warmth doesn't seep through the trees, and its light is muted by the black, twisted trees surrounding us. Our breath turns into puffs of white clouds in the frigid air, our exhalations and our footsteps the only sound in this cold, stale mausoleum.

Henry's hand tightens around mine. "If I remember correctly from my parents' maps, the threshold to the council chambers should be to the—"

"I know where it is."

"Right," Henry says, his cheeks turning red. "Of course you do."

Wind whispers through the trees, bringing with it voices only I can hear.

*Help us, Winter. Save us.*

I don't know if it's the wood or Uncle Joe messing with my mind or something else entirely. I still have so many questions, and it's all because of Joe. He took my father away. He owes me the answers my father can no longer give.

I turn to Henry, tears blurring my vision as I hide the coin in my palm. "I want you to know I lied. I do feel something between us. I wish we lived in a time where that wouldn't mean heartbreak and having to say good-bye, but we don't. I am the guardian of the wood. I have a duty here, and you have a duty to live out your life as you were meant to live it, in your own time." I let go of his hand, and by the time realization dawns on his face, I've already called the fireflies. "I'm sorry."

"Winter, no!" He lunges forward, but the little blue bugs

are already there, swarming him, zapping him back. "Do not do this!"

"Take him to the council threshold," I say.

"No!" He lunges at them again, his fists pounding into them. The smell of burnt hair sears my nostrils. "I will not let you do this."

"You don't have a choice."

"Winter!"

"When you get there, make sure you tell them everything. Don't try to protect me. They might not believe you if you don't tell them everything."

"Winter," he shouts. "Don't do this!"

His skin is red, blistering, and the fireflies are pushing him back, but he doesn't stop trying to break through them. I turn my back on him and start down the path, unable to bear the sight any longer, but I can still hear his flesh sizzling like eggs in a skillet as he rams himself into the bugs. He screams my name again and again, each time a little farther away as they push him toward the council threshold, until his words are muffled by the whispers in the trees and, somewhere to my left, the sound of flames crackling.

My mind is nothing but static, my heart a dead thing that hasn't pumped blood in years. I am unfeeling, robotic, cold, just like the man sitting on the bench in front of me, a gas lamp to his right, a stone fire pit in front of him, flames casting shadows across the planes of his face.

"Hello, Uncle Joe."

# XXXVIII

Joe cocks his head at me slowly, as if he has all the time in the world.

"Winter. What are you doing here?"

I expect him to sound as different as he looks to me now, but his voice is the same, and I want to believe it's not true. For a brief, guilt-ridden second, I want to act as if I don't know. I want to sit beside him and watch the fire and slip back into that place where Uncle Joe equals safety, protection, guidance. I have lost one father already, and there's a part of me—a spoiled, naive part—that doesn't want to lose another.

*But you already have*, I remind myself.

"First patrol," I say. "It's dawn."

Joe looks up at the pink-orange sky and sighs. "So it is."

"I found my father's journal."

He hesitates. "I wasn't aware he still kept the old thing."

"But you knew he kept one once," I say. "Why didn't you ever tell me to do the same?"

He waves off my question. "It's not really that important,

more of a tradition than an obligation. As long as you report to the council every week, there is a record of every traveler you've ever dealt with, and seeing as how you've never missed a meeting . . ."

"But that only guarantees a record in the council archives," I say. "What were the Parish guardians who came after me supposed to study? There would be a whole gap of information."

His eyes narrow. "Why so interested in posterity all of a sudden?"

I stare back at him, unflinching. "It's an interesting read, Dad's journal. Especially the last entry." I grit my teeth. "Were you with him the morning he disappeared?"

"No. Why would you say such a thing?" There are all the right tones of surprise and incredulity and concern in his voice, all the things that have lulled me into believing whatever he wanted me to believe in the past. But I feel them now, the lies underneath, the manipulation that flows from him like the Olentangy. I pick the lies apart like a loose thread, unwinding them until his words ring hollow in my ears. If only I could have done it sooner, all those times I should have questioned him about the wood, about my father, the words fizzling out on the tip of my tongue, all because I trusted him. Because I didn't think someone who supposedly loved me so much could ever hurt me.

"Dad seemed to think you were behind the conspiracy to overthrow the council," I say. "You wouldn't happen to know why he would think that, would you?"

Joe's expression is tired now, as if he's a very busy man who doesn't have time for my silly teenage musings. It's the same look he's worn for years, and only now do I see the cracks in it, the flicker of anger in his eyes, the slight curl of his lip. "Winter, you're in shock. You don't know what you're saying—"

"Bravo. Really, Unc, you should have gone into acting."

He stiffens. "Winter, listen to me. You're making a mistake—"

"No, you listen to me. I know, okay? I know *everything*. I read Dad's journal. I know you're the one who brought Varo back."

He stands, cracking his knuckles against his palms. "I didn't, actually," he says. "Varo was properly banished almost five hundred years ago. There was no way for him to return. But I was able to use his ideology to begin recruiting his old followers, and when your father discovered what I was doing, I knew it wouldn't be long before others noticed, too. I needed an alias, someone I could pretend to be to shift the focus off me. Varo seemed the perfect disguise, and glamours are such easy magic once you have the power of the wood bending to your control."

My heart stutters. I try to take in his words, but it's like trying to breathe underwater.

All this time, Joe was Varo. Every time Joe told me to stay out of it, it was just because he didn't want me discovering his secret. Not because he was worried about me.

"You killed Dad," I say, my voice small. "Didn't you?"

He rolls his neck and pulls down his shoulders, and when he looks back at me, it's with a mixture of sadness and defiance.

"I didn't want to," he says. "Your father left me no choice."

Hearing him say it knocks the air from my lungs. I stagger back, my heart pounding in my ears. "Why?" That one word slams through my head over and over again. *Why, why, why?* "Why did you have to drag us into it? Why couldn't you just leave us alone?"

"I didn't foresee it ending this way. I cared for your father very much—"

"Liar."

"Please don't look at me like that," he says. "Your father was a casualty in a war that has been brewing for hundreds of years."

Tears blur my vision. I shake my head to clear it, but all I can see is Dad, making my favorite cranberry cider on my birthday. Showing me how to roll the perfect snowball in the backyard. Saying prayers before tucking me in for the night.

And then the memories morph into future moments we'll never share. Me walking down the staircase in my prom dress while Dad permanently blinds me from the flash of his camera. Dad watching me graduate from high school, and maybe, with us sharing patrol duties, college. Dad walking me down the aisle on my wedding day. Meeting his grandchildren and making them cranberry cider and teaching them how to roll the perfect snowball.

Joe took every last piece of my father away from me.

I think of the meeting Henry and I walked in on the other night. I thought Varo had been alerted to our presence by Stoner Guy, but if it was Joe, if it's been Joe this whole time, he knew it was me because he heard my message. He sent his followers after us, even though we could have gotten hurt. And yesterday, in the wood—he separated Henry from me. Threatened me.

"Why did you send your followers after me? Were you going to kill me, too?" I ask, even though I remember him saying he wanted us to be taken alive.

He shakes his head as if I'm being ridiculous. "Of course I wasn't trying to kill you. I was trying to save you."

"I don't believe you."

"I merely wanted to frighten you so you would stay out of it," he says. "I tried to save your father, too. I *tried* to make him see reason. I didn't want any harm to come to him."

"Stop lying!"

"I'm not."

My eyes narrow. "You tried to save him?"

"Yes."

"Tell me *exactly* how you tried to save my father. Tell me what you did, what you said, that should have kept him here with me. Because the way I see it, you didn't try very hard."

"Please, sit down and I'll explain everything."

"I'd rather stand."

"Very well." He takes a deep breath. "You know Varo's story, but you do not know *my* intentions. You assume the worst of me like your father did, but please, for your own sake as well as mine, try to understand."

Listening to him is both the last thing I want to do and the only thing I want to do. I want to understand, but nothing he can say will ever make me understand. I want to stand here, unmoving, unchanging, forever. I want to be anywhere but here.

I cross my arms over my chest and nod. I do not sit, and I do not look away from him. I want him to know that at any second I could decide I've had enough. That at any second, I could drive my knife through his heart, and although I know it won't kill him, it'll feel good to do it all the same.

Joe clears his throat. "I was young when Varo came to power. Impressionable. I agreed with the council's banishment of him, thought he was crazy for even suggesting we could use the thresholds to change time. But the older I became, the more I realized the power of the wood was being ignored instead of utilized, and I started to wonder if my people—the Old Ones—if we were supposed to use the thresholds of our world to change events in the human world. I started to wonder: What if I could have stopped every single traveler from ever entering our wood, so that our way of life would never be threatened? Or what if I could go back in time and stop the countless wars that have left millions of humans dead from their own destructive tendencies? If I could have brought modern medicine to the plague, or stopped the genocide at the concentration camps—you can't tell me that's wrong."

It's true. He could have done a lot of good things for the world, but there's no telling what the ramifications would have been, and as terrible as it sounds, that's life. We can't change the past—no one person should have that power. I tell him so, but he laughs.

"You've been drinking the Kool-Aid, kid. That's just an excuse the council came up with to keep the wood a secret. They didn't want to share it with anyone else. *They* were the selfish ones, for not seeing the wood as the miracle it was. But Varo saw it. His supporters saw it. *They* had vision. And when I finally saw it, too, I couldn't stop thinking about the possibilities. As long as I went back to the exact right moment in history, I could stop every war, every famine, every outbreak of disease. There wouldn't have to be any suffering in our world or in yours. You can't tell me that is not a noble cause."

"What about us?" I ask. "What about the suffering you put my family through when you killed my father?"

"Like I said, he was an unfortunate casualty. I have every intention of bringing him back."

I freeze. "What did you just say?"

"Once I've overthrown the council, I will go back in time and save him, if I can."

"What do you mean, if you can?"

He shrugs. "Your father did not have to die. If he had just listened to me, if he had just seen reason, he could have joined me. We could have done this together. There's a chance I can go back and save him without changing the course of my future."

"That's not true. You know that's not true!"

"There is a chance, Winter—"

"Stop it!" I press my palms into my ears. "Stop talking!"

It isn't true—none of it. He's psychotic if he thinks he can go back in time and change anything in history without putting his own future in jeopardy. Time isn't meant to be messed with. Every time he would change something, he'd risk changing his own path. Altering any moment in history, even a tiny, seemingly insignificant one, could then change the lives of the people involved in that moment and the choices they make, which, down the line, could affect Joe in such a way that he never impersonates Varo in the first place. It could maybe even change him so much that he never gets assigned to be the intermediary for my family and he never kills Dad—

And then I get it. It's tempting, so, so tempting to let Joe do what he wants to do. To take that chance and hope those events in history don't change my family, that they only change Joe so that he leaves my family alone.

But I know it doesn't work that way. Time is a domino effect, and just as it would change the lives of every other person who ever lived, it would change mine as well. My father may have never met my mother. I may have never been born. Neither of *them* may have ever been born. I could disappear and it would be like I never existed at all.

That's why the council is necessary. That's why the guardian is so important.

I pull Dad's Swiss Army knife from my back pocket and flick it open. Sunlight dances across the blade.

"We can do this the easy way, or the hard way," I tell him through clenched teeth.

He sneers. "I am not some traveler you can command back to a threshold."

I grab hold of my coin, the leather straps taut against my skin. The coin's symbols glow with white fire. "Want to bet?"

"You don't want to do this, Winter."

"The thing is, I really do."

"You don't understand. You're too late. The attack on the council is already under way."

*Henry.*

I take a step back. "No."

I have to get to him. I have to make sure he's all right. I turn to run toward the council threshold, but Uncle Joe appears in front of me.

"I'm afraid I can't let you do that," he says.

"Let me go." I raise my knife, daring him to refuse me.

He sighs. "This is the path you have chosen, then? I cannot change your mind?"

My coin burns as Alban's frantic voice echoes through my mind. *The council is under attack. All guardians and intermediaries, come at once.* There's a scream in the background—male or female?—and then Alban's voice cuts off. My coin turns cold once more.

"Why would I choose to follow you?" I mutter, my eyes burning into Joe, finally seeing his true self after years of thinking I knew who this man was. Of thinking I could trust him. Turns out, I didn't know him at all. "You're a monster."

Disappointment flickers in his gaze. "Very well. I didn't want to do this, but you've given me no choice." He claps his hands and the canopy overhead thickens, blocking out the sun. Shadows glide from behind the trees, circling us.

"I will try to save you when this is all over. I promise." He gives me a sad smile. "See you in another life, Winnie girl."

# XXXIX

My fingers tighten around my coin.

"*Sahabri'el*," I cry as shadows rush me. Their fingers claw at my hair, nails digging into my scalp. They are the *cold, cold* burn of winter, the breath you take that feels like fire in your lungs and leaves ice crystals on your scarf. My muscles seize and my heart pumps faster, faster, trying to get blood to the parts of my body already shutting down, compartmentalizing the cold. I lunge out with my knife, but the shadows break apart like smoke. I pull my hand back and they re-form.

Their whispers clog my ears.

*Fresh meat so nice to eat. Skin like honey, skin like wine, skin in my mouth, so fine fine fine.*

I scream as they tear through my coat and peel a slice of skin from my arm, wriggling it in the air like a piece of bacon. A few of them fight over it, darting far enough away for me to see Uncle Joe, his face expressionless, his eyes dead coals.

"Have you changed your mind yet, Winter?"

"Go to hell," I spit as I reach into my coat pocket and pull out the flashlight hidden there. The beam is not very wide, but it's bright. I swing it around myself in circles. I'm not fast enough to keep them all back, but it does slow their progress.

Another long finger of smoke scratches a thin triangle into my bicep as the others circle me, trying to find a way in, a tornado of whispered voices and arctic air. The smoke seeps into the lines of the cut on my skin and *pulls*. I swing the flashlight on the Sentinel, but it's already gone. Two more shadows glide away from me as they fight over that piece, and somewhere a rational part of my brain thinks they could all just fillet me to death and get their fair share, that there's no point in fighting over every little piece, but maybe that is the point. Maybe it's all part of the fun, and meanwhile I stay alive. Stay fresh.

A ball of blue light sears the side of my vision. I glance through the hole left behind by the scuffling shadows. My fireflies are closing in. They'll save me. Tears spring to my eyes as I watch them. So fast, so loyal, so—

"*Balak'ahmeir*," Joe hisses, throwing up his hand.

My fireflies fall to the ground like fat raindrops, their lights extinguished, their tiny bodies unmoving.

"NO!" I run for them without thinking, and the shadows take their chance. They swarm me, knocking me to the ground. I try to shield myself with the flashlight, but now that I'm horizontal, I can't reach my entire body.

My cheek burns where another strip of skin is sliced off. Their lips smack against my ear as they chew. My fingers go numb from the cold, and distantly I realize my flashlight is no longer in my hand. But that can't be right . . . the light is still hovering over me. I just can't feel the handle in my grip anymore.

*Winter.*

Dad?

*Hold on.*

It hurts.

*I know. Just hold on a little longer, baby. You're my strong girl, remember?*

*Strong*, I think to myself. *I'm strong.* But I don't feel strong, and my eyes are closing, and I can't feel my legs anymore. It's too cold. It would feel so good to just close my eyes for a minute. When I open them, I'll be ready to fight, but right now they're so heavy, and I just . . . can't . . .

Joe's hand circles my wrist, wrenching me out from the shadows. The collar of my shirt digs into my windpipe, choking me as his fist gropes the fabric behind my neck. He sets me down. My body tenses to run, but he grips my wrist once more.

"Don't," he says. "They won't touch you so long as you stay here, next to me."

My eyes widen. *What sort of monster must he be, to terrify darkness itself?*

"I'm going to ask you again," he says, his voice soft, "now that you've seen the full extent of my power. Have you changed your mind?"

I try to speak, but I can't breathe. My lungs are frozen inside my chest. And then, *finally*, there—a little gasp of air sneaks into them. I try again, breathing deeper, and deeper. Blood seeps from the cut on my cheek, dripping into my mouth.

"No," I reply, the word thick as sludge on my thawing tongue. "I have not changed my mind."

"You're making a mistake."

"So you've said, but I'd rather die than join my father's murderer."

He grabs me by both arms, his fingers bruising my bones. "Stop calling me that," he shouts. "I'm going to bring him back!"

"Let go of me!"

"Please, Winter." His eyes are wild, frantic. "You have to believe me."

"I said, let go!" I swipe my knife at his forearm. The blade slices through his coat, nicking his skin, but there's no blood. The wound closes too fast for that. Still, it takes him by surprise, and I wrench out of his loosened grip.

The shadows are on me almost immediately, but this time I don't try to fight them. I just run. My joints are stiff from cold, and I feel like the Tin Man, in desperate need of oil, but adrenaline pushes me forward. Burns through my veins like battery acid. It isn't pretty, and every limp, every stumble, brings the Sentinels and Uncle Joe closer to me, but I can't give up.

I *won't* give up.

I keep the flashlight angled behind me. The light swings wildly with every pump of my arms, and some of the Sentinels manage to tangle their fingers in my coat, my hair. But I keep moving, driving my feet into the ground. Faster, faster, *faster*.

"You can't escape me, Winter," Uncle Joe says. He appears on the path in front of me, blocking my escape. "I *am* the wood."

I skid to a stop and double back. A few of the shadows swipe at me, but my skin is too cold to feel it being ripped away. I turn onto the next closest path, but Joe's already there.

"Give it up," he says, and there's a slight chuckle in his voice, as if he's enjoying himself. As if we were just playing a game. "Fighting is pointless."

He's right. I can't win—not like this. He's too strong, too

fast. He's everywhere. I wonder if he toyed with Dad like this, too. If I'm just repeating the same pattern. If Joe will go to my mom tonight and tell her he did everything he could to save me.

*I'm sorry, Mom.*

I slow down. Glance at the shadows behind me. A speck of an idea plants itself in my brain, grows into a sapling, and then taller, wider, branching off into a scurry of thoughts. It's insane, and most likely impossible. But I have nothing to lose.

I stop, my coin trapped in my palm. I keep my flashlight pointed up at me, but my legs are in the dark, and the shadows begin attacking my boots and jeans like starving piranhas. Their coldness seeps into my bones so I can hardly feel them, and it allows me to clear my mind completely, just like Dad taught me. I focus on the only thing that matters:

Controlling the Sentinels.

I don't know if it can be done, but there can be no doubt in my intention, or it won't work. Instead, I think about the fireflies, about the day I first called them to me. The day they fluttered against my cheeks and Dad told me it looked like they had taken a shine to me. I had been wanting to see them the moment I stepped in the wood. I focused on it so hard that a word popped into my mind, as if it had always been there even though it was a word I'd never heard before.

*Sahabri'el.*

I'd whispered it under my breath, trying it out on my tongue, and then the fireflies appeared. They were the only creature I'd ever tried it on, mostly because they were the only creature in the wood, aside from travelers, I'd ever seen. But if I could control them, why couldn't I control other creatures in the wood?

Of course, I've never read anything like it in the journals, but that doesn't mean it can't be done. Maybe no other Parish guardian has tried.

And this time, I'm not waiting for a word to come to me. I remember the word Varo—Uncle Joe—used to call the Sentinels to him that first day I saw him in the wood.

I focus on the shadows, on their long, amorphous bodies and the way they suck every last drop of warmth from the air, until the very ground beneath my feet is a sheet of ice. I focus on everything I know about them: from the way they smell, a sharp and piercing absence of life, like the wind on the coldest day of winter, to the way their laughter tinkles through the air. And then, I speak the language of the Old Ones:

"*Tierl'asi.*"

The shadows stop. Uncle Joe's lips part in surprise.

I meet his eyes, and then I issue one command. "Attack him."

The shadows do not hesitate.

Joe tries to call them off, but they are single-minded. Still, I'm certain it won't be long before he regains control, so I turn and run as soon as he's swarmed. Joe's screams echo off the trees, but I am not lucky enough for them to be screams of pain. Only screams of frustration.

*Just a little farther,* I tell myself. *Almost there.*

He's still screaming when I barrel through a threshold and come out the other side, my boots slapping the damp stone floor of council headquarters.

# XL

Headquarters is complete pandemonium. Joe's supporters (wearing their black cloaks, their hoods thrown back this time to reveal their faces) brandish a mixture of daggers, sabers, and short swords; the Old Ones and guardians fight back with the heavy broadswords that have always lined the walls.

I don't see Henry anywhere.

I grip my knife in my palm and enter the fray, my eyes scanning every face, searching for him. Several bodies lie unmoving on the floor. One bears the long, white hair of a council member. Another wears modern clothes. Either a guardian or an intermediary, but there's no time to look. All I know is it isn't Henry, so I keep moving.

Blades clash in front of me. Guardian Ballinger grimaces as he presses all his weight into his sword, refusing to let the cloaked figure in front of him gain the upper hand.

"Need some help?" I ask.

"If—you—don't—mind," Ballinger grinds out between his teeth.

I slice my knife forward, toward cloak guy's face, forcing him to break contact. Our eyes meet.

Septimus.

He knocks my knife away easily, raising his sword—

Ballinger carves his blade through Septimus's midsection. Just like what happened with Uncle Joe, the wound heals itself as quickly as it appears, but it shocks Septimus enough for Ballinger and me to get away unharmed.

"I don't know how much longer we can keep this up," Ballinger shouts over the clang of metal and the percussion of magic exploding all around us.

"The Old Ones can go on forever," I reply. "It's just us mortals who are in danger."

Ballinger shakes his head grimly. "Did you not see Tiberius on the floor? Their blades are tipped with dragon's bane."

*Oh, God. It's going to be a massacre.*

Everything slows. The guardians swirling their weapons through the air, fury and pride and fatigue all battling for precedence on their faces. The Old Ones staggering under the assault of their brothers-turned-enemies. The walls and ceiling crumbling all around us, leaching streams of lake water onto the floor. And then I see him.

Henry, wielding one of the broadswords like a vengeful angel, pushing Joe's supporters away from guardians and Old Ones alike before their poison-tipped blades can find their marks. Sweat dots his brow, but the strength with which he wields his weapon and the determination in his gaze make me think he could do this for another hour, at least.

I run to him, dodging blades and fists. Henry parries a thrust from a black cloak and kicks him square in the stomach, sending him flying into the wall.

"Henry," I say, laying my hand on his shoulder.

He turns his wild eyes on me, momentarily uncertain if I'm friend or foe. Then he exhales a huge gasp of air, as if he hasn't breathed since I left him in the wood. He wraps his free hand around my skull and pulls me to him, pressing his lips against my forehead.

"Thank God you're all right," he says.

"We need to get out of here. There's no winning this fight."

"Not until we've gotten everyone else out, too."

I glance around. Count our numbers against theirs. Nine guardians, three intermediaries, and six Old Ones versus four black cloaks. We have the numbers on our side, but if our Old Ones go down from the dragon's bane, the rest of us won't have a chance.

"Okay," I say, thinking. "Okay. We'll have to try to round everyone up into a circle and make our way toward the threshold. Then maybe we can—"

My coin blazes white-hot against my skin. I suck in a breath.

"Winter, what is it?" Henry asks.

Everyone stops at the sudden, burning sensation of their coins. Even the black cloaks. Joe's voice echoes through the room.

*I will give you one last chance,* he says. *If you join me now, peacefully, I can promise all of you safety and a place of power in this, our new world order. If you don't . . .* He pauses. *Any blood shed now will be on your hands.*

"We will never join you! We have all promised to protect the thresholds from any threat, including one from within,"

Guardian Kamali Okorie shouts back at him. The skin around her left eye is purple and swelling, and she spits a glob of dark blood onto the floor. "We will not break that promise."

*I'd be very careful taking that stance now,* Joe replies. *It is a choice from which you cannot return once it's made. If you do not decide to join us, then you are our enemy, and you will be treated as such.* His supporters lift their cloaks and spin, disintegrating into black dust that disappears midair. *I will give you an hour to decide.*

My coin immediately goes cold. Henry looks at me questioningly. He couldn't hear Joe's words.

Valentin, the guardian-in-training from Romania, slumps to the floor. "We're screwed, aren't we?"

The dead are laid on benches, white sheets thin as bridal veils shrouding their bodies. The wounded are taken to the dais, where Seral ministers to them with ladles of water and jars of foul-smelling ointment. No one speaks above a whisper. They are too shell-shocked, too lost in their thoughts. Too defeated.

There's something I'm supposed to say. Something I'm supposed to tell the council. But I can't stop staring at the bodies: two council members, Briel and Tiberius, who I have seen once a week for the past twenty months; and though they never spoke much, I can't imagine looking up at the dais and not seeing them there; Ballinger's intermediary, Tertia, who had been with Ballinger's family for hundreds of years, and Ballinger kneeling at her head, whispering something to her as a tear rolls down his cheek; and Guardian Anaya Kapoor, the girl from Bangalore who always smiled at me. Does she have a family waiting for her at home? Friends? An entire life, snuffed out in the flash of a blade.

Henry's fingers twine through mine, his palm sliding across

my palm, his lips pressing against my temple. I close my eyes, but I still see them. The lives Joe took. The lives he will take, if we don't give him what he wants.

Seral's voice murmurs through the static echoing in my ears, "If only Celia were here," and I remember what it is I'm supposed to say.

My eyes spring open and I turn to Seral. Watch her shake her head as she spreads the ointment on Valentin's shoulder.

"I know where Celia is," I say.

Alban snaps his attention to me. "What? Where?"

"Brussels. Joe tried to poison her and her husband with dragon's bane. We believe they were able to escape through the Brussels threshold."

"How do you know this?" he asks. "And who's 'we'?" He shifts his focus to Henry, narrowing his eyes. "I do not know you."

I step in front of Henry, shielding him. "I'll tell you everything, but we need to send for Augustus and Celia."

He hesitates, sucking in a breath—probably at my audacity for trying to order him around—but then he nods. I wait for him to send Kamali's intermediary, an Old One named Leok, to look for Henry's parents before beginning my story. The guardians and council members listen intently. Henry fills in the gaps, describing his upbringing, and how he knows so much about the wood. They look horrified when I tell them about the Sentinels, but not as horrified as when I tell them about letting Henry through to the modern world.

"He stayed with you?" one guardian shouts.

"For three days?" another joins in.

"Let her talk!" Kamali growls back at them.

"You have to understand," I say, "I would do anything for even just the slightest chance of finding out what happened to my father, and when Henry said he thought the disappearance of Augustus and Celia was connected to the disappearance of my father and this conspiracy to overthrow the council, I had to take him seriously. And it was a good thing I did, because he turned out to be right. My father did not walk off the path, as Joe and his supporters, who I'm guessing headed up the ridiculous investigation into my father's disappearance, led us to believe." I stop, my breath hitching in my throat.

"What happened to him?" Ballinger asks quietly.

I force the words out. "Joe threw him off the path," I say. "For knowing too much."

For a moment, no one says a word. Then—

"What if we give him what he wants?" Valentin asks. "Would it really be so bad?"

His mother, Remi, smacks him upside the head. "Of course it would be bad," she says. "This is the very thing we have sworn to keep from happening. No one should be able to use the thresholds for personal gain, and no one should attempt to change the past. It is too dangerous."

"If it's so dangerous—don't *hit* me, I'm just asking," Valentin says, "then why does Josiah think he can get away with it?"

"If he's anything like Varo once was, he thinks his power is stronger than the wood's." Alban's voice is quiet, resigned. "He sees himself as indestructible, infallible, which is the greatest mistake anyone can make."

"So, what do we do?" Seral asks, closing the lid of her ointment jar.

Kamali's eyes flash. "Isn't it obvious? We fight."

Seral stands. "They have the only poison known to kill us on their side. We will most likely lose."

"Well, we can't do *nothing*," Kamali growls. "What other choice do we have?"

Henry has moved to sit in the corner, his back against the wall. He digs idly at a hangnail on his thumb, staring at nothing. I leave the others to fight it out, crossing the room and pressing my spine against the damp stone, sliding down to the floor next to him. "Leok will find your parents. Kamali wouldn't have volunteered him to go if she didn't trust him."

He leans his head back against the wall and closes his eyes. "I know."

Now that I'm closer to him, and not distracted by the threat of death, I can see the burns on his face, neck, and hands. Red welts surrounding puffy white blisters. I reach my hand toward him, but touching him would hurt him even worse. "I'm sorry. I didn't want to see you get hurt—"

"You have a funny way of showing it," he says.

"I couldn't risk losing you, too."

He doesn't look at me.

"Henry." I breathe his name. My hand hovers in the space between us, and then, slowly, tentatively, I lace my fingers through his. He winces, but his fingers tighten around mine, and he breathes a little deeper. "I'm sorry."

He sighs, pulling his head forward so that his hair falls into his eyes. "You have nothing to apologize for. I would have done the same in your situation. Only . . ."

"Only?"

His eyes flick to mine. "Only I thought I'd never see you again, and I . . ."

"Yes?"

He shakes his head. "I did not want the last conversation we had to be in anger. I could not have lived with myself." He doesn't look at me as he says it, and I get the feeling this isn't the whole truth. I want to press it, but I haven't exactly given him the whole truth, either. I told him I felt something for him, but that's such an unworthy expression that can encompass so many different things: a short-lived crush, a passing attraction, an appreciation that doesn't really change you on any significant level.

But Henry *has* changed me, has made me want things that are impossible. For the first time since Dad disappeared, he made me feel safe. Whole. Alive. But how do you tell someone that? Where do you start?

I take a deep breath. "Henry, there's something I need to tell—"

"Henry?" a woman's voice murmurs softly, hopefully.

Henry glances up. "Mother! Father!" He pushes off the wall and runs across the room. I follow him with my eyes as he wraps his arms around a small, stocky woman with silver hair pulled back from her face and wide amber eyes, and then a tall, slim man with snow-white hair and a nose that used to fascinate me as a kid for the way it hooks down, like a hawk's beak.

Augustus and Celia.

They cling to each other. Augustus's shoulders shake. Celia runs her hands through Henry's hair, whispering something in his ear.

Alban strikes his gavel against the table, and they break apart, Celia still clutching Henry's arm.

"It seems we have a bit of trouble on our hands," Alban says. "You two wouldn't know anything about that, would you?"

# XLII

My stomach twists as Augustus and Celia give a detailed account of how they eavesdropped on a conversation in which they discovered Joe was the one behind the conspiracy to overthrow the council. They knew they could not bring such a claim to the council without hard evidence, or else Joe would be able, with the help of his supporters, to talk his way out of it, so they began searching for concrete proof of what they'd overheard.

But Joe had more eyes and ears than they had realized. He confronted them about it in the wood over a week ago.

"He was unrecognizable," Celia says. "His eyes were completely black, soulless, as if there were no goodness left inside of him. He told us we were standing in his way, and that if we refused to join him in his pursuit of the advancement of our people, then we would need to be silenced."

"He called the Sentinels on us then," Augustus continues, "and in the confusion, he nicked both of our arms with his dagger. We didn't understand, at first, why he didn't try to wound us more than that, but then he explained the dagger was tipped with dragon's bane."

He left them to die there, in the wood, but Celia used her healing powers to leach the poison out of their bodies. It seeped into the ground around them, infecting the wood instead. They tried to get to council headquarters, but they were too weak, so they fell through the nearest portal they could find. But first they left a clue behind for their son about where they'd gone, knowing he would probably come looking for them if they couldn't make it back to him soon.

"The threshold closed behind us, and our powers were too diminished to make it open again," Celia says. "We camped outside the threshold, waiting for it to open. We knew we would need our strength, not just to open the threshold, but to confront Josiah again, if he or one of his supporters found us before we could make it here."

"That's where I found them," Leok explains. "Just outside the threshold, trying to get through."

Alban sighs. "There is much in your story I would like to discuss with the both of you," he says. "Mainly the fact that you have adopted a human son and told him everything about us and the wood, going against our laws to do so. However, that matter will have to wait until we've dealt with Josiah."

"Yes, well, we were not just twiddling our thumbs in Brussels, waiting for the threshold to open," Augustus says. "We have a plan."

Alban's eyes widen. "By all means, let's hear it."

I listen with a cold numbness. They want to kill Joe with the very dragon's bane with which he tried to kill them, leaching it out of the ground and placing it into a weapon. The problem will be getting close enough to him.

"I can do it."

Everyone turns to me.

"I can get close enough," I say.

Henry shakes his head. "No."

"It isn't up for discussion."

"The hell it's not," Henry says.

I arch a brow at him. Henry stares back at me defiantly.

"He won't let anyone else get close," I say. "He has no reason to trust any of you, but he . . . he has a soft spot for me. If I can convince him I've decided to join him, he'll let me get close enough, and then if I can catch him off-guard, if he can be distracted for just a second, I can . . ." I close my eyes. "I can kill him."

The room is quiet.

Alban clears his throat. "Are you certain you are capable of doing such a thing?"

"He killed my father."

"That doesn't answer my question."

"Yes," I say, my voice a hard, dead thing. "It does."

Alban studies me. Then he nods, strikes his gavel, and says, "Very well. All those in favor of this plan?"

Everyone except Henry raises their hands.

"All those opposed?"

Henry raises his hand.

Alban says, "It is unanimous. Now then, Guardian Parish, what exactly did you have in mind?"

Celia and I cross over into the wood while the others wait a few more minutes to take their positions. I hand Celia my dad's knife. She holds it in one hand and touches a black, infected tree trunk with the other. I watch in amazement as the disease slowly bleeds from the tree, turning the blade of my knife black as polished obsidian.

"There," Celia says, handing back the knife. "That should be more than enough."

This process was already discussed at headquarters. At first, Celia wanted to rid the wood entirely of the disease as quickly as possible, but I pointed out that Joe would suspect something was up if the wood was suddenly one hundred percent healthy again, and so the healing of the wood will have to wait. *Besides, keeping the wood like this a little while longer has its advantages,* I think, palming my coin.

Celia slinks into the shadows, whispering, "Remember, dear, we'll be right behind you."

I know I should be thinking a million things as I move

through the wood, my boots sinking into the sandy muck that was once a dry path. I know I should be warring with myself over what I'm about to do, over how it will irrevocably change me—isn't that what killing someone is supposed to do? Shouldn't I be feeling *something*?—but all I can think about is my mom.

I wish now that I'd told her what I was doing. She wouldn't have let me leave the house, of course, and we would have had a huge fight; and I would have stormed out anyway, and she would have probably followed me, resulting in an even bigger mess and putting her life in danger; but in a selfish, childish way, all I want in this moment is for my mom to know where I am, what I'm doing. To know that I love her, and that I don't want to leave her.

It is my greatest fear, as I walk toward the place where instinct tells me Joe is waiting for me, that I will die in here, just like Dad, and Joe will tell my mom that I walked off the path, just like Dad. That she'll never know what really happened to me. That she'll drive herself insane with the not knowing.

Maybe that's why I'm so numb, because I don't really have a choice. This destiny has been laid out for me, and the only way I'm going to get home to the one person in the world who needs me more than anything is by not losing my nerve.

Joe stands in the same clearing I stood in just a few days ago, when I was trying to walk off the path. His supporters stand behind him, their blades flashing in the midday sunlight.

Joe's brow arches. "Where is everyone?"

*Breathe*, I tell myself. *Believe everything you're about to say, so he'll believe it, too.*

"At council headquarters," I reply. "I left them behind."

"Come to fight me on your own, Winnie girl?"

I grit my teeth. "Did you mean what you said? Can you really save him?"

Joe studies me. "Yes," he says. "I believe I can."

"Swear it to me," I say. "Swear to me you'll save my father, and I'll join you."

He smiles. "Not so much of a monster now, am I?"

"I wouldn't say that, but I know you loved my father. I know you wouldn't have done what you did if he'd"—I force the words out—"if he'd just listened to you. And I know you'll save him anyway, even though he didn't believe in you. My grief got in the way of seeing that, but I get it now, and if it means getting my dad back, I want to help you."

He hesitates.

Tears well in my eyes, and I don't have to tell myself to believe in what I'm about to say. It's been in my heart for twenty months and seven days, banging its fists against my valves, always making it so damn hard to breathe. "I can't keep going on without him, Uncle Joe. I die a little every day he's gone, and I'm afraid if it lasts any longer, there's going to be nothing left of me. I *need* him to come home. I'll do anything. Please, just . . . help me."

Joe's gaze softens. "Very well," he says, his voice soothing, like one of the times I fell off my bike and scraped my knee on the sidewalk. Joe carried me into the kitchen and spoke to me in that same hushed tone as he cleaned the scrape and used three *Sesame Street* Band-Aids to cover it. My mom and dad would have told me I was fine, that the cut wasn't that bad, but Joe was properly solemn about the whole thing, and I loved him for that. "But I want you to stand behind us, out of harm's way. Understand?"

"Yes, sir," I say, moving to stand behind him, my throat tight from the memory.

We don't have to wait long for the others to arrive. My eyes immediately find Henry. His parents keep trying to push him behind them, but he refuses. He stands next to them instead, and when he sees me, he doesn't look at anything else.

Alban leads them, and when Joe asks if they have come to their senses, Alban replies, "We've come to ask the same of you, Josiah. We are willing to give you this final chance to stop this nonsense."

Joe laughs. "You're giving *me* a final chance? You still don't get it, do you? I've already won." He claps his hands together, creating the same black smoke that choked out the sun the first day I saw him as Varo. "I do not wish for more bloodshed, but that does not mean I am not willing to do whatever it takes to make my vision a reality. Just remember, as you watch your friends and family die around you, that you chose this, and for what? For some ridiculous notion that our people could not use the thresholds that make up our world? That it would somehow break down the very fabric of time? We have been denying our legacy for over a thousand years. Well, no more. It ends today."

Joe's supporters pull out their weapons.

"It didn't have to be this way," Alban shouts back at him.

"You're right," Joe says. "It didn't."

He thrusts the black smoke into the sky, transforming day into night. The wood changes immediately, monsters seeping from the trees to join the fray as Joe's supporters rush the Old Ones, weapons drawn.

"Stay close to me, Winter," Joe says, glancing at me over his shoulder.

I take a step closer to him. I can't see anything past Joe, can only hear the screams of the Old Ones and the guardians as the Sentinels and other monstrous, nocturnal creatures descend upon them.

"Henry!" Celia shouts.

My heart leaps into my throat. My body tenses, every fiber of my being urging me to run to Henry, to find him, but I can't leave Joe's side without betraying my true allegiance. *Please let him be okay*, I pray, my eyes scanning the darkness, picking up nothing.

But then—there! A spark of light. Alban, the most ancient Old One on the council, must know at least some of Joe's tricks, because he holds the light in his palm. It grows into a shield, throwing up an arc of light that hovers over the council members, keeping the Sentinels back. I see Henry lying on the ground at his parents' feet, unmoving.

*He's all right*, I think. *He's all right, he's all right.*

I squeeze my coin between thumb and forefinger and whisper, "*Tierl'asi.*" The Sentinels change course immediately, attacking Joe's supporters instead. Thankfully, Joe assumes they are attacking his people to avoid Alban's light. He doesn't realize I'm controlling them.

But the Sentinels aren't the only thing attacking Joe's supporters now. The wood has come to life, paths turning into swirling eddies, growing larger and picking up speed. The trees try to grab at Joe's supporters and Alban's people alike, but their trunks are too rotten, and they shear in half, toppling to the ground. One of Joe's supporters shouts as his leg is crushed beneath a fallen tree.

A black cloak enters Alban's circle of light. Kamali lunges

for him, stumbling back into the darkness. Her foot catches in the path's whirlpool, pulling her legs out from under her. She screams. Ballinger tries to help her, but another black cloak is on them.

I have to end this. Before anyone else gets hurt.

I grip the knife in my palm, raise it high over my head. Joe doesn't notice; he's too busy watching the battle unfold. I could do it now—I *have* to do it now—and he wouldn't see it coming. But I hesitate, and in the fraction of a second between blinking my eyes closed and opening them again, he's turned his head to look at me. Time slows as his brows draw together. His lips thin, betrayal hardening his jaw. I thrust the knife down, but he's faster than me. One hand bracelets my wrist as the other circles my throat. A grim smile slashes his lips.

"I wanted so much more for you than this." He angles the knife toward me. "Do you realize," he says, so quietly I can barely hear him over the screams rending the air, "I could force your hand to cut your own heart out of your chest? That is what you are up against."

"You're forgetting . . . I have something . . . you don't," I say between gasps for breath.

"What's that?"

Henry appears behind Joe. "Friends," he says.

Joe's grip on me loosens as he turns toward Henry, but I don't give him the chance to gain the upper hand this time. All I have to do is nick him. I slash the black dagger through the air. It cuts a thin line across his neck, barely a scratch, but when my blade comes away, it's silver again. The veins in Joe's neck turn black as the poison courses through his body.

Joe lashes out at Henry, pushing him back. Henry flies

through the air, striking his head against one of the logs lining the path.

"HENRY."

I start to run to him, but Joe grabs me, pulling me back. I try to fight him off, but he cups my face with his hands and forces me to meet his gaze. I can't look away. He holds me prisoner with his stare as the veins in his eyes turn black.

Images swirl through my mind. Varo—the *real* Varo— standing trial in front of the council, still trying to convince them to change their minds even as they order his banishment. Joe sitting in the back, nodding along with the others, believing it to be a fair punishment for Varo's crime. No silver lines his hair, and there's an innocence in his eyes, as if he's still years away from becoming the man who would kill my father.

The image changes. Joe, wearing a tweed Edwardian suit, strolling past Orton Hall on Ohio State's campus. Did he take classes there? No—he's following someone. Walking a few paces, then stopping unexpectedly, shifting his gaze to a bench or a tree, as if it's the most interesting bench or tree he's ever seen. When he starts walking again, it takes me a moment to figure out who he's following, but then I see her. A woman wearing a white dress with a peach sash that matches the ribbon on her parasol, her golden hair swept into an elaborate knot beneath a pretty straw hat. She notices Joe and gives him a small, shy smile.

The memories fly past. Joe and this woman, spending more time together. Taking canoe trips down the Olentangy, picnicking in a park, sharing stolen kisses in darkened alleys and private gardens.

The woman coughing blood into her handkerchief. Looking pale and skeletal in a big, fluffy bed. Joe arguing with the doctor, telling him there must be something he can do. The doctor shaking his head and whispering those awful, inadequate words, "I'm sorry."

A casket topped with lilies. Mourners dressed in black, surrounding the tombstone, and Joe, watching them from afar, clutching a blood-splattered handkerchief in his fist. Only approaching the tombstone when everyone else has left. Tracing her name with his fingertips—*Elizabeth*.

Joe confronting Alban and the other council members. Begging them to do something for her. She wasn't meant to die, not yet. Not yet. They'd barely had any time together. It isn't fair. But they just remind him this is why they do not encourage relationships with mortals. It never ends well.

In his grief and frustration, Joe picks up Seral's ledger and hurls it across the room.

Years pass. Joe loses himself in his work, in the wood, trying to forget her. It works well enough, in the daylight. But he keeps her picture by his bed. Stares at it every night before he goes to sleep.

And then comes Dad, Joe's first real friend. I want to hate these memories flashing past, of Joe and Dad joking around in the wood, going to bars at night, watching football games together. But I feel it, that seed of hope, of love, that Joe feels for him. Undeniable in its purity. That seed grows when Dad meets Mom, and she and Joe develop a sibling-like friendship, and then grows again when I come along.

The love he feels for me the first time he holds me in the hospital is indescribable. I would have thought there was no greater love, if I hadn't felt the love he'd had for Elizabeth.

"Stop," I tell him. "I don't want to see this."

But it keeps coming. A Varo supporter, meeting Joe in the wood, telling him he doesn't need the council to bring her back. Joe secretly researching Varo in Dad's study and the council library. Someone unseen slipping Varo's manifesto, detailing his convictions, into Joe's hands. And slowly, over too-long nights and too-short days, Joe becoming obsessed with the idea that the thresholds could be used—no, *should* be used—by the Old Ones if they so wished. It is their birthright. The council cannot keep them from it.

Joe doesn't feel the darkness seeping into his heart as a plan forms in his mind—it happens too slowly—but I do. The righteous anger and overwhelming grief mixing with the dark magic he's begun performing in the wood, to increase his own magic and give himself all the power he needs to overthrow the council. Blackening his soul by the smallest of degrees. Changing him from the inside out. Leading him to—

"No!" I shout. "I don't want to see this!"

But it's too late. Dad confronting him. Joe trying to sway Dad, like he tried to sway me. Dad heading for council headquarters, intent on turning Joe in. Joe, in desperation, pushing Dad off the path.

For a brief, flickering moment, Joe feels it. The darkness inside of him. The way it's changed him. The *wrongness* of it. But then come the excuses—*he should have listened to me; he should have joined me*—and the twisted belief that he could undo the damage. *I can save him, I can save him*—*It'll all be worth it*—*Stick to the plan*—

"Winter." Joe breathes my name, and then, as if someone has flicked a switch in my brain, everything goes black.

# XLIV

When I come to, I'm lying flat on my back, the sun warming my face. Joe's corpse lies next to me, all skin and bones and spidery black veins. His eyes are glassy, unseeing, and his tongue hangs out of his mouth, black and bloated. I scramble away from it, furiously wiping at the tears on my cheeks.

*No*, I think, drawing my knees up to my chest and pressing my face against my crossed arms. *I won't cry for him. He doesn't deserve it.*

I take all the memories flooding my brain—Joe lifting me onto his shoulders at the zoo so I could see the animals better; dancing with me and Mom and Dad in the family room; playing Candy Land with me at the dining room table—and force them back into a dark corner of my mind. None of it matters. The happy memories I had with him don't make up for what he did to me, to my family. He was a monster, and he deserved a monstrous death.

I repeat it to myself over and over again, hoping it will make me believe it.

When I finally look up, I see another body. Henry's body.

At first I think he's still pretending, like we'd planned for him to do earlier, so he could slip into the trees and sneak around the side of the battle to get to Joe, but that can't be right. . . . Joe's dead, which means Henry already did that, and he's lying on the ground now because . . . because . . .

Because Joe pushed him. Because he hit his head.

*Henry.*

I push off the ground and run to him. His eyes are closed and his breathing's shallow. "Henry, wake up," I say, crouching next to him. I run the back of my hand over his face as he's done to me so many times. He's cold—should he be this cold?

I pull off my jacket and lay it on top of his chest. "Henry, come on. Wake up."

I'm distantly aware of Celia's magic healing the fallen guardians while the Old Ones bind Joe's supporters in shackles.

"Celia," I yell. "Celia, it's Henry!"

Her eyes meet mine, and then she sees Henry lying on the ground. She picks up her skirts and runs toward us.

"I'm sorry I lied to you," I whisper to him, pushing his hair off his brow. "I thought it would be easier. You were leaving no matter what—you still are—and I thought if I acted like I never felt anything for you, it would be better for us both. But the truth is I've never felt this way about anyone, so I need you to wake up, now, okay? I need you to wake up and show me you're not bleeding internally somewhere because this isn't your time, you hear me?"

Celia crouches down on his other side and places her hands on him. "He's all right, dear. Only a concussion." She takes a deep breath, and a bright green glow that reminds me of Henry's eyes appears underneath her hands. "*Medicor'ae.*"

Color seeps back into his face, and the burns from my fireflies fade away into small, shimmering scars, almost as if they were never there. His eyes roll behind their lids.

"Well," I say, laughter rising over my words as I wipe away the tears clinging to my lashes, "that's convenient."

Celia reaches for me. "May I?"

I look down at my arms, where dirt clings to the slices of skin the Sentinels ripped away. The wound on my face pinches, dried blood cracking and peeling and bleeding again.

I nod.

She places one hand on my shoulder, the other above my heart, and chants something beneath her breath. I watch my arms as the cuts slowly fade, new skin bubbling up into the cracks. It reminds me of the grout Mom used when she replaced the bathroom tiling.

I rub my hand over the new skin, the pearlescent scars. "Thank you."

She smiles.

Henry's lashes flutter. "Winter."

Celia looks at me. "It seems he's grown fond of you, my dear."

My cheeks warm.

Henry takes a deep breath, his eyes brightening. "What happened?"

"We did it," I say. "Joe's dead."

That word—*dead*—echoes through my mind. Dead, as in I'm never going to see him again. Dead, as in his immortal life, which was so permanent only twenty-four hours ago, has been irrevocably snuffed out.

*He did it to himself. He deserved it. It doesn't matter that he lost*

*someone, that he had his reasons. Everyone has their reasons to do hor-*
*rible things if they only think about them long enough.*

*Don't. Cry.*

"Are you all right?" Henry asks. He reaches up, brushing a strand of hair off my face, and his eyes are so full of concern, I feel something break inside.

"Yeah," I say. "I'm fine."

"Alban has called for an emergency meeting tomorrow morning to discuss the sentences of the prisoners and council's next steps, but for now he wants the guardians to return home and rest," Celia says. "There's nothing more you can do today. The council members, however, are a different story." She glances at Henry. "They want us to return to headquarters for questioning."

"What sort of questioning?" I ask.

Celia's lips thin. "About Henry, about us adopting him and teaching him about the wood."

"But—" The trees in front of me blur. I shake my head, trying to make sense of what she's saying. "But he'll be all right, won't he? I mean, the council wouldn't do anything to—to hurt him, would they?"

"Of course not," Celia says, "but we may be put under restriction, and, well, Henry will most likely be forbidden from ever setting foot in the wood again."

I knew this was going to happen, regardless of whether it was a decree from the council or not. He has to live in his own time— he *has* to—that's it. End of story. So why does it feel like such a shock?

Celia stands. "I'll give you two a moment to say good-bye."

"Good-bye? But I'm not—"

"You're not what, Parish?" Henry asks as he pushes himself

up onto his elbows. Celia gives us a knowing look, disappearing into the crowd of guardians and council members speaking in hushed tones.

I swallow. "I'm not ready to say good-bye to you."

He grins. "Are you finally ready to admit you will miss me?"

My eyes burn. I squeeze them shut, but it doesn't help. "Yes," I say. "I'll miss you."

He smiles, but it's a sad smile. A good-bye smile. "You are a remarkable woman, Winter Parish, and an even more remarkable guardian. I have never met anyone who could have done the things you have done this day. No matter what fate has in store for us, know I will never forget you."

He presses his lips to mine. The kiss is salty from my tears and his jaw is hard as if he's trying not to cry, too, and it's the worst kiss I've ever had in my entire life because in it is written everything I feel for him and it's not enough to make him stay.

He breaks the kiss and squeezes my hand. "Come," he says, standing. "We will walk you home before we leave."

I wipe the backs of my hands across my eyes. "Don't your parents need me to guide them to headquarters?"

"They were born here, remember? I imagine they know the way better than you."

"Oh. Right."

Henry grabs his parents, and together we walk through the wood, toward my threshold. Too soon, I see the kitchen windows through the trees. I turn back to Henry and his parents. "Please, before you go, just tell me"—I take a deep breath, steeling myself—"what exactly happened to my father? When he was pushed off the path?"

Augustus's frown lines deepen. "The wood is not meant for mortals. You know that as well as anyone."

"So he's—I mean, is he . . ." I can't say the word. It's too final.

Augustus seems to hear it anyway. "Death may not be the right word for what he has become. The wood will have embraced him. His life force will have seeped into it, becoming a part of it. He *is* the wood, now. He is all around you when you are in here, just not as you remember him. But he can never be returned to you. He is gone, my dear."

I inhale, and it feels like the first breath I have truly taken in twenty months. It isn't the answer I was hoping for, and I know a part of me will always be looking for Dad to appear outside our threshold through the kitchen windows, but to not have to wonder all the time about what happened to him, where he is, if he needs me to find him, is freeing in its own horrible way.

"Thank you," I say. "I know I can't get him back but . . . it helps. To know he's still out here, in some way. Maybe even watching over me."

Augustus squeezes my shoulder. "He is; I guarantee that."

Henry wraps me in his arms. Whispers, "I wanted to find him for you."

"I know." I stand there a moment longer, breathing him in, memorizing his scent, the feeling of his shirt against my cheek. Then I force myself to take a step back, because if I don't do it now, I may never be able to. "Take care of yourself, okay?"

"And you, as well."

I nod. I begin to turn away from him, but he takes my face in his hands and kisses me. It's a soft kiss, and I want to melt into it, to keep him here, but his father clears his throat and Henry pulls away from me. We stare at each other a moment longer, hoping this moment will last us a lifetime.

Turning away from him is the hardest thing I've ever done. Walking away from him would be even worse, except I see Mom on the back porch. She gives me the strength to step forward.

My toes hesitate on the edge of the threshold. I glance over my shoulder. "Are you sure you'll make it—"

But they're already gone, and now that the Old Ones are working on ridding the wood of dragon's bane once more, I have to believe they'll be safe from anything still lurking in the darkness. And yet . . .

*Dad?*

Deep inside my heart, I hear him say, *Yeah, munchkin?* And I don't know if it's real, but I want to believe it is.

*Watch over them*, I think. *Keep them safe.*

# XLV

I tell Mom everything, not that she gives me much choice. I tell her about Henry, and his parents, and that I think I heard Dad's voice telling me to hold on while the Sentinels tried to kill me. But telling her about Joe is the hardest part. How do you tell someone that the man who was like a brother to her is the one responsible for killing her husband, and almost killing her daughter? How do you lessen the pain of that? The betrayal?

I wish I had the answers to those questions. Wish I could make this easier on her, so she doesn't have to feel the utter devastation and hopelessness choking my heart. But, in the end, all I can do is tell her every last truth. That the man we thought we knew changed right in front of our eyes, and we trusted him too much to see it. That he made us, our family, collateral damage in his downward spiral.

I don't doubt that Uncle Joe loved us. I felt that love in his last, dying moments. But he chose the darkness, let it corrupt his soul until nothing else mattered. Not us, the family he once cared for so much. Not the fate of the world. Nothing but his own selfishness and ego and dark sense of entitlement.

I wish I could say that the fact that he started out with good intentions makes it better somehow, but it doesn't. Joe destroyed every last piece of my life. Nothing will ever be the same, because of him.

And all I feel for him now is hate.

I expect Mom to have a meltdown, to tell me I'm never going into the wood again and this time she means it. I expect her to ground me for going after Joe on my own.

Instead, she's very quiet. Flames crackle in the fireplace, and she's been holding her cup of coffee for so long without taking a sip that it has to be ice cold.

When I can't take it anymore, I blurt, "Mom, say something. Please."

"He's really gone," Mom murmurs. "That man, Henry's father . . ."

"Augustus?"

She nods. "He confirmed it." She sucks in a shaky breath. "All this time, I thought maybe he was still out there. Maybe one day you would find him, and you'd both appear on the path next to that rock. It's stupid, but—" The tears come fast now. She chokes on them. "It's like losing him all over again."

I wrap my arms around her and we stay like that, tangled up in our loss, for hours.

❧

The next morning, I wake on the couch, sunlight streaming across my face and catching on the sparkly threads of one of Grandma's knitted blankets. The whole house smells like bacon and melted butter and biscuits baking in the oven.

I sit up, rub the sleep from my eyes. Mom brings out a pitcher of orange juice and sets it on the dining room table.

"Good morning," she says.

"G'morning," I croak.

"Breakfast will be another ten minutes, if you want to get ready for school."

I stare at her. It takes me a moment to remember it's Monday. Back to school. Back to business as usual. As if my whole life didn't change over the span of a weekend.

"Uh, yeah," I say. "Sure thing."

I head upstairs. Brush my teeth and change into a long-sleeve T and a pair of jeans. I grab my backpack off the floor and reach for the books on my desk.

I freeze.

A black composition book taken from the stack in my closet—one of about a dozen Mom picked up during a back-to-school sale—sits on top of my other books. Across the white space is my name written in calligraphy. My breath catches at the beauty of it, the delicate whorls and swirls. A lump the size of a baseball lodges in my throat as I crack open the spine.

*The best guardian deserves the best journal. Unfortunately, this pathetic excuse was all I could find, and so it is given in the hope you will someday replace it with one far superior. Until then, I pray you find it useful. Eternally Yours, Henry.*

He must have done this the night I helped Meredith study. Before our first kiss. Before our fight. Before good-bye. I trail my fingers over his name, smiling even as tears prick my eyes. I hug the composition book to my chest, then slip it inside my backpack along with the rest of my books. Later, I'll put it in the study, where I will sit night after night, recording the day's events, but, right now, with the ghost of Henry's good-bye still on my lips, I can't quite bring myself to leave it behind.

I head back downstairs, making a beeline for the kitchen, and pull up short.

The dining table is set for two.

It breaks my heart and repairs it somehow, all in the same breath. I help Mom bring the dishes to the table—enough bacon for two, a couple links of sausage, a small fruit salad. Mom places two over easy eggs on each plate and sets them on the table.

We sit down and stare at the chair that used to be Dad's. And then Mom squeezes my hand and asks, "Anything special going on at school this week?"

And even though I don't know what will happen now that the council knows I harbored a traveler in the modern world, and even though I don't know if the wood will ever go back to normal, none of it seems that important right now. Because we have this.

We have each other, and for the first time in a long time, it feels like enough.

# Acknowledgments

While writing in and of itself is often a solitary venture, the arduous journey of getting a book published could not be completed—and should not even be attempted—without a strong support system. I am fortunate enough to have many people in my life who helped make this dream of mine a reality.

First and foremost, I want to thank my Lord and Savior, Jesus Christ, for leading me through the darkest parts of the wood and bringing me out safely on the other side. You are my peace, my comfort, my strength. Apart from You, I can do nothing.

To my editor, Anna Roberto, for believing in me, and for taking my weird little book and transforming it into what I always imagined it could be. Also, to my publisher, Jean Feiwel, and to everyone at Feiwel and Friends and Macmillan, who have worked so tirelessly to make my book the best it could possibly be. I am forever grateful to you all. And to my amazing agent, Andrea Somberg, for being my consummate cheerleader, publishing warrior, and trusted friend. I have absolutely no idea what I'd do without you.

To my critique partners, who help me see the forest for the trees and who have talked me into not giving up more times than I can count. To Lori Goldstein, for always providing insightful critiques, industry knowledge, and encouraging e-mails whenever I need them, and for doing your best to turn me into a plotter. (I'm not at your level yet, but I'm a lot closer than I used to be!) You're like the big sister who went to college before me and then taught me all your tricks on how to survive, and I couldn't be more thankful for that! To Natalie Knaub, for always challenging me to dig deeper, go darker, and push myself, both through your critiques and through your own writing, which tends to inspire both unfathomable awe and supreme jealousy in equal measure. One of these days I won't feel totally inferior when I read your work! To Naomi Hughes, for filling my manuscripts with encouraging notes, funny reactions, smiley faces, and truly brilliant suggestions. Thanks for being an awesome critique partner, and an even more awesome friend. And to May Robertson, for the coffee meet-ups, life catch-ups, book talks, and Harry Potter nerd-outs. You're the best!

To the writing community, both online and off, which is chock-full of the nicest people a girl could ever meet. I am astounded by all the support out there to help fellow authors succeed. Particularly I want to thank Miss Snark's First Victim for helping me grow as a writer through her many contests and peer critiques. I also want to thank Brenda Drake, whose annual writing contest, Pitch Wars, started me down the path to signing with my dream agent. As for the offline writing community, I want to thank Thurber House in Columbus, Ohio, for providing such wonderful classes and opportunities for writers, and I would like to thank young adult author Lisa Klein, who taught the class at Thurber House that made me believe I could not only write an entire book, but someday become an actual published author.

To Jane, for seeing an advertisement for Lisa Klein's class and for making it possible for me to attend. If it weren't for this extremely special act of love and kindness, I don't know if I would have had the courage to take my passion for writing and actually make a career out of it.

To my mom, for teaching me to love books in the first place, for always encouraging me, and for too many other life lessons to count. In so many different ways, I wouldn't be the person I am today if it weren't for you. I am honored to be your daughter. To my grandma, for making up stories whenever I asked, and for teaching me to love history, which is, at its heart, stories of people who were just trying to live their lives among different circumstances than our own. You turned me into a storyteller. And to my dad, for always supporting my dreams, whatever they happened to be at the time. You always made sure I knew nothing was out of my reach if I worked hard enough and never gave up. (You were right!)

And, finally, to Nathan—my love, my light, my best friend, my soul mate. For all the times you believed in me when I didn't believe in myself. For all the times you celebrated with me, consoled me, and cheered me on whenever I needed encouragement. This book would not exist if it weren't for your unending love and support. It belongs to you just as much as it belongs to me. Thank you. I love you.

Thank you for reading this
Feiwel and Friends book.

The friends who made

THE

WOOD

possible are:

Jean Feiwel, *Publisher*

Liz Szabla, *Associate Publisher*

Rich Deas, *Senior Creative Director*

Holly West, *Editor*

Alexei Esikoff, *Senior Managing Editor*

Kim Waymer, *Senior Production Manager*

Anna Roberto, *Editor*

Christine Barcellona, *Associate Editor*

Kat Brzozowski, *Editor*

Anna Poon, *Assistant Editor*

Emily Settle, *Administrative Assistant*

Rebecca Syracuse, *Junior Designer*

Ilana Worrell, *Production Editor*

Follow us on Facebook or visit us online at fiercereads.com.
Our books are friends for life.